Faceless
A Mystery

Dawn Kopman Whidden

BRIGHTON PUBLISHING LLC
435 N. HARRIS DRIVE
MESA, ARIZONA 85203

FACELESS
A Mystery

DAWN KOPMAN WHIDDEN

PUBLISHED
BY
BRIGHTON PUBLISHING LLC
435 N. HARRIS DRIVE
MESA, ARIZONA 85203
BRIGHTONPUBLISHING.COM

COPYRIGHT © 2013

ISBN 13: 978-1-62183-140-2
ISBN 10:1-62183-140-X

PRINTED IN THE UNITED STATES OF AMERICA

FIRST EDITION

COVER DESIGN: TOM RODRIGUEZ

All rights reserved. This is a work of fiction. All the characters in this book are fictitious and the creation of the author's imagination. Any resemblance to persons living or dead is purely coincidental. No part of this publication may be reproduced or transmitted in any form or by any means, electronic or mechanical, including photocopy, recording, or any information storage retrieval system, without permission in writing from the copyright owner.

Acknowledgements

I would be remiss if I didn't thank the following people for their role in making this book a reality.

Once again, I need to thank Jean Whitley for jump-starting my lifetime dream to write and for being my biggest supporter and best friend; and not to leave out her husband, Wilbur, who puts up with us both!

To Tammy Sanders, for being the first person in Bell to download *A Child is Torn*, and for insisting that everyone in town buy it as well.

To Don Rosenthal, my toughest critic, who pushed me and gave me the encouragement to make it right.

To Tawnya Jenkins, who not only is the best hairstylist on the east coast, but the sweetest person in the whole world. You have been an inspiration and the reason, I know, that I can keep on going.

To Mary Jo Padilla, who has been one of my biggest cheerleaders, and a great friend and neighbor. I don't know where I would be without you!

To Greg Marciano, who was relentless in helping me promote my first novel, *A Child is Torn*. Greg, I am so proud of the man you grew up to be. Ann would be proud. She missed the best of you.

To Gail Bennett, for being the first of the DEEPDALE/BEECH HILLS group to believe in me, and one of the first to download the eBOOK.

To Peri Nusbaum Kolakowski, for being tireless in promoting *A Child is Torn*, and for helping and encouraging me in this, and future, endeavors.

To Faith Johns, for buying every copy in Alabama!

To Don and Kathie McGuire and the Brighton Publishing editors, for taking another chance on me, and for working tirelessly to get it right.

FACELESS: A MYSTERY ~ DAWN KOPMAN WHIDDEN

To all my friends and neighbors, if I didn't mention your name, it's because there are so many to thank. Hopefully, I will continue to produce enough books to make you all a part of the story! I LOVE YOU ALL.

∼

OTHER BOOKS BY DAWN KOPMAN WHIDDEN

A Child is Torn "Innocence Lost"

DEDICATION

This book is dedicated to my family.

To my husband, Horace, who has been the rock and mortar that helped build this wonderful life we have made together.

My nephew, Steven; his lovely wife, Ashley; and son, Taylor.

My niece Stacie.

Mason Walker Ivey and Morgan Sydney Simpson, my grandchildren.

To my stepdaughter, Shavon, who has lived through the worst that life has to offer.

To the other members of my family too numerous to mention, you know who you are.

You light up my heart. May your journey in life be filled with only sweet things and love. I wish that all of your dreams come true.

May the road to happiness be the only road you find yourself on, and may it have nothing but wonderful experiences on that journey of life.

This book is also dedicated to the memory of Jean Friedman, Betty Goldfarb Katz, and Naomi Trost: Three of the strongest women that walked on this planet.

To the wisest woman: Esther Kopman.

To the sweetest woman: Faye Migdal.

To my DADDY: a man who had all of those qualities and so much more.

I HOPE I'VE MADE ALL OF YOU PROUD

PROLOGUE

She thought she heard someone in the brush behind her. Glancing around, she couldn't spot anything or anyone. *Probably just a raccoon,* she thought as she continued through the dark woods, looking for her friend.

She wasn't scared to walk alone through the forest with only the moonlight and a flashlight to make her path visible, but she was pissed at Jamie for running off. Now, because the girl was pulling one of her drama acts, she found herself tramping through the woods looking for her, instead of being back at the house partying with the others.

Her shrill scream penetrated the dark night. She didn't hear the others approach from the woods until they reached the spot where she stood. They had heard her screaming and immediately made their way to her location.

She stood staring at what lay on the ground before her. She heard one of the others cry out. "Come on," she heard someone say. "Let's get out of here!"

Chapter One

Wednesday Evening/Thursday Morning

When you're a homicide detective as well as a mother and the phone rings at three a.m., your first instinct is to take inventory of your children. When the dispatcher requests your attendance at a crime scene, you try to calculate whether your children could possibly be anywhere in that vicinity.

Shaking off my sleepy fog-like consciousness, I took a deep breath as the dispatcher read off the address. I asked her to repeat it as I clumsily reached for the switch on my bedside lamp, my fingers feeling their way in the dark. Suddenly, I heard a soft pop and saw a flash of light .I jerked my hand away as the bulb chose that moment to burn out, almost as if in protest.

I waited until my eyes adjusted to the darkness and I resigned myself to working in just the dim moonlight that made its way through the slats in the window blinds. I grabbed the pen and pad sitting on my nightstand. As I sat up and cradled the phone between my neck and shoulder, I felt my husband Glenn's strong fingers start to massage the other side. He was barely awake, yet he was trying to help me relax. He knows all too well that these calls can lead to emotionally draining days and weeks ahead.

"125 Cedar Hill Road, detective," she told me. "I tried to reach Detective Moran, but he isn't returning my calls."

"It's okay, Wendy, I'll take it," I told her, just before I hung up the phone. Now I had another concern and now I had something else to worry about. Where was my partner of seven years?

Was Joe sleeping off an alcoholic stupor? Maybe it was better that he wasn't answering his calls.

"What's up?" Glenn asked me, rubbing the sleep from his eyes. He started to lean over to get his glasses, but I stopped him. "I've got to go. Go back to sleep, honey." I pushed the button on my watch. It gave off a purple glow, allowing me to read the time.

"I probably won't be back in time to get Bethany off to school.

1

FACELESS: A MYSTERY ~ DAWN KOPMAN WHIDDEN

Can you take her? She's got that science project and it would be awkward for her to take it on the bus."

I am not much of a multi-tasker and I was trying hard to coordinate getting dressed in the dark and thinking of all the things that I was not going to be able to do that day. I knew it was going to happen, and I tried hard to avoid the inevitable, but damn if I didn't stub my toe on the iron leg at corner of the bed.

"Damn! Damn!" I cried, tears welling up in my eyes as the pain shot up my leg. It didn't last long, because I bit my tongue the moment I grabbed my foot to rub it. Now the tears were flowing down my cheek. If there were any doubts in my mind at this moment, they were no longer part of the equation. It was not going to be a good day.

Suddenly, the room filled with a burst of light. In my exasperated state, I didn't realize that Glenn had gotten up and flipped on the wall switch.

"You know, Jean, turning on the light isn't going to ruin my sleep any more than you screaming in agony. Your trying to be considerate sometimes costs us both," he declared, pretending to be stern while trying to keep a smile from betraying his amusement at my pain.

I couldn't help but smile at him. It never failed to surprise me how calming his voice was. After almost twenty years of marriage, I still found myself deeply in love with him. His deep and sexy vocal tone was enough to make me melt, yet visually, he had so much more of an effect on me. His deep-set green eyes and thick, black eyelashes (which any woman would die for), combined with his chiseled facial features (which were probably a throwback to his one-sixteenth American Indian ancestry) would make any pain seem to fade away. How easy it was giving birth to my two children when I found myself staring into those gorgeous green eyes so many years ago.

"Sorry," I offered as I gave him a quick kiss on the lips. Taking a little bit more care now, I took my police-issued Glock 22 out of its lockbox and positioned it in my shoulder holster.

"Be careful out there, Jean—you're not easily replaced." His tone reflected his fatigue.

"Go back to sleep," I told him as I walked out the bedroom door. I walked down the hallway, and then stopped and backed up a bit as I passed my daughter's room. I took a peek and laughed to myself as I saw her spread diagonally across her canopied bed. She never did sleep from one end of the bed to the other. Even as a baby, she would lie across the crib corner to corner, as if she was compelled to take up the most space.

When she did crawl into bed with Glenn and me, we inevitably would end up sleeping on the living room couch, leaving her to enjoy our bed. I decided that if her father ever allowed her to grow up and get married, I would buy a king size bed for her and her husband. It would be a requirement for her to have a successful marriage.

I stepped over Roxy, the four-legged family member, who barely raised an eyebrow as I walked out of the house through the kitchen door. I pulled out of the garage, hoping that the squeal of the automatic door would not disturb my neighbors.

A full moon hung in the sky, illuminating my driveway, which is probably why I didn't notice that my headlights weren't on until I started driving down my street. I turned the knob on the dashboard and my headlights came on, spooking a cottontail, which sprinted in front of me. I barely missed turning it into road kill.

I didn't know what I was going to find at 125 Cedar Hill Road, but I knew it wasn't going to be pretty. Dead bodies usually aren't. I also didn't know whether I was going to find my partner, Joe, there—and if I did, what condition he would be in.

A light mist hit my windshield as the dark road loomed before me. These mountain roads were hazardous in the daylight, but at this time of the night, they could be downright treacherous. Too many fatalities happened on this very stretch of road, and I didn't intend to end up a statistic—tonight or any other night.

A cloud must have passed by and blocked the moon's light, so I turned on my high beams. The shafts of light looked like two colorless kaleidoscopes leading me down an endless dark tunnel.

One twenty-five Cedar Hill Road was on the outskirts of town, where the population of the town of Fallsburg is sparse, but affluent. A few of the homes could be considered mini-mansions. Several of them sat on the edge of the mountain with a view of the small city of Monticello below.

I was so intent on watching the road, fearing that a deer would decide it was a perfect time to cross the highway that I hadn't noticed the creature that was crawling up my right thigh. I felt the tickle first, and then I spied the damn thing creeping up my leg. I knew I shouldn't overreact—it was just a bug—but I was petrified.

Afraid to take my eyes of the road, and with my hands locked onto the steering wheel in a death grip, I used my peripheral vision to track it. This had to be the biggest roach I'd ever laid eyes on, and it was on me. My stomach was now in knots as I realized this creature had wings. I had to do something quick, before it took flight and landed on my face.

Taking a deep breath and trying not to take my eyes off the road, I took one hand off the wheel and made a fist. My jaw clenched and my stomach turned as my fist smashed down on my thigh and I felt the crunch under the base of my hand.

It was everything I could do not to scream in disgust as I rubbed my hand against my pants, trying to get the bug's outer shell and guts off my skin. Shuddering, I finally let my breath loose. I was feeling relieved, but that lasted for just a second. At that moment, my cell phone rang and shattered the silence.

Fumbling around, I grabbed the cell from my purse.

"Whitley," I blurted out my name.

"Jean, it's Marty, what's your ETA?"

"I'm just about there, Marty. They called you in?" I questioned him, my thoughts still drifting to the remains of the roach on my pants.

"They couldn't get hold of Joe," he told me almost apologetically. "I suppose I'm the next best thing." He paused for a second, and then, as if he carefully made a conscious decision how much he should say over the phone, he continued. "It's not pretty…well, you'll see when you get here."

I offered him a quick goodbye. I liked and respected Marty, but I was disappointed and angry that my partner was A.W.O.L. I was hoping Joe would pull himself together and get back on track.

It broke my heart that my best friend and mentor was on the verge of losing everything, but from his perspective, he already had. It had been two years since his wife, Connie, had died suddenly of cardiac arrest.

Connie and Joe were just about to celebrate their twenty-fifth anniversary when she succumbed to an undetected heart condition. Connie was like a sister to me and a surrogate aunt to my children, so a part of my world was shattered that day, as well.

Joe's daughter, Annie, was stationed in Afghanistan at the time, and returned to duty shortly after her mother's funeral. She was scheduled to return home to the states six weeks later, when Taliban militants ambushed her Humvee.

She survived, but suffered brain damage, and was still hospitalized at a VA hospital in Riviera Beach, Florida. The prognosis was sketchy, however, we held out some hope that Annie would be able to overcome an array of disabilities.

Now Joe was angry at the world, but more importantly, he was angry with God. When Connie was alive, she would drag Joe to church every chance she got, and although he bitched and moaned about it, I knew he felt a strong connection to his Catholic upbringing.

In the beginning, when Connie passed away, he found himself going to church on his days off. Instead of going to the Lion's Den, the local pub that served as a meeting place for off-duty cops, he found himself going to St. Mary's Church, where Connie and Joe were married over twenty-seven years ago. It was where his only daughter, Annie, was baptized and christened, and finally, where Connie was eulogized.

He admitted to me that he felt comfort and solace there, and that he felt his wife's spirit there—that is, until he got word of Annie's injuries. After that, as far as Joe was concerned, the devil had not only won more than his share of battles, the devil had won the war, and Joe was just another casualty.

My thoughts of Joe were interrupted as I came around a curve to 125 Cedar Hill Road. There I was met with an array of activity, illuminated by flashing red and blue lights of scattered official vehicles, some of them with their motors still running and their exhausts spitting out fumes.

Crime scene technicians were making their way into the woods and I followed closely behind them. Within a few minutes, I found myself in the mist of more activity. Yellow tape and evidence placards were strategically placed throughout the wooded area. I carefully walked a few steps forward praying it was only weeds and dirt I was stepping on. A few steps more brought me to a small clearing and there it was. Two officers were erecting a small pop-up canopy over a gray tarpaulin. I squinted, trying to get a more accurate view of what lay under the tarp. The moon was full and the glow from it seemed directly targeted on the spot and illuminating the area.

FACELESS: A MYSTERY ~ DAWN KOPMAN WHIDDEN

I closed my eyes, hoping that when I opened them, I would realize my first assumption was wrong. It wasn't too hard to imagine that underneath the tarp lay something or someone of small stature. I prayed silently that what had been discovered was not the body of a child.

My arrival had caught Detective Marty Keal's attention, and he made his way toward me.

Although the man may have been awakened from a dead sleep and been called in to work unexpectedly, Marty looked like he stepped out of a modeling photo shoot. He was 6'3" and broad-shouldered, with a body fat index which, I guessed, measured in the negative range. His physique was complemented by a mass of thick, black hair that fell in waves outlining a perfectly formed face dotted with dimples that stayed hidden until he smiled.

His physical beauty was only just a bonus to his warm personality. Detective Marty Keal was just a hell of a nice guy, and a pleasure to work with.

As luck would have it, Marty had been spending the night at his girlfriend's place when his cell phone rang. The address that the dispatcher gave him was less than a ten-minute drive from Hope's house. If he had spent the night at home with his dad, affectionately known by all as the "Captain" a name the old man had acquired while working as a corrections officer at the state penitentiary, it would have taken him three times as long to get to the scene.

He reached his destination pulling his unmarked car behind Officer Patricia Beck's cruiser, and grabbed a flashlight from the glove compartment.

Although a few large estates were scattered throughout the area, this particular spot was just on the outskirts of a wooded section. The full moon was shining brightly in the night sky, but a forest of tall pine trees cast dark shadows on the ground, making it difficult to see.

To make matters worse, and although Marty would deny it vehemently if asked, he suffered from ophidiophobia. Nothing could make Marty's skin crawl faster than a slimy, long reptile that made rattling and hissing noises.

Ten yards from the road, he spotted Officer Beck. She stood directly across from a young girl who seemed to be in emotional distress. He could hear Officer Beck's own voice quavering as she attempted to calm the girl down. As he got closer, he noticed two other girls standing in the shadows.

It was apparent that Beck, who was the first officer to arrive at the scene, was a little shell-shocked. She appeared to be desperately in need of reassurance. Even in the dim lighting, Marty could see that the pint-sized rookie's face was a ghostly white, with a slight green tint. She looked as if she was trying hard to keep whatever she had for dinner from making a re-appearance.

Marty couldn't blame her. He recalled puking in some bushes at a gory crime scene not that long ago.

"Patty, what do we have?" he asked as he tried inconspicuously to shine the flashlight across the faces of the three girls. He pegged them to be most likely high school age.

Grabbing hold of the crook of Marty's arm, Officer Beck turned to the girls. "We'll be right back, please try and relax…just stay right here." She turned back to Marty.

"It's bad, Detective Keal—real bad."

She turned on her flashlight, establishing a bright LED path ahead of them, and she led him toward the tree line. The sound of the weeds and small rocks beneath their shoes seemed to echo throughout the woods. Each crunch beneath their feet seemed to be magnified tenfold as they walked down an overgrown footpath.

Officer Beck stopped abruptly, causing Marty to bump into her.

"There." She pointed with her light a few feet ahead.

Marty followed the ray of the young officer's flashlight with his eyes.

He could make out a small body lying face up, surrounded by a mound of broken twigs and weeds. Naked from the waist up, the small exposed white breasts assured him that his first assumption of it being a female was correct. He shined his flashlight slowly up from the torso toward her head, which lay at an angle facing away from them.

Something seemed to be placed over her face, because he couldn't make out any of her features. He walked closer in order to get a better look.

His first thought was that someone had placed a blanket over her, or that she was wearing a mask of some sort, but he wasn't sure. He finally understood what it was as he caught a whiff of it. There was no mistaking it now; it was the distinct odor of burnt hair and flesh.

There was no mask and there was no blanket: whoever this was no longer had a face. Instead, there was just a charcoal mass of melted skin and muscle tissue.

He turned back to Officer Beck who was kneeling now, head between her knees, trying hard not to be sick.

Marty walked over and knelt next to her, his large palm gently rubbing her tiny back.

"Hey, you okay?" he asked, as he tried to swallow some bile of his own.

She nodded as her top teeth bit down on her bottom lip. It reminded him of that thing that Hope would do if she thought she was going to start to cry.

"Do you know who she is, Patty?" he asked her, still rubbing her back. "Do those girls know who she is?"

His hand rose and fell as he felt her inhale and exhale.

"They said that she is a friend of theirs, they all came up here together and she got separated from them. They went looking for her and…"

As they heard the sound of backup vehicles arriving they immediately both let out a sigh of relief.

"Come on," he said as he led her back down the path to where they had left the three girls. He could see the other officers and crime scene investigators exiting their cars as they reached the opening of the woods.

Somehow, he managed to go on autopilot and began the task of directing crime scene techs and officers to maintain the integrity of the crime scene. This was his first major case, and he knew that this would make or break his reputation as a Homicide Detective. He was determined to do everything right.

Yet there was more at stake here than his reputation. Everything he did from this moment on would be key to finding the animal that murdered the girl now lying faceless in the woods.

He prayed silently that Jean would arrive quickly. Marty knew that there was nothing better than the voice of experience.

Chapter Two

Jean

"What do we have, Marty?" I asked as he lifted the yellow crime scene tape so I could join him under the canopy.

I could tell by his expression that whatever it was had disturbed him.

Being an officer of the law, he had come upon death in many forms, including car wrecks or death caused by some illness. This was the second time he had come upon a very unnatural death.

Two years earlier, when Marty was still in uniform, he had been dispatched to a home for a well-care visit where he discovered ten-year-old Brad Madison covered in blood, playing a video game, while his parents lay bludgeoned to death in their upstairs bedroom.

It was the call that changed Marty's life. It was how he met Dr. Hope Rubin, his girlfriend. It also was the experience that inspired him to take the Detective's Exam—something that had previously only been a fleeting thought.

If I had to work with anyone besides Joe, I was happy that it was Marty. Marty didn't have the experience and knowledge that Joe had accumulated over his twenty-eight years in law enforcement, which I had always depended on. However, Marty was turning out to be a fast learner, and I hoped I could be even half the teacher and mentor to him that Joe was to me.

A couple of the techs muttered a tired hello to me and I nodded in reply. I glanced down as Marty knelt down and lifted the tarp. My stomach did flip-flops and the taste of vomit shot up my throat. Whoever it was no longer had a face.

I waited until Marty pulled the cover down lower. It appeared to be a young girl, naked from the waist up.

Marty dropped the cloth and stood up shaking his head.

"Do we know who she is?" I asked him. "Does she have any ID on her?"

"We didn't find anything in her possession, except for what appears to be a house key. Her friends say her name is Jamie Camp, age sixteen."

"Friends?" I looked at him, bewildered. As I turned, I realized that about thirty feet away from where we stood was a group of girls. In the dark, I had assumed everyone here was law enforcement.

"Yeah, the girls claim they were just messing around near the Forester house when one of them came up missing." He indicated by nodding his head in the direction of the assembly of young women.

"What do you mean, 'messing around'? What the hell were they doing out here in the middle of the night?" I shook my head in disgust as I started to walk over to the teenagers. I could hear a female officer trying hard to calm one of them down.

Even in the low light, I was able to recognize the officer by her slight figure. She was a rookie—Patricia Beck, barely five feet tall and weighing all of one hundred pounds in full dress uniform. Two of the girls she was talking with towered over her. But at this moment, it didn't matter that she herself looked like a teenager. The girls were looking at her for comfort and support.

Beck turned when she heard our footsteps approaching.

"Detective Whitley," she greeted me. I heard a slight tremor in her voice.

"Officer Beck, thank you, I'll take it from here." Apparently, she had been putting up a brave front for the girls, but I could see in her eyes that she was seconds away from losing it.

"Do you have any blankets in your vehicle, Officer Beck?" I asked her.

"Yes, ma'am."

"Why don't you gather up a few for the girls?" I suggested. "It's a little chilly."

"Yes, ma'am." She gave me a grateful look as she turned to the girls and told them that she would be right back.

I turned to Marty.

"Did you notify their parents yet?" I asked.

"No, I thought we would do that once we get back to the station," he replied. "I didn't want to drag any distraught parent out on these dark roads in the middle of the night."

"Good thinking, Marty. Let me just ask them a few questions and then why don't you get them back to the station. Call their parents and have them meet you there."

I turned to look at the girls again, only this time I took a good look. Two of them looked familiar to me, but I just couldn't place them.

The girl closest to me was about five foot four. A lone patch of her shoulder-length dark brown hair was streaked with a highlight of hot pink. A small diamond stud sparkled from her right nostril. She was the one who seemed the most distraught, and the one that Officer Beck was having the most difficulty trying to calm down.

The girl was sucking on her fingers, and as I got closer, I could see that each nail was well manicured and polished in black. Her thick black mascara was smeared below her eyes. The whites of her eyes had turned a pale pink, which emphasized the gray tint of her irises.

She was standing directly in front of a large rotting log, one of many that were scattered throughout the woods. I took her hand and sat down on the log, gently giving her arm a tug so that she would sit down with me. The thought briefly crossed my mind that I might be inviting a host of chiggers to join me as well.

"Honey, what's your name?" I fished through my purse, found a pack of Kleenex, and handed it to her. She wasn't looking at me, but had her eyes locked intently on the tallest of the three girls. I nudged her shoulder; it seemed to get her attention.

Looking down at the package of tissues, she took the pack. As she leaned over, I got a whiff of a strong fragrance on her clothes. It was apparent that she was trying to mask the odor of marijuana. I also caught a faint scent of alcohol on her breath.

"What's your name?" I asked.

"My name?" she said, repeating the question, as if she was confused.

"Yeah, your name—what's your name?" I repeated. She was obviously a bit disoriented.

"Lisa Padilla," she answered me this time, but kept her eyes on her friend, as if she was taking some sort of silent instruction from the taller girl.

After a moment, she answered me as if the other girl sent her some sort of cosmic message. "My name is Lisa Padilla; I want to go home, please." Her voice quivered. I wondered whether it was more of a reaction to the chill in the air than nerves.

"Lisa, can you tell me what happened here tonight? What were you girls doing out here this late?"

She didn't answer. I tried another question. "How did you get here?" I looked around, my eyes searching for a means of transportation. "Do you have a car?" I glanced at Detective Keal. He shook his head, indicating to me that there didn't seem to be a vehicle around.

Once again, I saw the tallest of the three make eye contact with Lisa. Again, she seemed to be sending her some kind of silent message.

"We...um...we hitchhiked up here." I thought I detected a slight wheeze in her breathing and her voice started to break as if she was starting to cry.

At that moment, Officer Beck came back with the blankets and gently laid one over Lisa's shoulders. She handed the other girls blankets as well. No one bothered to say "Thank you".

There was something so familiar about the taller girl. I felt that I had seen her before.

"What's your name?" I stood up and faced her.

"Katie Hepburn, my stepdad's Mayor Knox." She spoke with her mouth twisted in a sneer.

I could see that this took Marty by surprise. He looked at me and shrugged those broad shoulders of his. Apparently, this was news to him, as she hadn't given him that information before now.

"My parents are divorced, I live with my mother. I gave him my mother's address and phone number," she indicated, gesturing toward Marty.

She had a cocky attitude about her, as if she and her friends had been caught shoplifting instead of discovering her friends' faceless dead body lying in the woods, partially naked.

"And you?" I said, turning to the third girl. Smaller and slightly thicker in her waist than the other two, she seemed to be in some sort of stupor. When she didn't answer, I got up and walked over to her.

"What's your name?" I asked again.

She was looking straight at me, but I don't think she saw or heard a word I said.

I gently touched her arm.

"Her name is Tiffany." Katie answered for her.

This time it was my turn to speak in silent code. I sent Miss Katie Hepburn a stern look.

I guess she got the message, because Ms. Hepburn didn't speak again.

"Tiffany, do you have a last name?" I made an effort to sound compassionate, though my patience was running thin.

She nodded but didn't reply. I had to coax her.

"Tiffany…Tiffany what?"

"Bennett," she answered, but her eyes were focused over my shoulder at Katie Hepburn.

I tried to reposition myself so that she had to look at me alone.

"Tell me about your friend. Did you come up here with Jamie?"

She nodded a yes, her eyes drifting as if she was trying to connect with Katie. She seemed to be putting a lot of effort into not looking at me directly.

She kept making a slight movement with the right side of her mouth. It seemed Tiffany Bennett had some sort of nervous tic.

I turned my focus back to Marty.

"Marty, get the girls back to the station and call their parents." I leaned over and whispered to him to keep them separated. I received a nod from him before I even finished what I was going to say, letting me know that he understood.

Marty and I hadn't worked too many cases together, and until recently, homicides in our town were relatively scarce, but we seemed to have an uncanny ability to read each other's mind.

"Give me the name and address of the dead girl's family, I'll notify them."

I could tell by the look on his face that he was grateful that he didn't have to perform that duty. It was the part of the job that we all hated the most.

It was then that I realized just how angry I was with my missing partner. Joe always took the lead and gave the families the bad news. Now I had to tell some poor woman that her daughter was never coming home. I had to tell her that she would never plant another kiss on what was once her daughter's face. I had to be the one to inform her that her daughter probably spent her last minutes on this earth scared to death and in pain.

"Damn it, Joe, where the hell are you?" I thought I said it under my breath, but I must have been louder than I thought, because Marty heard me, and it prompted a reaction from him.

"Justin's working the graveyard shift and on patrol tonight. Do you want me to radio him and have him go to Detective Moran's house? See if he's okay?"

"No, he'll show up..." I replied.

I heard the sound of a vehicle approaching. The medical examiner's van had arrived. "I'll see you back at the station, I'm going to talk to the ME. I'll stop off on the way into town and get some breakfast burritos or something. I have a feeling it's going to be a long night."

I looked up as the moon started to fade behind a cloud and corrected that statement. "Long day. It's going to be a long day."

I turned my attention back to the leader of the pack.

"Katie, do you know if Jamie's family belongs to any church?" It always helped to have a minister, priest or rabbi with you when you informed the family, especially if it was a child that had died.

Maybe she was getting tired, or maybe I had gotten the wrong impression before, but now she answered me without the attitude. She almost sounded humble.

"Yes, ma'am, they belong to St. Mary's. Her mother is the secretary there."

"Thank you," I told her as Marty guided the girls into his vehicle for the ride back to the station.

Now it came to me why everyone looked so familiar. All these girls belonged to the same school and youth group at St. Mary's that my daughter Bethany belonged to. Now not only did I have to break the news to that poor girl's parents, I had to tell my daughter once again that something terrible had happened to someone she knew.

She still hadn't come to grips with the death of Joe's wife. Connie had been like a second mother to her. Then Annie came back from Afghanistan with a devastating brain injury and my daughter, who was twelve at the time, fell into that dark hole they call depression. Glenn and I were so concerned that we enlisted the help of Marty's girlfriend Hope, a child psychiatrist.

My daughter was now also feeling the loss of her "Uncle Joe," who was so wrapped up in his own sorrow that he couldn't see he was breaking my daughter's heart.

On top of that, Bethany's hero, her big brother Cliff, had gone off to college and she was having trouble adjusting to his absence.

I didn't relish coming home and giving her the news. I looked at my watch. It was almost five a.m. She would still be asleep and unaware of how her day would begin. I toyed with the idea of having Glenn keep her home from school. News of the girl's murder would spread like fleas in a kennel. I didn't want her to hear about it at school, but I had a job to do, and I couldn't shelter my child from the realities of life forever.

I turned to one of the officers who were just hanging around waiting for something to do.

"Rick, get the number of St. Mary's Parish and give Father Murphy a call. Explain to him what happened and have him call me."

I walked over to the medical examiner, deciding that when I was done here, I would call Glenn and have him make the decision of how we would inform my daughter about what had happened.

Robert Lyons served as the town's medical examiner. He was a fifty-four-year-old confirmed bachelor with a Harvard education, a throwback to the sixties era with a hippie persona. He had returned to his childhood home after becoming disillusioned while working in the trauma department at one of Boston's inner-city hospitals. He told me once that he couldn't deal with the expiration of someone's physical and spiritual being, but that he believed that the science of discovering why that person ceased to exist within our reality was his preordained future.

His vernacular was usually wasted on the majority of us cops while he performed his duties, but put a drink or two in him, or, as I sometimes suspected, a toke of some illegal substance, and he spoke just like the rest of us: "It sucks, watching someone die—especially a kid."

It boiled down to the fact that watching gang members, mostly children, shooting the crap out of each other had taken a toll on this sensitive man. Although he often was able to repair the damage inflicted on so many of these kids and save their lives, there was a percentage of those who did not survive. Watching those kids die in such a senseless way was not his cup of tea.

Anyway, Boston's loss was the town of Fallsburg's gain.

I got to him just as he was lifting the gray tarp that covered Jamie Camp's now-faceless body. He tossed it aside as you would a blanket getting out of bed. The girl now lay fully exposed. I saw several of the officers turn their faces, in either respect for the partially nude child or just in horror of what had been done to her. One or two seemed fixated on what they were seeing, drawn to it as a deer is to headlights.

When the ME lifted the gray tarp and exposed the body, the first thing my eyes were drawn to, was what at one time had been her face. The acrid scent of burnt flesh and hair still lingered in the air. Charred skin reminded me of a toasted marshmallow that was left in the fire a bit too long.

As Lyons knelt down and began a preliminary examination, taking her liver temperature to determine the time of death, and looking for other signs of injuries, my own eyes slowly took inventory of Jamie Camp's other physical attributes. She was petite— I guessed her to be five feet tall, maybe ninety-five pounds, if that much. Not flat-chested, but with small firm adolescent breasts. The bottom half of her body was attired in a pair of blue jeans that sat low on her waist, showing her to have a slight hourglass figure. Her belly button was adorned with a diamond stud that acted like a tiny prism, reflecting off the car high beams, which were aimed at her body to provide adequate light. She wore socks and a popular and expensive brand of leather sneakers. This very same type of sneaker sat in the bottom of my own daughter's bedroom closet.

I was just about to ask Lyons if he could determine the cause of death when Tommy Sullivan, known affectionately as Sully, approached us.

"Detective Whitley, we found a half-empty can of lighter fluid under some brush about thirty yards from here. We have it marked off and photographed, but I'm waiting for someone to get some material to make casts of what look like shoe prints. Do you want me to bag it and label it, or do you want to check it out first?"

"Leave it, Tommy, I'll be right there. Thanks," I told him.

"Sure, detective, no problem. Damn crazy people out there," he muttered as his teddy bear physique and signature duck walk carried him back in the direction from which he came.

I started to turn back to the ME as Tommy waddled away. I looked back in Tommy's direction.

"Hey," I called after him. "What about her blouse? Bra?"

He shrugged with what a decade ago had once been broad shoulders, but now appeared rounded and tired.

"Nothing," he answered me, shaking his head as he kept walking, never turning around.

"Do you think that's what caused the burns to her face, Rob? Does that look like burns from lighter fluid?" I asked Robert, who was standing now. His tall, lanky body reminded me of an overcooked green bean. His skin fell in deep creases, taking on the look of worn leather. His hair was tied back and woven into what had to be at least three feet of gray braid that swayed back in forth as he moved. I found myself picturing him playing the part of an aging surfer dude in one of those "Beach Blanket Bingo" flicks with Troy Donahue and Sandra Dee or Annette Funicello.

"Can't say with any degree of certainty, but it is categorically a distinct possibility that lighter fluid, a highly flammable, colorless liquid, could be the culprit. Sure as hell smells like it."

I smiled at his answer. Lyon's was so meticulous in his wording until the end, when he spoke in plain old English.

"What about cause of death? Any ideas?" I asked.

I wasn't an expert in forensics, but experience and a lack of blood on or around the girl's body made me fairly confident that Jamie Camp did not meet her demise by the use of a gun or knife.

'I would rather not presume anything at this point, detective." Kneeling back down, he carefully cradled the girl's head, gently lifting her neck back, trying to expose skin that was unaffected by the burns.

"There are no obvious ligature marks, no discoloration around her throat, but it's hard to tell, with the residue of the burns. Normally I would look for petechiae in the eyes, but her lids are burnt shut." His upper lip curled up in what I took to be a sign of disgust.

He gently laid her head down back on the ground. The way he did it reminded me of the care Glenn would take when Bethany was just an infant and he was laying her down in her crib. I pictured my daughter's tiny head cupped in the palm of her father's hand.

As he stood up, I heard a loud snap as he took off the latex gloves that protected his hands. He was a few years older than me, but you couldn't tell it by looking at his hands. His fingers were long and thin, almost feminine. In the shadow of the moonlight and with the lights coming from the high beams, I had perfect visibility. As hard as I tried, I couldn't find a blemish on them. It was as if the man's hands didn't belong with the rest of his body.

"Let's get her on the table; I prefer not to make any assumptions," he reiterated, adding, "I would make an educated guess, though, since rigor mortis is in full bloom, she has been deceased anywhere from one to four hours."

The officer that I had instructed to call St Mary's walked over to us. "Detective," he handed me his cell. "Father Murphy is on the line."

I mouthed a word of thanks as I took the phone from him.

"Sorry to bother you this early, Father, but I thought it would help for you to accompany me to the girl's home. Can you meet me there in about forty-five minutes?" I asked as I tried to make out the time on my wrist- watch. The face of the watch appeared blurry.

I hated to admit it, but this was becoming more and more of a problem. I knew it would be just a matter of time before I joined that group of aging baby boomers that I often saw turning the display of reading glasses in Wal-Mart.

I could hear the sleepiness in his voice when he answered me, but I could tell from the noises in the background that he was already in the process of getting dressed.

Father Murphy was what my mother would have described as a dapper young man. I knew many of his female congregation, of which I was a part, thought that the church's gain was every single woman's loss. Since I was suffering from a lack of sleep and that often made me a little slaphappy, I got giddy at the thought of the good Father stepping into his tighty-whities. Annoyed with my lack of professionalism and maturity, I compelled myself to visualize him placing the clerical collar around his neck instead.

I started to give him the address, but he informed me that he didn't need it. He reminded me that Jamie's mother was not only a parishioner, but also an employee. Before hanging up, he echoed my own feelings, "This is the part of the job I hate the most."

"Yeah, me too," I told him, before I handed the phone back to the officer.

I turned back to the medical examiner.

"Okay, Rob," I said. "I need to go inform her parents. Take care of her, will you?"

I knew he would. I knew that although he appeared to be emotionally detached because of his highly intelligent persona, it was just a defense mechanism. I had caught him tearing up and sniffling on more than one occasion, often blaming the distinct smell of death for his watery eyes.

Although we all try to hide our feelings sometimes, our body language betrays us, and we cannot conceal our emotions. Robert Lyons had trouble concealing his sadness. It was written all over his face.

I checked the time on my cell phone. The digital numbers were bigger and were much easier to read. I realized that by the time I got to the Camp's home, the family would be probably getting up and starting their day. I wondered if they even knew that their daughter was not safely tucked into her bed.

Shaking the thought from my mind, I walked over to where Tommy Sullivan was waiting for me with a crime scene technician. I glanced down at the can of lighter fluid. If there hadn't been a body lying a few yards away, it would seem perfectly natural, just the result of some careless litterbug disposing of his garbage in the woods…nothing out of the ordinary.

But this might not be just some ordinary can. This particular piece of trash could be the reason Jamie Camp's parents would not be able to have an open casket as they said goodbye to their daughter. This seemingly harmless eight-ounce can of Zippo brand lighter fluid could be the accelerant used to cause this child's mutilation.

Then it occurred to me— "Who the hell uses lighter fluid

anymore, anyway?" I didn't know they still sold the stuff. I thought that those flip-top style fluid lighters were as extinct as the dinosaur and eight-track tapes.

I was willing to bet that the three girls who came to the woods with Jamie Camp and found themselves leaving without her wouldn't have a clue what the can was, much less what it was used for.

Nevertheless, I could be wrong. At this point, taking a cue from Robert Lyons, I wasn't going to make any assumptions.

Besides, it wasn't even established that this can had held the accelerant that had caused Jamie's facial burns. It could be just some discarded trash.

I looked up at Tommy. A large, round head adorned the teddy-bear physique. His eyes had a weird form to them, almost triangular. Paint him orange, and he could get lost in a pumpkin patch.

"Okay, bag it and label it, Tommy. Assign an officer to protect the crime scene, and as soon as the sun is up, let's get a team out here and go over this area with a fine-tooth comb. Tommy, find out if anyone is presently residing in the Forester house, or if they have a caretaker. I'll see you guys later."

Stepping over weeds and sand spurs, which were grabbing onto the cuffs of my pants like a gaggle of Pac Mans, I made my way back to my car. I started to sit down, but I had a sudden vision enter my thoughts and I stopped abruptly. I decided to take a good look at the interior. It wouldn't hurt to make sure that the big, brown, ugly cockroach I killed didn't have a companion. Let's face it, I wasn't an entomologist, and I had no clue when roach-mating season was.

After a brief visual scan, I was somewhat satisfied that I was safe from any unwanted hitchhikers. With the key in the ignition, and feeling satisfied that I wouldn't be subjected to any more creepy-crawlers, I started my engine and headed back toward town to meet Father Murphy at the Camp residence.

Chapter Three

Thursday Morning

Fortunately, I arrived about a minute before the good Father. I was concerned that someone in the Camp family would notice the well- known and well-worn blue Lincoln that served as St. Mary's official vehicle sitting in front of their home. It's never a good sign to have an unexpected visit from the clergy or law enforcement.

My white unmarked Dodge could blend in easily on the quiet, tree-lined street, especially since the sun was just barely making its appearance in the eastern sky.

Even though I dreaded parallel parking, I chose a spot in front of an empty lot at the end of the block, leaving Father Murphy the convenience of parking in the Camp's driveway.

He chose instead to park directly across from me. I noticed a small, amber light being extinguished and a faint swirl of smoke as he made his way out of the car. He looked at me, embarrassed that I caught him smoking, but Father Murphy could charm the pants off an old maid, and he knew it.

"Remember, Jean," he looked at me brushing ashes off his overcoat. "I know all your deep, dark secrets."

"Your secret is safe with me, Father," I assured him. We both knew he was tossing out idle threats, since I hadn't been to confession since eighth grade, and we both knew it. However, the task ahead was daunting and a bit of humor was what we both needed right now.

For the next five minutes, I gave him only the pertinent details of the horrific condition in which we had found Jamie Camp. Even though everything I said to him would be confidential in nature, I didn't feel the necessity to give him information that needed to remain available to only the investigators of the case. The case was a homicide, and the department could not afford to leak any information that might make it more difficult to arrest and convict the monster that did this.

Father Murphy needed as much detail as possible in order to

comfort the family after I left. If it had been my precious daughter lying in the morgue, I would want answers. No—I would demand answers.

"Ready?" I asked him as we started up the path that led to a charming two-story redbrick home. As I spoke, a light appeared in what looked to be an upstairs bathroom.

"As ready as one can be under the circumstances, Jean." He took a deep breath and rang the doorbell.

It was a musical chime and the tune "Memories" came floating through the air. The sound was muffled through the door, yet I could still make out a woman's voice rising in volume as she headed toward the front door. As she came closer, I could make out what she was saying. She was calling out to her husband. "Garrett, someone's at the door. Garrett!"

I figured it was probably Garrett who turned on the upstairs bathroom light. I prayed silently that Garrett would join the woman before she opened the door.

Another light came on in the house and I saw a hand lifting one of the slats of the venetian blinds that hung over the front window. Mrs. Camp peered out, trying to see who was ringing her doorbell at 6:15 in the morning. She must have recognized either Father Murphy or me, because she didn't bother to ask who was knocking at this ungodly hour. She immediately undid the deadbolt and opened the door.

Her first thought was that her elderly neighbor, Mrs. Thomas, who had been stricken with pancreatic cancer, had passed away and the priest was here to ask her help comforting the woman's husband. It was almost as if she was expecting him. She smiled at me, but didn't seem concerned with my appearance.

"Father Murphy, good morning." She clutched her robe tightly, now embarrassed that she had come to the door still in a nightgown. She made an effort to fix her unruly hair by patting it down with her hand.

"Is it Mrs. Thomas?" she asked Father Murphy. Without waiting for an answer, she continued talking. "Poor man...I'll get dressed and get right over there."

"Who is it, Patty?" Garrett, slightly balding and at least a foot taller than his wife, walked down the stairs buttoning a recently dry-cleaned white shirt. Mrs. Camp, noticing the dry cleaning tag was still attached to her husband's collar, walked over and gave it a tug, removing it. She stuck the tag it in her robe pocket.

Garrett, slightly embarrassed by his wife's action, nodded to Father Murphy and then looked at me. It was obvious by his expression that he recognized me, although he wasn't quite sure from where.

"It's Father Murphy, Garrett. Poor Mrs. Thomas passed on…"

"Patty, may we come in?" Father Murphy asked her, but keeping his eyes on her husband Garrett. It didn't go unnoticed by her husband.

"Oh, yes…sorry, where are my manners? Please." She opened the door wide.

"When did it happen?" Mrs. Camp asked him. "Can I get you something to drink? Garrett, can you make Father Murphy some coffee?" She turned to me, not questioning my appearance, as if it was perfectly natural.

"No, thank you, no. Mrs. Camp…" I started to tell the woman the bad news when was interrupted by Father Murphy. What normally my missing partner would do, the good Father did, and gave me a reprieve.

"Patty, can we sit somewhere?" he asked, looking around. A modern pit sofa of brown leather took up a good deal of the living room area.

I could tell that the woman was starting to realize that she had been mistaken, and our visit was not about the elderly woman next door.

Her face showed signs of being thoroughly confused now. She glanced over at me and then at her husband. Garrett gently put his hand on his wife's back.

"What is it?" he asked, now looking directly at me.

"Please, Garrett—is there somewhere we can sit down?" Father Murphy repeated.

Garrett's other hand gestured for us to go in front of him and directed us to find a seat on the sofa.

Mrs. Camp sat down opposite us. Leaning forward, she took her husband's hand. He remained standing.

"Father, what is it? What's wrong?" Now the poor woman was starting to think that it was the priest who was in need of her support.

"Patty, I'm sorry." He took her other hand in his. "I am afraid this is about Jamie."

Her head jerked back in surprise. Her chin seemed to become more prominent "Jamie? What are you talking about, Father?"

"I am afraid Patty, that there has been an…"

He started to stutter. I could tell he was going to say "accident," but thought better of it.

"A terrible tragedy," he continued.

Patty exhaled. She let out a small chuckle; now realizing it was all some sort of mix-up.

"Jamie's fine, Father…she's still sound asleep." She turned to her husband. "Honey, go wake up Jamie." She glanced at a wall clock. "It's time she got up for school, anyway."

Garrett didn't move. She repeated herself.

"Garrett, go wake up Jamie." This time it sounded more like a demand.

"She's not in her room; I thought she was down here." He answered her, his eyes never leaving mine.

"Don't be ridiculous. Of course, she is in her room…Jamie, come down here!" she hollered.

When she got no reply, I noticed her facial expression changed and she started to panic. She turned her attention back to me.

"What's going on?" She stood up, calling her daughter's name again. Getting no answer, she walked briskly to the stairway leading to her daughter's bedroom. "Jamie, Jamie, come down here." This time she was sounding a little more panicked. Still getting no answer, she ran up the stairs, her husband right behind her.

Frantic now, she called her daughter's name a few more times. After standing on the landing, motionless and confused for a few moments, she finally made her way back down the stairs.

"Where is she?" She turned to me, her eyes shooting darts in my direction, demanding an answer. Her husband tried to lead her back to the couch. She violently brushed his hand away.

"I'm sorry, Mrs. Camp, Jamie's body was found a few hours ago in some woods outside of town. I am afraid she was murdered. I am so sorry." I was fighting so hard for my throat not to close. I felt my vocal chords tightening, and my eyes were beginning to burn.

"There must be some mistake." She shook her head, her hand clutching the small silver cross that hung from her neck.

She was still looking for one of us to tell her that it couldn't be true.

Father Murphy got up just in time. The poor woman suddenly turned white as a sheet and collapsed. He caught her just before she hit the floor.

I kicked myself for not having had the foresight to see that something like this would happen.

I should have realized that I would be delayed in getting back to the station. I called Marty and asked him to start interviewing the girls. I was a little worried about this being his first major interview in what might turn out to be an important homicide case, but I had no other choice. I had a lot of faith in the young detective, but he was not an experienced interviewer, and even one small mistake could have incredibly disastrous repercussions.

Although Mr. Camp, a CPA by trade, was as shocked and grief-stricken as his wife, he managed to take control of the situation in a way that only a mathematician can. Logically and in a precise manner, he managed to call paramedics for his wife. Begging our forgiveness, he spent the next half hour making phone calls.

He called in a friend and neighbor to come over to help tend to Jamie's four-year old brother, who was still sleeping soundly in a bedroom upstairs, and his own brother to inform the rest of his family of the tragedy that had struck like a tornado in the middle of the night.

The house became a flurry of activity in no time, with Mr. Camp directing the now present EMTs and the concerned and inquisitive friends and neighbors like a stage manager in a Broadway play.

Once he was convinced that his wife was out of physical danger, he joined us in the kitchen, where Father Murphy and I had gone to allow the EMTs to care for Mrs. Camp.

"I'm sorry if I have ignored you, I can assure you that it wasn't my intention, it's just..." his voice broke.

"No apologies are necessary, Mr. Camp, you are doing what you need to do for your family. Is your wife going to be okay?" I knew the woman would never again be okay, but I hoped he realized I was talking about her immediate physical condition.

"Patty has a slight heart murmur, which is a concern of ours, but they gave her a pretty strong sedative. Right now she is sleeping, but I wonder if sedating her was a good idea. I don't want her waking up thinking this was nothing more than some nightmare."

Father Murphy and I nodded in unison.

"I know this is a very difficult time Mr. Camp, but do you think you can answer a few questions for me?"

He looked around the kitchen and then turned his attention back to me.

"Can I get you some coffee? I need some coffee. Um, Father? Detective? We have one of those single-cup things. Tea?"

"Yes, coffee would be fine, thank you," I answered him.

"Garrett," Father Murphy stood up. "Why don't you let me do that? Please relax, sit down before you fall down."

Mr. Camp gestured for the priest to remain seated.

"No, Father, please—I need to do this, I need to stay busy. I'm afraid that if I stop moving, I will crash. I can't afford to do that."

Reluctantly, Father Murphy sat back down. "Okay Garrett, coffee…just black, please," he said.

Mr. Camp turned to me, looking for my preference.

"Cream and one sugar, please," I told him.

I could see his hands were trembling as he prepared the coffee. He managed to get all three mugs to the table without spilling a drop.

I waited until he was seated and took his first sip before I started my interview.

"I got the feeling that you and Mrs. Camp were surprised that Jamie was not at home last night, is that right?"

He nodded his head. He lifted his right hand, pinched the bridge of his nose, and then spread his thumb and index finger across the bones below his eyes.

"Yes…she…I thought she was in her bed; when I looked in her room this morning and didn't see her, I just thought she got up early and was downstairs having breakfast or on the computer. We don't allow her to use the computer in her room, we are very…well, we like to keep an eye on…"

He stopped mid-sentence. He reached into his pocket and took out a handkerchief to wipe his eyes.

"I know it's kind of futile, trying to keep her from using the computer without our knowledge, but we try to keep abreast of what she is doing and what she is looking at. We hear so many horror stories."

I could tell by the expression on his face that he just made some sort of connection. One of those horror stories had just become more than a story, it had become reality.

"What happened? What happened to my daughter? You said she was murdered. How? Why? Are you sure that it's Jamie? I need to see her. Where is she?"

I knew there really was no way I was going to soften the blow for this man, so I just was as honest and as forthcoming as possible.

"She was found in the woods at the northern end of town, not far from Route 42, near the Forester mansion. Her friends said she came up missing, so they went looking for her. They found her body just at the edge of the woods."

"Her friends? What friends? What the hell is going on?" He had his hand wrapped around his coffee mug, his knuckles were turning white his grip was so tight. "What was my daughter doing up there? I thought she was in bed."

He raised the coffee mug to his mouth, but he was trembling so hard that some of the liquid splashed out and stained the neatly pressed white business shirt that he had put on just an hour ago. Immediately he made an effort to wipe the brown liquid from staining the shirt, but gave up after a few seconds.

I looked at my notebook and read him the names of the three girls that were now with Marty. I didn't see much of a reaction when I read off Tiffany Bennett and Lisa Padilla's names, but I did seem to get some reaction when the name Katie Hepburn was mentioned.

"Mr. Camp? Do you know these girls?"

"Yeah, I know them. Tiffany and Lisa have been friends with Jamie for years. Katie was…I didn't know that they had reconciled. There was an incident awhile back, and Katie and my daughter weren't getting along."

"What kind of incident, Mr. Camp?" I asked, my interest in his answer now piqued.

"What the hell were they doing up there? How did they get there? None of those girls drive, do they?" He looked at me for answers—answers I knew I couldn't give him.

I repeated my question. "What kind of incident, Mr. Camp?"

"Oh, I'm sorry, I didn't mean to ignore the question, I just…this is just so…"

"I know Mr. Camp, I completely understand, please take your time."

He turned his attention to Father Murphy. The distraught father's eyes seemed to be speaking a language of their own. It was times like these that people with faith would just cling onto their beliefs for dear life, or fall by the wayside, like my partner Joe had now done.

I got the impression from the look that Mr. Camp was now giving Father Murphy is that he would fall into that first category, and hang onto his faith like a captain on his ship during a ferocious storm.

"Some boy Jamie and Katie had some sort of falling out over a boy. I think that Katie was giving Jamie a hard time about this kid. My wife knows more about it than I do. Apparently, they actually got into some sort of physical brawl over him. They both got suspended from school for a week. My daughter was punished and she missed out on one of her modeling jobs because she was grounded. She was not a happy camper."

He started to smile at his own joke, an expression that the family probably used often, and then, once again, reality slapped him in the face.

"Your daughter was a model?" At that moment, it had occurred to me that I had not seen any photographs of Jamie or her family in the two rooms that I had been in. The living room walls were adorned in what appeared to be expensive oil paintings. The kitchen in which we now sat had on one wall a clock and a calendar. An intricately carved large wooden spoon and fork decorated another.

I turned around to see if I could see back into the living area. A rounded archway separated the two rooms. From where I sat, I could just make out the edge of one of the oil paintings of a landscape. Other than that, the walls were barren.

I found it odd that there were no family photos. In my home, dozens of photographs of my kids' faces adorned the walls and any other spot a frame could occupy.

If Jamie's face had not been so horribly disfigured, I probably would have had the same feeling that I had had with the other girls, that she looked familiar. But now I realized that I had no idea what Jamie Camp had looked like in life.

"Yes, Detective, Jamie was just starting to get some work as a model. She was hoping to earn enough money to buy a car. My wife and I tried to dissuade her from that type of career, because we didn't want her to become shallow and vain, but we didn't want to keep her from pursuing her dreams. Jamie was blessed with a natural beauty, but we want our children to be more than what she was on the outside. She's…she was beautiful…isn't she, Father?"

I couldn't help but notice that he kept on mixing up his tenses. He was having trouble referring to his daughter in the past tense.

"Do you have a picture of your daughter, Mr. Camp?" I asked him.

"You didn't see her?" I saw a spark of hope in his eyes. "Then how do you know it's Jamie? Look, I want to see my daughter; I want to make sure you have the right girl. Maybe you're mistaken."

He pulled out his wallet from his back pocket and handed it to me. It was opened to a wallet-sized picture of his daughter.

It wasn't just a father's bias talking when he said his daughter was pretty. The girl was stunning. Long blond hair framed a heart-shaped face. Her cheekbones were prominent, but not too sharp. A mouthful of perfectly straight white teeth made up a captivating smile. It now was that much more real to me, as I was saddened by what was taken from this family.

I turned to Father Murphy, hoping that he would answer the man.

"Garrett." He took the other man's hand in his. "Garrett, something terrible was done to Jamie, something beyond explanation. I'm afraid that seeing her would not be a wise idea."

Mr. Camp looked bewildered. "What are you talking about Father, what did they do to her?"

"I'm afraid that Jamie was burned, Garrett. Someone burned your daughter's face beyond recognition."

It was at that moment that all the self-control that Mr. Camp had showed until this point had abruptly slipped away. The man let out a deep and agonizing howl, and then broke into sobs that were so intense that they violently shook the table. I found myself holding down the table to stop the coffee from spilling out of my mug.

CHAPTER FOUR

MARTY
Thursday Morning

Marty decided to start his interview with what he considered the top of this particular teenage hierarchy.

The statuesque and somewhat exotic looking Miss Katie Hepburn seemed to be the leader of the pack, and Marty wanted her away from the other girls as soon as possible.

He had been uncomfortable with the teenager's behavior from the moment he arrived at the scene. He couldn't shake the feeling that the girl was not being completely up-front with her answers. He also had a nagging feeling that she was acting a bit flirtatious.

He found her behavior suspicious for a young girl who had just found her friend not only dead, but also in an extremely grotesque condition.

He walked her into an interrogation room.

"Why don't you have a seat? I'll be right back," he told her, and then asked, "Can I get you a soft drink or some coffee, Katie?"

He flashed a dimpled smile at her. If she was going to flirt with him, he was going to take full advantage of any vulnerability he could find, just in case she had some knowledge about her friend's death.

She looked around the room as if she was judging the furnishings. She pulled a chair away from elongated table in the middle of the room, using the very tips of her carefully manicured fingers, as if she was afraid she would catch a disease from the seat.

Katie nodded her head. "I'll have a Diet Coke."

And, as if she had an afterthought "Can I have my cell phone back? I think I should call my mother."

One of the first things that Marty did when he arrived at the scene was to separate all three girls from their phones. He wanted to be in control of whom the girls spoke to before he got a chance to interview them. He knew that legally he couldn't interview them without a lawyer or parent present, but he wanted to make sure no one else was able to speak to the three girls before he had the opportunity.

Marty turned back and looked at her.

"We've notified your parents, Katie, they're on their way." He stopped as he held the door open. "You'll get your phone back before you leave."

"You called my dad?" she asked him as she twirled a strand of her long dark hair around her finger. For the first time, a spark of real emotion crossed her face.

"I'm sorry…we called your mom and your stepdad. Would you like us to call your father, Katie? Does he live in town?"

"No, don't bother." She turned back around, clearly disappointed.

There were times Marty wished he had his girlfriend Hope's ability to read body language, but he was pretty sure that he was reading Miss Hepburn's correctly. It took just the mention of her father to evoke a real emotional response. For a brief moment, a look of real pain traveled across her face, but just as fast as it appeared, it seemed to disappear, leaving her with a cold, blank expression.

"I'll be right back," he said again as he walked out, gently closing the door behind him. Not paying too much attention to his surroundings, he walked immediately into the brick wall otherwise known as Detective Frank Robinson.

"You scared the crap out of me Frank! Could you be a little more obvious, and not walk around like a damned cat?"

Marty could never grasp how someone with Frank's build could float around a room like a ghost. The six-foot-two-inch, 215-pound detective worked out a minimum of two hours a day, and his body reflected it. The Brooklyn native, a product of a mixed marriage between a Caucasian mother and black father, had a dark toasted-almond complexion that stretched tightly over his chiseled physique like a surgeon's latex glove

The man walked around constantly flexing his pecs as if they were dancing to the rhythm of a tune only he could hear. As big as he was, though, Frank had an uncanny ability to enter or leave a room without being noticed.

"Sorry, buddy," he told the younger detective. "His Honor, the

Mayor, and the first lady are in the building, and they are demanding to see their daughter."

He deliberately over-emphasized his Brooklyn accent as he spoke. It was apparent to Marty that the mayor or his wife had said something to tick Frank off.

∽

Thursday Morning

Leaving Father Murphy behind with the distraught family, I started to get into my vehicle when it hit me that I hadn't called home.

I looked at my watch; it was just a quarter past eight. My daughter was probably sitting at the kitchen table, finishing up her Lucky Charms and arguing with her father about her choice of wardrobe for the day.

We had taken her out of the public school system because Glenn and I felt that they lacked what she needed academically and emotionally. She was now at St. Mary's Parochial School. The school no longer required the students to wear the plaid school uniforms of the past, so sometimes wardrobe choice was a bit of a battle.

I knew I had about five minutes to spare before he took off to bring her to school, science project and all.

I was glad my husband answered, and not Bethany.

"Hey, we are just on our way out the door," he greeted me.

"Tell her she doesn't have to go to school today," I said. "Um, can you go in late? Actually, do you think you can take the day off?"

I heard him put something down. I heard my daughter's voice in the background. A muffled sound told me he placed his hand over the mouthpiece, but I could still hear as he called out to Bethany. "I'll be right there, honey."

"What's going on?" he asked, adjusting his volume so he wouldn't be yelling into the phone, yet loud enough that I could hear and my daughter couldn't.

"One of the girls from Bethany's school was murdered. I think she may know her, but even if she doesn't, I just would prefer that we, or you, tell her and she doesn't hear about it at school."

"How? Do we know the family?" he asked.

"Her mother, Patty Camp, is a secretary at St Mary's. I've…"

"Garrett Camp?" he interrupted me.

"You know him?" It hadn't even occurred to me that my husband might know the family.

"I went to school with him, we played golf together just last week. Oh my God, what happened?"

I heard my daughter's voice again. Again, he covered the phone with the palm of his hand.

"Can you handle this, Glenn?" I asked him. I was really starting to feel guilty that I was abandoning my maternal obligations.

"Yeah, babe, it'll be okay, I got it," he assured me.

Maybe if this were any other man, or any other father, I would have hesitated to have him talk to a fourteen-and-a-half-year-old about the murder of someone she knew. But I was confident that Glenn would handle the situation with sensitivity and courage.

I often felt jealous of the ability he had in discussing sensitive issues with our daughter. Too many times lately, whenever I would talk to Bethany, it would erupt into an argument.

After one of those recent arguments, I pictured her newly acquired hormones emitting hundreds of star-like particles, bursting out from her developing body like a sparkler on the Fourth of July. In response, my tired body was retaliating with its aging hormones, fighting them off like that arcade game "Asteroids" we used to play as a kid.

"Okay, I'll call you later. Thanks. I love you, Glenn."

"I love you too, Jean." He must have heard the concern in my voice. "Don't worry, she'll be fine."

"I know," I said, trying to believe it myself as I disconnected the call.

∾

I arrived at the squad room just as the shifts were changing. Normally the men and women who worked the graveyard shift would scurry to get into their personal vehicles and take off for home. Today, I noticed that they were all lingering, trying to get as much information about the murder as possible.

The three girls who arrived with Marty stirred up their curiosity, and the place was buzzing with theories and suspicions. Several of them had kids that went to St. Mary's, so their curiosity was a little bit more personal.

"So where are those breakfast burritos you told Marty you were going to bring in?"

I turned to Kathy, the department's only other female veteran plainclothes detective. She was six feet tall and liked to refer to herself as "big boned." Sometimes I think she intimidated the suspects more than some of our male counterparts, and she took great delight in doing it.

"Crap, sorry, I completely forgot. Is there anybody we can send out?"

"Already did," she replied. "They're on the coffee table in the chief's room. I had to threaten some of the guys with bodily harm if they didn't leave you something."

"Thanks, you're the best, Kathy." I walked into the chief's office and grabbed a breakfast burrito off the desk. I knew it would be cold, but I was disappointed just the same.

I grabbed a coffee cup off the makeshift table that served as my boss's own personal dining area. The chief brought in his own fresh coffee beans from Starbucks and it was forbidden for any of us to help ourselves to his personal stash, but what the man didn't know wouldn't hurt him.

"Oh, yeah," she continued, "the chief just called in…he's at the school with Father Thomas and the school board members. They decided to close the school for the day. Some of the teachers volunteered to stay with kids who aren't able to go home because they don't have anyplace to go until their parents come get them. Someone said that they got hold of Marty's girlfriend to do some grief counseling."

I was glad to hear that they were bringing in someone with Dr. Hope Rubin's experience. Marty's girlfriend, whom I considered a good friend, was a child psychiatrist who worked at the Armistice Mental Health Institution for Children. The hospital was a facility that housed children with violent and criminal behaviors. She was well prepared to deal with the type of emotional reaction that some of the kids at the school were bound to experience.

I just hoped my daughter wouldn't require her services again—

which brought up a question I wasn't sure I wanted to know the answer to, but before I made my way upstairs to see how Marty was making out, I turned to Kathy.

"Has anyone heard from Moran?"

She looked at me, her eyes wide in surprise.

"You don't know?" she asked.

"Know what?" I looked around the squad room. Everyone was still milling around.

Kathy walked over and shut the door.

"What's going on, Kathy? Come on, I can't take any more crap today. I'm tired."

"I'm sorry, Jean, I thought you knew. I thought someone told you. I thought Joe would have told you." She pushed a few papers out of the way and sat her large frame on the boss's desk.

"What?" I was bracing myself for more bad news.

"Joe called up the chief yesterday and told him he needed some time off. He was on his way the VA hospital in West Palm Beach. His daughter tried to take her own life yesterday, but they stopped it just in time. I guess the injuries she sustained in Afghanistan and the PTSD just became too overwhelming. I'm sorry, Jean...I know how close you all are."

Now it was my time to sit down. Kathy's foot was resting on the arm of one of the chairs that was in front of the chief's desk. She pushed it toward me with her shoe, rolling it close enough for me to grab. I pulled it toward me and sat down. The cheap vinyl seat let out a whoosh as I landed.

I couldn't understand why Joe didn't confide in me. It hurt to realize that Kathy knew all of this, and I didn't. He was my partner...my best friend...or at least, that is what we once were to each other. Next to Glenn, there was no one I trusted in this world more.

I just didn't know anymore. I didn't know whether to be angry or feel compassion for the man. Yes, his world was torn apart and turned upside down, but didn't he realize that mine was, too. Yes, he lost Connie, his wife of twenty-five years, yes, his only daughter was terribly injured while serving her country, yes, he lost them both.

But I had lost all three of them, I thought selfishly. I lost him, I lost my best friend to liquor and anger and bitterness.

I stood up. I knew I had to get my act together and now concentrate on finding the creep that killed this young girl.

"What's going on with the girls? Did anybody else but Marty interview them?" I asked her, totally changing the subject.

"Frank is working with him." She must have thought the expression on my face pertained to Frank, because she tried to defend him. "Frank's a good interviewer, Jean."

"Yeah, I know." I told her, still disturbed by what she told me about Annie. It should have been Joe that told me. Once upon a time, he would have confided in me. I realized she was still talking.

"The mayor is here and he's making some demands. This thing is going to be one hell of a mess, Jean. It had better resolve itself quickly, or heads are going to roll. The reporters have shown up already. I think I convinced them to head over to the school—let the chief deal with them."

"Good idea," I replied. "I don't need them here right now, we have enough to deal with. I'm going to see what's doing upstairs. Maybe Marty got some answers."

She gave me a sympathetic look and put her hand on my back as she followed me out the door.

"Joe will come around, Jean. Give him some time. Connie was his world, and Annie is his universe. He'll come around."

She was trying to convince me, but I knew she really was as worried about Joe as I was .We both knew that he was in a world of pain and his behavior and drinking were spiraling out of control.

I didn't say anything else, because there was nothing more to say. I headed up the stairs to the turmoil that awaited me next. As I climbed the stairs, each step seemed to have swollen to twice its normal size. I was physically and emotionally drained.

I used to love this job. I used to take situations like this in stride. Cases like this would get my adrenaline churning resulting in a burst of energy. A murder like this should have incited my anger and made me anxious to solve the case and put away some crazy freak for the rest of his or her natural life.

But I wasn't feeling angry or anxious. I was feeling downright depressed, and I was lacking my usual confidence. I knew I needed to shake it off, so before I got all the way up the stairs I took a deep breath, gritted my teeth and said a few expletives under my breath. Joe would have told me to chill out…but Joe wasn't here.

CHAPTER FIVE

MARTY

Marty heard the mayor before he saw him.

The man's voice trumpeted through the hallway like a bull elephant's cry in the jungle. Turning from Frank, who gave him a look of despair, he caught sight of His Honor making his way up the stairwell, pushing one of the uniformed officers to the side. Behind him was the first lady of Fallsburg, looking mortified.

"Don't give me this crap, officer, I demand to see my stepdaughter!"

"Mr. Mayor, please..." The officer tried to block his way, but the husky politician was having no part of it.

"Get out of my way, kid, before I have your job!" he hollered, spraying spittle in the officer's face.

Marty stood at the top of the stairs, looking down at the bad comb job the mayor used to hide his balding and lumpy scalp. He figured that this was as good a time as any to come to the officer's rescue.

"That's not necessary, mayor. Marty called out, trying to be as diplomatic as possible.

The mayor, who was as wide as he was tall, had a tendency to try and throw his weight around. Marty knew that Paul Knox was more hot air than substance, and he knew that the mayor knew that he knew it.

The minute Knox saw Marty at the top of the stairs, his whole attitude changed.

"Marty! Good, you're here. This imbecile won't let us see my stepdaughter. She needs her mother right now."

Katie's mother stood behind him, looking intimidated. Although Marty was well acquainted with Paul Knox, he had never met the mayor's second wife. The platinum blonde was at least three inches taller than her husband, even though she was wearing flats.

Marty nodded to the young officer who had been trying to keep the mayor from gaining access to the interrogation room.

"It's okay, Stiskin, I got this."

Relieved, the young officer made his way back down the stairs, deliberately bumping the husky politician as he passed him on the narrow stairwell, tipping his hat to the mayor's wife as he descended.

The mayor watched intently and waited for the officer to get out of sight before he climbed to the top of the landing in an unsuccessful effort to appear closer to Marty's eye level.

"What the hell happened, Keal, what is this about Katie being a witness to a murder?"

He must have recalled at that moment he was with his wife, who appeared frozen a few steps below him, because he suddenly turned his attention to her. He climbed back down a few steps and placed one chubby palm under her elbow, guiding her up the rest of the stairs.

"Your stepdaughter is fine, Paul. I was just going to get her a soft drink. Can I get something for either of you? Mrs. Knox?"

"No, nothing, thank you. Can I see my daughter?" the blonde asked him.

Marty took a good look at the woman. She had the same exotic features that made her daughter so striking and conceded that the woman was probably quite beautiful once herself. But now the mayor's wife looked tired and worn. He could hear his father's voice as he recalled one of the old man's favorite expressions, "Rode hard and put up wet." It seemed a fitting way to describe the lady.

Marty turned to Frank, who had been standing on the sidelines watching the exchange.

"Frank, could you bring a few refreshments up? I'll bring them to see Katie."

"Yeah, sure, Marty. Mayor, can I get you a soda?"

With a smile and a wink, Frank signaled to Marty that the older and more experienced detective wasn't insulted that Marty was taking the lead in the investigation.

Turning back to the mayor and the second Mrs. Knox, Marty motioned for them to follow him.

"Tell me what's going on, Marty." He once again resorted to acting passive and friendly. Paul Knox, the career politician and occasional attorney, was never without a motive. The mayor calculated that the familiarity would allow Marty to speak more freely.

Marty turned and leaned his back against the door of the room where Katie waited.

"One of Katie's friends was murdered last night, Paul; we're trying to find out what happened."

"Who?" Katie's mother grabbed her husband's hand. "What friend?"

"A girl named Jamie Camp. Do you know her?" Marty asked looking directly at the blonde woman.

She gasped, bringing her hand to cover her mouth. "Oh my God—Jamie? How?"

"What does this have to do with Katie, Marty?" The mayor put a protective arm around his wife.

"Did either of you know that Katie wasn't home last night?" He once again directed his question to the girl's mother.

"She said she was spending the night at Tiffany's. I didn't think that Katie had anything to do with Jam…" she stopped midsentence and turned to her husband. Marty could see the woman getting exceedingly nervous.

"Well, how about we go in and ask Katie what she knows? Maybe she can shed some light on what happened last night."

Marty opened the door and noticed Katie's relieved expression immediately when she saw her mother. The relieved expression disappeared just as fast when she saw who accompanied her.

Getting up, the girl quickly turned her attention back toward her mother and fell into the older woman's arms. Marty, watching the scene unfold, noticed that although Katie seemed to find comfort in her mother's embrace, her eyes seemed to be riveted on her mother's husband.

Mrs. Knox took her daughter's face in her hands and pushed some stray hairs away that had fallen over the girl's right eye. Suddenly Katie's dry eyes began filling up with moisture, and fresh tears began to fall. Her mother wiped them away, gently kissing her daughter's cheeks.

"Oh, my poor baby, what happened, honey?" The older woman asked, taking a seat at the table, as if she was in too much emotional stress to continue standing.

Frank came back into the room at that moment and handed Katie her Diet Coke. The teenager took a seat next to her mother, once again using just the tips of her fingers to move the chair into position.

Once she was seated, the mayor found a seat at the head of the table, as if to make sure he was in a position of authority. Behind the mayor's back, Frank sent Marty a look, rolling his eyes in a way Marty assumed to mean that the other detective had little use for the chubby politician.

Marty pulled out a chair opposite Katie. He pulled a small digital recorder out of his pocket and laid it on the center of the table.

"Do you mind, Katie, if we record this conversation?" he asked her. "It may help you remember later some of the things you say here. Sometimes when we experience a trauma, our mind will block things out or things get foggy."

The mayor turned his attention to Marty. His jowls jiggled like a bowl of Jell-O.

"Is this necessary, Marty? It's obvious that Katie has been through some trauma. Why don't you and I discuss this outside?" He started to get up from his seat when Marty motioned for him to sit.

"Yes, Paul, I'm afraid it is necessary. A young girl is lying in the morgue, and Katie may be able to help us find out why."

Marty turned his attention back to Katie. The tone of his voice softened when he spoke.

"Katie, can you tell me exactly what happened? What were you girls doing up in the woods in the middle of the night?"

"We just wanted to hang out." Her voice was hardly audible across the table.

"Katie, can you speak up a little bit? I didn't hear you." Marty gave her a soft smile, trying to make her feel a little less anxious.

"We just went to hang out. We thought it would be fun…sneaking out." She spoke a little louder, a bit more self-assured.

"Did you all go up there together? All four of you?"

Katie nodded.

"Can you speak up, Katie?" Marty reminded her of the recording by glancing at the small electronic device.

"Yes," she answered this time slightly leaning toward the machine.

"How did you get there, Katie?" he questioned her. "It's too far to walk."

She hesitated, as if she needed time to formulate an answer.

"We hitchhiked." Realizing that she was still speaking softly she repeated herself, this time a little bit louder. "We hitchhiked."

Realizing that this might be an important piece of information and might even lead to a suspect, Marty leaned closer, making an effort to make her feel like he could be trusted. He took great care, though, not to get too close. He didn't want to make her uncomfortable by getting into her personal space.

"Who picked you up, Katie? Was it someone you know?" Marty glanced over at Frank. From the other detective's expression, he also appeared to be thinking along the same lines.

Quickly, maybe too quickly, Katie answered him.

"No."

"No what?" Marty asked.

"No, I didn't know who it was. It was just a stranger," she elaborated.

Disappointed by the girl's answer, Marty leaned his chair back, its front legs lifted off the floor. His fingers tapped nervously in frustration on the arm of the chair.

"Are you sure, Katie?"

She nodded her head. "Yes," she said out loud, remembering the recorder.

Marty quickly turned around and grabbed a pen and pad sitting on the cabinet behind him.

"Can you describe the car?"

"No. I don't remember," she answered, leaning back in her chair, closing her eyes.

"What color was it?" he asked her.

"I don't know, it was dark."

"Can you describe the driver?" Marty asked, trying not to let her hear the anger in his tone.

"No. I want to go home. Mom, I want to go home, please." Turning to her mother, her voice took on noticeable desperation.

Fearing that the girl was going to clam up, Marty tried another angle. Taking on a more sympathetic attitude, he turned off the recorder, and placed the pen down.

"Katie, this is really important. We need to find the person responsible for doing this to your friend. We need to stop this person, make sure no one else gets hurt."

Mayor Knox suddenly became alert, as if he suddenly thought of something that hadn't crossed his mind just seconds earlier.

"What are you saying, Keal? Are you saying there may be a serial killer out there?"

"No, Paul, that's not what I am saying. Let's not get ahead of ourselves. We have absolutely no reason to believe that's even a remote possibility." *That's all he needed*, Marty thought to himself; the mayor spreading panic throughout the city.

"Katie, please, this is very important." Marty turned back to the teenager. "You must remember something about the person that picked you up. Was it just one person? Man or woman?"

"Um…man," she answered, but her eyes were cast down at the table, avoiding Marty's gaze.

"How old?"

"I don't know…Mom, please," she said, turning to her mother, pleading.

"Look, Keal, that's enough, I'm taking her home!" Spittle came out the side of his mouth as the mayor raised his voice, making an awkward attempt to take control of the situation.

"Sit down, Paul." Marty stood up, his body towering over the fat politician, getting within inches of the shorter man's face.

"I've got a dead kid lying in the morgue, and your stepdaughter may be a material witness." His voice was starting to show signs of impatience. He turned back to Katie, frustrated by her lack of cooperation and now, evidently, lying.

Humiliation was something that the mayor did not take in stride, especially in front of his wife and stepdaughter. His face turned tomato red and he started to perspire profusely. He was just about to pull the "I am the mayor" card and throw his weight around when the door to the interview room opened.

Marty let out a sigh of relief the second Jean walked through the door.

∽

I felt the tension in the air the moment I walked in. Marty looked like he wanted to take a swing at His Honor, the mayor. I had seen that look on my partner Moran's face in regard to this same individual more than once. There was something about the tubby politician that got on everyone's nerves, and I was not exempt from those feelings.

The crime scene photographer had printed up a few digital photos of the scene and I had run into him a few moments earlier. I was holding a manila folder in my hands. Inside were those photos.

I handed Marty the folder, which he quickly opened and then passed on to Frank. I didn't know what kind of information he had been able to obtain from the teenage girl, but I was reasonably sure by the look on his face and the vibes he was giving off that he wasn't having too much success.

Realizing that the temperature in the room was getting tropical and something needed to be defused, I called Marty outside.

"I'm sorry to interrupt, mayor. I need a few minutes with Detective Keal." I dropped the closed folder on the table in front of Detective Robinson.

I heard His Honor mumble something under his breath, something about "teaching the kid manners." I smiled politely, pretending not to hear.

Before Marty followed me out the door, he turned to the mayor, a strange smirk on his face.

"Hey, Paul, how's Cameron?" he asked, not waiting for a reply. Marty kicked the door shut behind him with the back of his heel.

I looked at Marty inquisitively.

"Long story…some other time," he told me.

I let it go.

"She give you anything?" I already knew the answer, but I had to ask.

"She still says that they hitchhiked up there, but she has no clue who picked them up, doesn't know the make of the car, doesn't remember anything—just that it was some man."

"You think she's lying?" I asked him.

"Damn straight she's lying. Did you speak to the other girls yet? Maybe they were a little bit more observant about who gave them a ride."

"No, I just got back from the Camp's house." I turned to look through the window of the interrogation room, where I could see the mayor bending Frank's ear.

"Apparently there was some sort of physical altercation between our victim and Ms. Hepburn a few weeks back. They got into it over some boy and they were both suspended from school. I take it from the look on your face that she didn't bother to tell you that?"

He ran his hand through a mass of black hair, his fingers disappearing in the thickness of it for a few moments. It was a habit he had.

"So we go from material witness to suspect. That should rattle His Honor's feathers." He turned around, glaring at the mayor through the window.

"Why don't you try and rattle one of the other girls?" I told him. "Try working Tiffany. She seems the most vulnerable right now. I'll go play bad cop with Ms. Hepburn in there, maybe shake her memory loose."

"Jean, do you think that these girls could have done this?" Marty asked.

I could see he was starting to toy with the idea, but my telling him about the girls fight wasn't the catalyst. It had already crossed his mind, but Marty was still green and hadn't been doing this long enough to become jaded. He had seen ugly, but sometimes ugly has to keep slapping you in the face before you really recognize it. Marty still saw monsters that looked like monsters. I knew that it wouldn't be too long before he realized that monsters came in all shapes and colors, and soon he would be able to recognize the pretty monsters as well. One of them might be seated only a few feet away.

"I would like to see the look on her face when you confront her about them fighting," he remarked.

I gave him a look, hoping he wouldn't fight me on changing tactics and would go to speak to the other girl. He smiled, his dimples making an appearance.

"You want to keep Frank?" he asked me. It was his way of acknowledging that he was accepting the change of course of the interview.

"Yeah." I glanced through the window. "Looks like slimeball and Frank have bonded." I said sarcastically.

"Good luck," he said as he walked away.

"Yeah, you too." I turned the doorknob with a twist of my wrist and walked back into the room.

When I entered, it was apparent to me that His Honor the Mayor was trying to play upon Detective Robinson's pseudo good nature. What he didn't know was that Frank was a first rate actor, and played his role of good cop and sympathetic cop to the hilt.

Detective Robinson was far from a fan, but was giving the mayor an Oscar-winning performance.

"Yeah, you're right, Mayor Knox, that young detective is a little over the top. I agree with you that the guy is probably a little overzealous, this being his first major case and all, but maybe if we can give him something, I can talk him into letting you guys go home."

In an effort to appear bored, so the small group would consider him less of a threat than Detective Keal, he began doodling on a blank piece of scrap paper that he found in front of him.

Glancing down, I was sure that the overweight cartoon-like character with horns he created was a caricature of the mayor himself, but the mayor would be too vain to recognize it. If he was starting to catch on, his attention was diverted when I walked into the room.

"Sorry about that, Mayor, Mrs. Knox. Detective Keal needed to go speak with Tiffany. She would only talk to him."

I turned to Frank. "I guess it's those baby blues, huh, Frank?" I commented. "That boy's got a way with the women."

Shrugging my shoulders, I took a seat across from Katie. I looked to see if she showed any sign of being threatened by my news. If she was disturbed by it, she was doing a good job of covering it up.

I started out the interview acting sympathetic.

"Katie, I know you're tired and upset, but the sooner you can give us some answers, the sooner you can go home. Can you think a little harder and try and remember who picked you up?"

"No, I told the other detective, I don't remember. It was just some man!" Her eyes darted from one target to another, unable to focus on anything or anyone .She began looking around the room, as if planning her escape.

Suddenly, as if she had a flash of memory, she turned to me.

"Um…he was old, and I think he had gray hair…yeah, yeah—he was old."

"How old do you think, Katie?" I had picked up the folder with the crime scene photos and shuffled it back and forth between my hands.

"I don't know," she told me, shrugging her shoulders.

"Take a guess—sixty? Seventy? Was he older than me? Younger than me?"

I knew I wasn't imagining it; she had a smirk on her face when she answered.

"I don't know, maybe sixty, younger than you," she answered, as if she was getting bored.

I wanted to slap the smirk right off the little brat's face. I was tired and cranky and some sixteen-year-old girl was lying in the morgue with her beautiful face burnt off, her parents devastated, and this kid was being flippant.

I knew what I was about to do next would probably end the interview right then and there, but I lost my cool. I opened up the folder and took the photos of Jamie Camp's body and laid them down on the table. Mrs. Knox put her hand to her mouth and tried unsuccessfully to muffle a scream of horror. The mayor turned his fat face away in disgust. Katie looked down at the photos for a second and then turned and stared back in my direction.

"Do you want to tell me about the fight you and Jamie had, Katie?" I asked.

"That's it! This interview is over." The mayor turned back around and slammed his chubby hand down on the table. "I'm calling my attorney. Katie, don't you say another word!" he ordered her.

I picked up the photos and with a deliberate slowness, I placed them back in the folder.

"Suit yourself, mayor. Maybe the other girls will be a little bit more forthcoming and tell us exactly what happened in the woods last night."

The mayor grabbed his wife's arm.

"Let's go, Donna," he said, as he practically pulled his wife out of the chair.

"You have no reason to hold my stepdaughter here. You have any more questions, they can be directed to my attorney," he told us. His teeth were clenched tight, but somehow spittle still managed to escape before his jaw locked shut.

He was right. I didn't have any proof that his stepdaughter was guilty of anything. All we had was what the three girls had told the first officer who responded to the 911 calls.

All three girls had told Officer Beck the same story. Jamie Camp had wandered off and they were concerned, so they went looking for her. When they found her, she was already dead.

Unless we were able to get one of them to tell us something different, I had no reason to hold any of them.

I threw the folder down on the table in frustration.

"Maybe after a good night's sleep, Katie, your memory will be a little clearer," I told her, my eyes targeting hers.

Her eyes were almond-shaped, and in contrast to her dark lashes and the long, dark hair, they reminded me of the sky-blue crayon in a Crayola box. As annoyed as I was with the girl, I could not help but acknowledge how beautiful she was. Her skin was flawless, and even seemed to glow as if it had been airbrushed.

She looked over to her mother and then to her stepfather. I had a feeling she wanted to mouth off to me, but thought twice about it.

"Can I have my cell phone back?" she asked snidely.

I turned to Frank.

"Give her the damn phone back, and mayor, I expect you aren't going to be planning any family vacations?"

He didn't bother to answer me, just guided his wife and stepdaughter out of the room.

I did notice that Katie was straining her neck as they walked out of the room in what I thought to be an effort to locate her two friends, from whom she had been separated.

∾

It wasn't more than five minutes later when Marty came out of one of the other interview rooms. He glanced up and gave me a shrug. Apparently, he hadn't had too much success, either.

He was standing next to Tiffany Bennett's parents. The girl's father, a tall, dark-haired man looked to be lecturing Marty as if he were a disobedient child, but Marty just stood there, nodding his head as if he was agreeing. (It was a cop trick, just pretend you are submissive and the aggressor will eventually say something stupid.)

It took only a second for me to recognize the man as an acquaintance of my husband Glenn. The man was a successful and prominent defense attorney who had a well-established law firm in the nearby town of Monticello.

The girl's mother looked familiar to me, yet I couldn't quite place her. She was tall, although her stilettos gave her an additional few inches. Unlike her daughter, Mrs. Bennett was quite attractive and was well proportioned. She was wearing what I assumed to be a pair of two hundred dollar jeans that fit her like a glove and a long car coat. It was apparent that under the coat Tiffany's mother, who I guessed to be about my age, had a figure that could very well be found on the front cover of fashion magazines.

I subconsciously looked down at my unattractive cop shoes and compared them to what could be no less than a $600 fashion statement that the woman had on her feet.

I comforted myself when I looked up at Mrs. Bennett and saw the sour expression on her face. Either she was uncomfortable having to pick up her daughter at the local precinct who was being questioned about a murder in the middle of the night, or her shoes were killing her. I chose to guess that it was the shoes that made her look as if she was constipated.

Now that I saw some of the adult participants of the puzzle, and with whom I would have to deal, I realized that if these girls were in any way responsible for the death and mutilation of Jamie Camp, it was going to be an uphill battle getting a conviction.

These girls weren't your average teenagers; they were born into privilege and money. These girls were to this town as the Kennedy clan was to Boston. Even if we could tie them to the murder, trying to get one of them convicted in this town was going to be tough. My mood was getting darker with each passing minute.

Kathy came out of another room, followed by the third girl, Lisa Padilla, and an older couple that I also recognized from St Mary's Church. They appeared to be a little bit too old to be her parents, and I faintly remembered hearing that the couple had taken in their three grandchildren recently. The grandchildren had been removed from their parents' home after an investigation by the Department of Children and Families found them to be neglected and abused.

Rumor had it that a family friend had sexually abused the oldest two female children, who at the time were twelve and fifteen. The story I had heard was that the children's parents were crack addicts and were convicted of actually selling their daughters in return for drugs.

The third child, a six-year-old boy, had been neglected and beaten so badly that he had been hospitalized for two weeks before he was able to join his older sisters in his grandparents' home.

The older woman hovered over Lisa, who appeared to be in some sort of respiratory distress. Her grandmother was holding an inhaler and Lisa took a long and intense drag on the portable device, her eyes focused on her grandmother in what looked like real panic.

Kathy walked over to me.

"Asthma attack. I asked them if they wanted me to call an ambulance, but they said no, they had it under control. My kid brother's son has asthma and it's frightening to watch."

"She didn't happen to confess to killing her friend, did she?" I asked, in a futile attempt to be funny.

"Nope, just that she was a fan of Jeff Dahmner and wanted to be just like him."

Her attempt at humor was just as poor as mine.

"No," Kathy said, and then added, "she's standing by her story. They all went up there together, they realized Jamie was missing, and they went looking for her."

"Mysterious driver picked them up, no distinguishing features…just a man?" I asked as I watched the threesome walk down the stairwell and exit the building.

"Yeah, but that's when she had the asthma attack. The minute I brought up the driver, she started to wheeze. Thought it was a little obvious. She might be the most vulnerable, Jean—I would lean on her."

I looked at my watch. It was almost eleven a.m. and I had been at it since three this morning. Nothing more was going to be accomplished today, since it was still too early to get back the autopsy report from the ME and I was worried about my own daughter at home.

I looked around to see if I could spot Marty. He was nowhere in sight.

"I'm going to call it a day, Kathy. Can you tell Marty I will speak to him later?"

I didn't even wait for her to give me an answer. I grabbed my purse hanging on the chair of my desk and headed for home.

Chapter Six

Thursday Afternoon

By the time Marty walked out of the building, the pain in his head had become a constant throb. As soon as he got into his car, he reached into his console and grabbed a bottle of generic painkillers. Popping into his mouth two red and white capsules, he took a slug of what remained of his cold coffee.

He had had every intention last night of waking up this morning and sneaking into the kitchen to fix Hope his version of a gourmet breakfast. He had gone shopping before she had gotten home and had hidden the ingredients in the back of the refrigerator, hoping to surprise her with a Keal omelet when she woke up.

It would have been the start of a special day that he had planned for them both. He leaned over in the bucket seat a few inches in order to maneuver the small navy blue velvet-covered box from his pocket. Opening it up with the thumb of his right hand, he sat and stared at the Princess cut diamond engagement ring that Hope's friend Diane had helped him pick out just two days earlier.

Hoping the pain in his head would subside, he stared blankly at the rainbow of brilliant colors that the ring dispersed, reflecting off the thin chrome that trimmed the car's windshield.

He wondered now if it had been a mistake to buy the ring. They had never actually discussed marriage. He knew that she had been burned badly by her husband Richard's philandering ways. Although he had never met the guy, he wanted to slam his face into a wall for hurting her.

Hope seemed to be perfectly content with their arrangement as it was, having Marty as a guest in her home a few nights a week, spending long weekends together, and occasionally getting together with Justin and Diane and their new baby, Christopher.

Justin and Diane had been the catalyst that had brought Marty and Hope together. For that, he would be forever grateful. Hope seemed genuinely happy for her best friend and his best friend when they made it official and got married six months after they all met that fateful night at the Lion's Den.

He had gone to the pub that night just to be Justin's wingman. Justin had a date with Diane, someone he had recently met, but she was bringing a friend for security and Justin dragged Marty along to make it a foursome. He had been surprised to see who his blind date was. He had met Dr. Hope Rubin briefly before; the beautiful child psychiatrist had been assigned to treat Brad Madison, the ten-year-old boy he discovered in the home where his parents had been murdered.

Marty and Hope, both stubborn and strong willed, had gotten off to a rocky start as a couple, but they now had fallen into a familiar and comfortable arrangement. There was no question in Marty's mind that this woman was someone he could never afford to lose. She made him feel so satisfied and complete. He knew in his heart she felt the same way. He felt it odd, that neither he nor Hope had ever really verbalized aloud how they really felt.

Time was passing them by. Marty's father and his seven brothers, seven sisters-in-law, one sister and numerous friends and co-workers were getting on his case about starting a family of his own.

He agreed with them. He was fast approaching thirty-five and had never been married. In hindsight, he had never been in love. Yes, he thought, he had been attracted and lusted wildly after a few women in his past, but never did he feel the strong connection that he felt with Hope.

He used to think that the expression, soul mate, was a crock, until he fell in love with this green-eyed beauty with the hair the color of chocolate pudding.

Looking at the ring, he realized that he was scared to death.

What if she says no?

"What if?" he said out loud to himself. "What if Richard screwed up her head so bad that she says no?"

He leaned back in his seat, returning the small velvet box to his pants pocket. His headache was starting to ease off and he jumped, startled, when a loud horn blared from a car waiting for his parking spot.

Marty let his foot off the brake and pressed lightly on the accelerator. He decided to head for home—the one he shared with his father, to get some sleep. He had been at it since almost three o'clock this morning and the day he had planned was shot to hell because some crazy bastard decided to take some young girl's life.

Besides, he thought to himself. *Maybe today wouldn't be a good day to show Hope the ring. Maybe getting that call this morning was an omen, and not a good one at that.*

Thursday Afternoon

As anxious as I was to get home, I was also dreading it. I did not relish the thought of explaining to Bethany what had happened to one of her schoolmates. She was an extremely bright and articulate child, and I believed she was somewhat wise beyond her years.

Glenn and I had always tried to be honest and up front with both our children, but I always tried to give them information that I felt was appropriate for their maturity levels. I always found it necessary to give Bethany more information than her older brother, who seemed to take things more in stride and required less detail.

Bethany was more like me; she needed to know every little thing. She would insist on knowing every little detail in order to understand what she was being presented with. I often wondered if it was more of a female trait than it was a personality difference between the two children.

The world had changed since I was a child. I was brought up in a world where sad and ugly things were whispered about behind closed doors. I was led to believe there were very few dark and horrific things that happened, unless it was in the make-believe world of cinema and the arts. It was there, of course, but not quite as abundant as it is today, and was definitely not available for children to witness or hear.

My children, on the other hand, were brought up in a world where they watched on a continuous loop the death and destruction of thousands of innocent men, women and children by madmen on that fatal September 11, 2001 morning. My children were raised thinking that a child's picture on a milk carton was as normal as their class pictures, and that Amber Alerts were part of the landscape of a normal day.

When I grew up, a crime spree consisted of the boys in the neighborhood taking joyrides with someone else's Schwinn or scrawling graffiti in the bathroom stalls in school. A bully would call you a name and you would retaliate by calling them one back. Talking back to a parent would result in a mouthful of Ivory Soap, or a good whipping.

Today, children were slaughtering their classmates and then killing themselves in order to escape punishment. They had no coping skills whatsoever. Parents today were constrained from employing punishments that once were accepted as part of normal disciplinary actions. We received corporal punishments that, in hindsight, I realize were probably well deserved.

∽

I realized that I was probably overthinking the task at hand when I pulled into the driveway. It was a beautiful spring day, and Glenn had decided to take advantage of the day off. This day would be as good a day as any to clean out the garage, something I had been pestering him about since Cliff had left for college.

My husband and daughter had boxes strewn all around, with memories half in and half out of what once were neatly packaged cardboard containers.

Bethany and Glenn would open a carton and suddenly find something that would spark a memory, and the two would stop midway and reminisce. I arrived just moments after Bethany pulled out her pink sparkly hula-hoop. It was now making its way down Glenn's well-toned legs as my daughter watched, doubled over in laughter, and Roxy, our mutt, ran around them both in circles.

"Hey, be careful." I said as I shut the car door behind me. "Last thing I need is you falling on your ass."

"Mom, he sucks at this, you know!" she managed to cry out between giggles. "But he can do a pretty mean Yo-Yo."

"Won the Duncan Yo Yo Walk the Dog award three years in a row in elementary school!" my husband blurted out with a look of pure pride and absolutely no embarrassment.

"Let me see that." I grabbed the pink Hula Hoop from his hands, the beads inside making a familiar sound, and slung it over my head with one arm, throwing my purse to my daughter at the same time.

Fifteen tries and fifteen minutes later, I was out of breath, my heart was racing and I was begging for a glass of water as we all walked back inside the house.

Glenn handed me a glass of ice water and I took that moment to take a good look at my daughter's face. Her eyes were a little puffy and the little makeup I allowed her to wear had run. It was a sure sign that she had been crying. I leaned over, dipped a napkin into my glass of water and wiped away a faint line of black.

"Did you know her, Bethany?" I asked, taking a strand of hair that was falling in front of her face and tucking it behind her ear.

"She was in my science class. She had to repeat it. She failed last year," she told me as she played with the discarded tissue, not looking at me. She hesitated for a moment and then, looking up, she continued.

"She wasn't very nice, actually." Again, she paused. "She was a real bitch."

"Bethany!" I didn't know whether to be surprised or angry. It wasn't like her to use that kind of tone or language.

She shrugged her shoulders. "I'm sorry, Mom, but she wasn't exactly the nicest person and not too many people liked her. She was really stuck up."

Well I was flabbergasted. Here I thought my daughter was going to be devastated and possibly in need of professional intervention. I quickly glanced at Glenn, who raised his one eyebrow letting me know he was just as surprised at her reaction.

My daughter loved everyone, and everyone loved my daughter. From the time she had first been able to communicate, she could turn the biggest sourpuss into a smiling fool. If we were in a long line at the supermarket and some cranky old man was giving the cashier a hard time, one smile or remark from Bethany would defuse the situation. It was so unlike her to say anything derogatory about anyone. She always found something to compliment about the least pleasant person.

"Can I go over to Melanie's house?"

I shook my head. "Honey, what do you mean she wasn't nice? Did she have any friends?" I felt a pang of guilt, but it didn't stop me. I went from concerned mother to detective. I was questioning my own daughter as if she was a material witness.

"She was just really mean to a lot of kids. You know, she would pick on them, call them names—stuff like that."

"You mean she was a bully?" I asked her

"Guess so," she replied, turning her face away from me and

looking down, her hair falling over her eyes.

"What about Katie Hepburn, do you know her?"

"Yes, I know Katie, everyone knows Katie. She used to be Dylan's girlfriend." My daughter was in honors classes, and honors students were assigned to tutor other classmates who weren't doing well in subjects that they themselves excelled in. My daughter had mentioned tutoring someone named Dylan previously.

"The boy you tutor?" I questioned

"Yes," she answered.

"Is Katie a bully, too?" I asked, leaning over, trying to get her to look me in the eye.

She shook her head. "Not really, she's too into herself. She doesn't pay anyone else too much attention."

"How about Tiffany Bennett and Lisa Padilla?" I questioned her.

"They're okay. Why are you asking? They weren't hurt too, were they?" She looked up at me, suddenly concerned.

"No, honey, they're fine—well, sort of—they are the one's that found Jamie's body."

I looked up at her father. "How much did you tell her?"

"Just about everything you told me," he answered me.

I turned back to my daughter. "Did you know anything about a disagreement that Katie and Jamie had about a boy, Bethany? Was it this boy Dylan?"

She didn't answer my question; instead, she asked one of her own.

"You don't think Katie killed Jamie, Mom? She wouldn't do that. You're way off base." I thought I heard a hint of anger in her voice.

"Right now, honey, I don't know much of anything. I know a beautiful young girl's life was ended last night. I know a family is mourning their child and they need to know why this happened and who did this to her. They need to know that this person will never hurt anyone again."

"I asked you a question. Do you know about the argument that Katie and Jamie had over this boy Dylan?"

"I don't know." She got out of her seat. "I have to study for a history test, may I be excused?"

I was exhausted and I knew where this might lead, so I chose to let it go.

"Yes, but we'll talk later, okay?"

She mumbled a "yeah, sure" as she hastily made her way up to her bedroom.

I looked at Glenn, totally perplexed.

"Where is my daughter, and who is that creature pretending to be her?" I asked.

He totally ignored what I had just said.

"Tell you what—why don't you go upstairs and take a nap? I'll throw a few steaks on the grill and I'll wake you up when it's time for dinner."

I just stared at him.

"Let it go, Jeannie," he urged. "Maybe it's just too much for her right now."

"Okay, but only because I am tired and I can't get that picture of you and that Hula Hoop out of my head."

I grabbed my purse and made my way upstairs to get into a hot bath and take a much-needed nap.

∽

THE MORGUE

Friday Morning

The ME's workspace was in the sub cellar of St. Katherine's Medical Center. I took the elevator down two floors and when the doors opened, I was reminded just how much this place gave me the creeps.

Unlike the upper floors of the hospital, this area was desolate and eerie. Fluorescent lighting gave a ghostly tint to the walls, which were painted a dull battleship gray. Exposed plumbing pipes were painted the same dull gray in a poor effort to make them blend in. The floor was covered with a freshly waxed beige tile that caused my rubber soles to stick. With each step I took, a sucking sound reverberated off the walls. The acoustics made each step sound like a marching band had followed close behind me.

Outside the autopsy room was a metal bench that was bolted to the wall, as if the hospital was afraid that someone would bother to steal it. Next to the bench was a metal closet that should have been bolted down, because it looked as if it would topple over the minute someone opened its flimsy doors. I opened it up and grabbed one of the white lab coats that hung on a broken rod held together with duct tape.

Above the rod was a shelf that held a lone blue plastic container of Vicks VapoRub, a staple of any autopsy room. I often wondered which was worse, the smell of a decaying body or the burst of menthol that the Vicks offered. I chose the Vicks and dabbed some under my nose as I pushed the heavy steel door open with my right hip.

As I entered the room, my left hand felt something in the pocket of the coat. I realized what it was as soon as I saw Rob Lyons and Marty standing over the body. What I was touching was a plastic medical mask, a clone of the ones they were wearing to avoid having any body fluids splattering in their faces. Both of them turned to look at me and I noticed that the blue plastic that covered the gauzelike material of the mask was the exact shade of Marty's eyes.

I stopped to put the mask on before I got any further into the room.

I tried not to look at the extensive injuries that Jamie had sustained to her face, but I couldn't help myself. Her thick blonde mane was now blackened and brittle, leaving part of her scalp exposed. Parts of her facial skin had literally melted off, exposing her nasal septum and charred cheekbones. Her lips were just a mass of blisters that seemed to trail down her chin.

It was not the girl's face that Marty and Rob were focused on. Robert Lyons had the girl's right arm lifted in the air, exposing her armpit.

The ME called me over to where he was standing. His voice was slightly muffled because of the mask.

"Here, Jean, come look at this." With a latex-gloved finger, he pointed to an area that was covered with small, red, swollen lumps. Still keeping Jamie's arm vertical, he shifted her wrist over to Marty to hold as he leaned over to get a pair of small tweezers from a metal tray that held his instruments.

"What is that?" I asked, as I leaned in to take a closer look.

Not answering, but applying the tweezers to the flesh of one of the nodules, he gently pulled something out. It looked like a tiny pubic hair to me.

"If I am not mistaken, this is a stinger from a species of Hymenoptera, commonly known as the honeybee. It appears that we have at least half a dozen stings in this area. I would take an educated guess and say this kid died of anaphylactic shock, an allergic reaction to melittin, the most prevalent chemical in the venom of the honeybee. Do you happen to know if her family was aware she was allergic to bee stings?"

"Easy enough to find out," I answered, as I looked at him, bewildered.

"You're telling me this wasn't a homicide? What about the burns on her face?" I asked.

"I'm not saying that this is not a homicide," he replied. "Can you see this?"

His finger traced a red mark that seemed to circle the swollen areas. Taking out a ruler, he measured it.

"The diameter of the circle measures exactly two inches, or precisely the measurement of a Smucker's Jelly jar." He stopped and walked toward a refrigerator that was in the back of the room. I caught a glimpse of the inside. It contained some jars with bizarre-looking substances, a couple of cans of Coke, and what looked like a hero sandwich in the familiar green-and-white Subway wrapper.

From the shelf of the refrigerator door, he pulled out a jar of grape Smucker's Jelly and twisted off the cap. Wiping off the top of the jar with a moistened paper towel, he measured it. He was right; it was exactly two inches in diameter.

"Looks to me like someone deliberately caused this kid to get stung," he said.

He wiped some jelly off that had gotten on his finger. "The burns are post-mortem—an afterthought. Apparently, watching her die wasn't enough for this sadistic bastard. He or she would have watched as this girl began to have difficulty breathing. Her face and throat would have become swollen and she would have had difficulty swallowing. She would have experienced an immediate drop in blood pressure, leading to shock, and eventually cardiac arrest. This kid suffered a horrific death. I don't know if whoever did this knew she was allergic, but I am guessing that he had at least six honeybees in a small jar, and it was the method used to inject her with the venom."

He nodded to Marty, who was still holding Jamie's arm upright. Marty carefully placed the arm back down next to the girl's body.

"What about the facial burns?" I asked him.

"Most likely the Zippo lighter fluid is the chemical that was used to accelerate the fire that caused the damage to her face."

I removed the gloves and then the mask from my face. "Well, I guess we have to find out who knew she was allergic to bees. It's a start," I said.

"Do you think they burned her face to make identification difficult?" I threw out the question; not really thinking it was a possibility or a motive.

Neither man answered. I didn't really expect them to.

I turned my attention to Marty. "Let's go talk to Lisa Padilla again. Maybe they bonded over their allergies."

I discarded the gloves and mask in a nearby wastebasket. "Thanks, Rob. Let me know if you come up with anything else."

He nodded as Marty and I walked over to the sink and moistened some paper towels to wipe the Vicks from our noses.

"Get the bastard, Jean," he added, as Marty opened the door letting us exit the room. I turned back to Rob and gave him a silent reply with a nod of my head.

After leaving the autopsy room and the lifeless body of Jamie Camp, the desolate hallway took on a different aura. What had appeared a half hour earlier to be quiet and spooky now seemed serene and tranquil to me. The sound of our shoes stomping down the empty corridor was comforting. At least I had gotten some answers…we got the cause of death answered. Now we just had to figure out who did this to the girl, and why?

Chapter Seven

Friday Evening

Marty was behind the wheel. We drove for several miles in silence. I don't know what Marty had on his mind, but I had a multitude of thoughts bombarding my brain cells all at once. Did any or all of the three girls know Jamie was allergic to bee stings? Could our teenage threesome be a group of sociopathic murderers? Who did they catch a lift from, and did they really not know who the driver was? I didn't think so.

Marty was right about one thing. Miss Katie Hepburn and her two friends were being less than honest with us. As far as I was concerned, we gave them way too much latitude when we had the chance to get answers. Now, with them lawyering up, we might have screwed ourselves.

I started to question my own ability to handle this case with the same brilliance that Joe would have conducted it. Now I was in charge, and Marty was dependent on me to lead the investigation. It would be totally on me if something went wrong, and I wasn't feeling too adequate at the moment. I murmured a strong expletive under my breath.

"I don't think I ever heard you cuss, Jean," Marty said, glancing in the rearview mirror as he changed lanes in preparation to exit the highway.

We were headed to Lisa Padilla's grandparents' home. The older couple had recently sold their large colonial family home and moved into a fifty-plus gated community only a stone's throw from the high school that two of their grandchildren attended. They had downsized with the anticipation and prospect of traveling, now that they had both retired from teaching school. Lisa's grandfather had been the vice principal of the elementary school since its inception thirty years ago, and her grandmother taught art at the Community College in the town of Loch Sheldrake, a few miles away. Their plans of retiring and enjoying the golden years were shot to hell when they assumed custody of Lisa and her siblings.

I suddenly realized that Marty was probably waiting for me to reply to his statement about my language.

"Sorry, I'm just so damn pissed at Joe for taking off without a word. I mean, how much effort does it take to make a friggin' phone call?"

I guess he knew that I really wasn't expecting an answer, because he didn't give me one.

Marty showed his badge to the elderly uniformed guard at the gate. It tickled me how a geriatric wanna-be cop could give the residents a false sense of security. This particular guard bore a striking resemblance to Barney Fife from *The Andy Griffith Show*, making it seem even more absurd.

The second we pulled into a guest parking spot in front of Lisa's grandparent's residence, both our cell phones rang, using the same exact ringtone. I finished my conversation and waited patiently until Marty concluded his.

Marty spoke up first.

"That was Sully. He says that there is a caretaker living at the Forester place. Claims he was home asleep the night of the murder and didn't hear a thing." His fingers danced nervously on the back of his cell phone, as if he was deep in thought. He let out a snort.

"What?" I demanded. I hate when men do that…have a thought and, instead of vocalizing it, they keep it to themselves. When a thought crosses a female's mind, she says it out loud. Men—they sit there in total silence, their brains calculating, their mouths clamped as if they were glued shut. You have to pry it out of them. My partner Joe would do the same thing to me. Sometimes I felt like a dentist instead of a cop. Getting them to speak up was like pulling teeth.

"Oh, sorry," he apologized, realizing I couldn't hear his thoughts.

"The caretaker." He paused for a second. "It's Cameron Knox."

"Any relation to our esteemed mayor?" I asked him.

"Yeah, he is. Cameron is Paul's son, from his first marriage, or at least I think it was his first."

'The mayor has a son? Why didn't I know that?" I replied, surprised at my own ignorance about the man.

"Yup," he answered, as he unbuckled his seat belt and got out of the car. He started down a narrow path that was bordered with a variety of shrubbery and foliage. It led to row of coral-colored block townhouses, each one an exact duplicate of the one next to it.

Joining him on the sidewalk, I suddenly recalled his exchange with the mayor the other day. Marty had asked Mayor Knox how Cameron was doing, but there seemed to be a hint of animosity in the exchange.

"I didn't know he had a son—at least, I didn't think I knew." I tried to take a glimpse into my memory bank. This information wasn't sounding the least bit familiar.

"He moved to Connecticut with his mother when his parents got divorced. That was years ago…at least ten years ago, maybe more." We reached Lisa's house. He rang the doorbell.

"Well, apparently he's back," I remarked, as I looked up at Marty. He had a faraway look in his eyes. I wondered if the mayor's son and Marty had some sort of personal connection.

"What? What is it?" I prodded. Yes, men are all the same; it was like trying to pull teeth.

He didn't answer, because at that very moment, the door opened and the woman I recognized as Lisa's grandmother was standing there.

She looked to be about sixty, give or take a few years. Her hair looked like it had been recently coiffed. Unlike most women her age, it was uncolored, and I could understand why. It was a unique shade of gray that matched her eyes perfectly. I recalled my first meeting with her granddaughter and taking notice of her eyes as well.

"Mrs. Padilla? I'm Detective Whitley, this is my partner, Detective Keal." It sounded a little foreign to me, calling Marty my partner, but I guessed I could get used to it. "We'd like to have a few words with Lisa, if that is all right with you."

"Yes, please come in." She opened the door wider. A long foyer led to an enormous living area. Glass and black Formica were everywhere. A long black-and-white sofa sat flush against the wall and on the opposite wall, a large, sleek LED flat-paneled TV was on, but the sound was muted. I recognized my late mother's favorite soap opera on the screen.

"She's upstairs. We kept her home from school today. I didn't think it was a good idea for her to go back yet. It's just too soon. Her asthma is really bad this time of the year, and stress makes it even worse. Please sit down."

She waited until we were seated and then took a seat on a luxurious white suede recliner opposite us. I thought she must have gone shopping for new furniture long before she had any inkling that she would be raising her three grandchildren.

"Has Lisa told you anything about what happened, Mrs. Padilla?"

"Please, call me Mary Jo, I like to reserve 'Mrs. Padilla' for my husband's mother," she told us, as a sweet smile crossed her face. I liked this woman. I immediately got the feeling that she was genuine and I wouldn't have to worry about her being honest with us.

"Mayor Knox told us that we shouldn't talk to the police without an attorney present." She hesitated for a moment.

"But personally I don't like or trust that man," she said. Her mouth made a gesture as if she was eating a lemon.

I smiled, letting her know that our feelings were mutual.

"Actually, I was waiting for my husband Frank, to come home and we were going to come back into the police station. Let me call Lisa downstairs, I think she needs to be the one to tell you herself."

She got up and walked to the stairway. She called out her granddaughter's name and then turned and looked at Marty and me. "She's scared to death, please understand that. This has been very traumatic for her. This poor child has been through an awful lot in such a short period of time. I could kill my son and daughter-in-law for that. I don't know what happened to that boy; he was such a good boy until he met her."

The last few words she said, she spoke in a whisper. Lisa had appeared at the top of the stairwell and her grandmother didn't want her to hear what she was saying.

"Yes, Me–Ma?" Lisa appeared at the top of the landing. Even from this distance, I could see her eyes were red and puffy.

"Lisa, can you come down here? The police are here, and they want to ask you a few questions." I saw a visual exchange between the young girl and grandmother. I recognized the look as something that had often been passed between my daughter and myself. It was the look of "I know you're scared, honey, but it's going to be all right. I am here. I will protect you."

Faceless: A Mystery ~ Dawn Kopman Whidden

When Lisa came down, I noticed that the streak of hot pink that had previously adorned her hair was now gone. Her black nail polish was also gone, and her nails were now short. The diamond stud in her nose was also gone. It was as if she had made a conscious effort to wash away what had happened by simply changing her appearance.

She didn't say anything, but I could tell she was obviously shaken up. She sat down on the chair that her grandmother had previously occupied. She started to scratch a design in the suede like material on the arm of the chair.

"How are you feeling, Lisa?" I asked.

She shrugged her shoulders.

"Lisa, answer the lady properly," her grandmother, who was now standing behind her, interjected. I could tell that even though the woman was stern, her words had certain warmth to them.

"I guess I'm okay." She sat back in the chair and started to rock gently.

"Lisa, are you ready to tell us what happened the night Jamie died? Can you tell me how you got up to the woods? Can you describe the car and driver?"

She turned to look at her grandmother, who nodded, her hand now resting on Lisa's shoulder.

"I didn't tell you the truth," she said, looking straight at Marty. "We didn't hitchhike up there." Her eyes fell to her lap. Without looking back up, she continued.

"Dylan drove us up there."

"Dylan? Dylan who? What's his last name?" I recognized the first name immediately, but I wanted to make sure we were talking about the same person.

"Silver...Dylan Silver," she replied.

"Is this Dylan Katie's boyfriend?" I questioned her.

"Well, sometimes. They're really close, they date sometimes. They're more like brother and sister, but they go out with other people. Dylan and Jamie were together that night, but they got into a fight. That's why she took off."

Marty leaned closer.

"Lisa, why wasn't Dylan there when Officer Beck arrived?" he asked. "It was just the three of you. Where did Dylan go?" He had taken a small notebook from his side pocket and opened it. He fumbled around for a pen so he could write down the boy's name. Mrs. Padilla noticed and handed him one that was on the coffee table.

The girl took a deep breath and continued her story.

"Katie told him to leave, she was afraid that he would get into trouble. So she made up this story about us hitchhiking up there. Dylan was scared that the police would think he hurt Jamie, 'cause they were fighting. After we found her, Katie told him to go home so no one would even know he was there."

"What were you doing up there, Lisa? Why there?" Marty asked her.

"Katie's stepbrother told us to come up. He was going to let us go into the hot tub at the mansion he was taking care of. He…" she looked back up at her grandmother. Again, the woman nodded. "He got us some wine coolers and pot. We thought it would be fun."

I noticed the poor woman's eyes rise to the sky. I could tell she was silently pleading with God for something.

"Cameron Knox? Is that who we are talking about, Lisa?" I asked.

"Yes." Her voice dipped, making it hard to hear her.

"Did you see Cameron that night, Lisa? Did you ever go to the house?" I questioned her further.

She shook her head. "Afterwards, we all did. I don't really remember much. I had a couple of wine coolers."

"Did Jamie go into the house, Lisa?" Marty quizzed her.

"No, I don't think so. Dylan and Jamie got into a fight on the way up there. When he stopped the car, she ran out into the woods. That's when we went looking for her."

"What were they fighting about, Lisa?" I prodded her to give us more.

"Just stuff. Jamie was being a bitch and Dylan was getting pissed at her."

"What time did you get there? Do you remember?" I asked her.

"I'm not sure, I think about ten o'clock. I wasn't wearing a watch." Her eyes shifted from me to her grandmother and back to Marty.

"How long did it take for you to find her? Who actually found Jamie first?" Marty asked this time.

"Tiffany found her. We heard her screaming. She was hollering for us to come. I was with Dylan and Katie was with Cameron."

She put three of her fingers in her mouth and started to suck them. She looked like she was going to cry. "Am I in trouble?" she asked.

"Not if you're telling us the truth, Lisa. Are you telling us the truth?" I tried to sound more maternal than official.

"Yes ma'am. I swear, I'm telling you the truth."

I had heard enough. We thanked them and I let Mrs. Padilla know how we appreciated her cooperation.

We were about to walk out of the house when I remembered something important.

"Lisa, do you know if Jamie had any allergies? Like you, with your asthma?"

She nodded.

"Yes ma'am. Jamie was allergic to bees. She usually carried an epinephrine pen in her bag, in case she got stung."

∽

We left the Padilla's house ten minutes later, after arranging for Lisa to come in and give a written statement.

When we got back to the car, I turned and looked at Marty. "Was Jamie's purse found at the scene?"

He pulled out a sheet of paper and scanned through it.

"Nope."

"Okay, who first? Dylan, Cameron, or Katie?"

"How about we have this kid Dylan picked up while we go talk to Cameron?" he suggested as he got into the vehicle. By the time I got into the passenger side, he had already radioed someone to have them pick up Dylan Silver.

"Let's go find out why Cameron lied to Sully," he said, pulling out of the parking spot.

"So what do you know about the mayor's kid? What's the long story you were going to tell me?"

"First off, he's no kid. He's a few years younger than me. He's my little brother Danny's age."

"Which is?"

"Thirty, Danny just turned thirty this year," he answered after some thought.

"What the hell is a thirty-year-old doing hanging out with sixteen and seventeen year olds?" I was nauseated at the thought.

"Cameron Knox is a piece of work. He has a problem keeping his pants zipped."

"He's an exhibitionist?" I shot out in disbelief. Now this was getting interesting.

"Among other things, but daddy always called in some favors and kept him out of trouble. The reason he moved to live with his mother in Connecticut was that he was being accused of statutory rape. They paid off the girl's mother and the problem went away. He liked—or should I say, likes—them young."

"Is this just speculation, Marty? Or do you know it for a fact?" I could tell he noticed the doubt I was feeling about his remark.

"The girl that he was sleeping with was Danny's wife's niece. It's true."

"Are you saying the mayor's kid is a pedophile, Marty? That's a pretty big accusation."

"I'm saying the guy's a horse's ass, and I wouldn't put anything past him."

"Including murder?" I prodded him.

"That I can't tell you. Cameron Knox is an embarrassment and thorn in his father's side. I never thought he was too bright. Cameron was, or is, more of an impulsive type. I can't see him planning anything quite so elaborate. Hope would have some sort of psychiatric medical term for it. I'm getting vibes telling me that Jamie's murder was definitely premeditated and well thought out. If the medical examiner is right, Jean, somebody had to have collected those bees, found an empty jar and put them in it...somebody who obviously knew that she would have an allergic reaction."

"Knox is not going to like this, Marty…two of his family members being suspects in a high-profile case…he's not going to like it at all. You're right, let's take a ride over to the Forester place. Maybe we can have a little talk with Junior, before the mayor finds out and calls in any favors."

It was getting late, and rush-hour traffic was starting. We both had the same thought at the same moment. I sat back as he pulled out the blue globe and placed it on the dash and hit the siren. Neither of us felt there was any sense in wasting time.

On the way to find Cameron Knox, Marty made a few phone calls and did a little fishing for information on the mayor's son. Unlike me, Marty had grown up in this town. That tended to be an advantage in our line of work. Even though I had been living here for over twenty years and raised a family here, I wasn't privy to old family gossip. I was still an outsider.

~

Just before we got to our destination, Marty filled me in on the history of the Forester home.

The Forester estate was built on land that used to be owned by the Armistace Family. Five thousand acres of prime real estate had been sold off in ten-and twenty-acre lots when Alexander and Rebecca Armistace passed on and left their numerous assets to their only surviving child a son, Skylar.

Skylar Armistace, now an old man himself, kept the main house and fifty or so acres, and deeded a good deal of the property to the state hospital for children with mental and emotional disorders, most of them violent in nature. That is where Marty's girlfriend Hope worked as a clinical child psychiatrist.

The Forester place was a three-story Victorian style home built in the 1980s by Herman Forester as a wedding present for his new wife, Claire. In order to make the transition easier for his wife, he had the house built as an exact replica of her childhood home in New Orleans. The new Mrs. Forester reluctantly left her home and family and joined her new husband in the mountains of New York State, where he pioneered a computer software company. What was supposed to be their main residence soon became just a summer home. The Foresters' business had become quite successful, enabling the couple to spend their lives jet setting around the world.

Being a lifelong card-carrying Republican, Herman Forester and Mayor Paul Knox became steadfast friends and maintained political ties.

Marty found out through some mutual acquaintances that Mayor Knox had arranged for his son Cameron to be offered use of a small cottage on the property rent-free in exchange for caretaking duties. His main job was to make sure the gardeners and groundskeepers were doing what was required of them.

He was to vacate the premises for three weeks in the summer when Mr. and Mrs. Forester returned from Europe, or Asia, or wherever their travels had taken them. According to Marty's sources, the arrangement was fine with Cameron. He could always go stay with his father, his new wife, and the hot stepsister for those three weeks.

The Forester mansion was about 500 feet back from the wooded area where Jamie's body had been found. A long driveway led to a clearing that was beautifully landscaped with seasonal foliage of all kinds and faux waterfalls and ponds. The small cottage just northeast of the main house reminded me of the cover of the picture book I used to read to Bethany when she was a toddler. I had never actually been back here before, and I found it breathtaking.

Marty pointed out a dark green Harley Davidson that was parked in front of the cottage.

"That's Cameron's bike."

"Do you think this guy is dangerous, Marty? Should we call for backup?" My hand immediately went to my weapon. I looked around; the area was beautiful, but desolate.

I would say he made an ugly face, but with Marty that would have been impossible. I don't care how hard he tried to screw up his face, there was no way the man could look bad. It was a curse.

"He's about as dangerous as Silly Putty, or at least he used to be. Just keep your eyes and ears open. No reason to be too lax."

We just pulled up next to the bike when a shirtless, tall, well-built man walked out of the cottage. He headed over to his bike to get something out of the saddlebag when he noticed he had company. He had a pair of shades sitting on his head and dropped them over his eyes to keep the glare of the setting sun from blinding him when he turned in our direction.

He seemed to recognize Marty immediately. If he was disturbed that we were here and were about to question him about his part in a homicide, and why he had lied to the cops, he wasn't letting on.

"Hey Keal, that you?" He smiled, reaching out a hand to shake, as if they were longtime buddies.

"Cameron." Marty made nice and accepted the handshake. "Do you mind if we ask you a few questions?"

The mayor's son glanced over at me. I don't know what I was expecting, but he wasn't at all what my mind had envisioned after the description Marty had given to me. He was not bad looking at all. Sandy blond hair fell loosely to his shoulders. Dark eyelashes emphasized a pair of muddy brown deep-set eyes. In his own way he was quite attractive, not to mention he was drowning in sex appeal.

"I don't think we've met," he offered me his hand. "Cameron Knox, and you are…?"

"Detective Whitley. Mr. Knox, do you mind if we join you inside, it's getting a little buggy out here. Mosquitoes and I don't get along."

I was hoping to get a look inside without needing a search warrant.

"Sure, come on in. So, Marty, how have you been? I hear Danny is on his third kid. Is he trying to compete with the Captain?"

The cottage was just a one-bedroom bungalow, with a large kitchen and dining area. Under a bay window in the room was a small, worn-out sofa. I grabbed a seat on the sofa; Marty took one of the wooden dining chairs.

"Can I get either of you a refreshment? I've got some wine coolers and beer." He didn't appear nervous at all. He was either feeling very confident or totally oblivious to what kind of trouble he just invited into his home.

"No, thanks, Mr. Knox," I answered him, deliberately looking around

"Cameron—please," he said, shooting me a smile. It was obvious someone had spent a lot of money on his dental work.

"Cameron, do you mind if we ask you a few questions?" I asked him, trying not to sound too invasive.

"Is this about that poor girl getting killed? Yeah, that's so sad. One of your officers was already here, asking me questions. I told him I'm as clueless as the rest of you. They came banging at my door when they found her."

He pulled out a pack of cigarettes and smacked the pack against the edge of his palm of his hand twice. "Do you mind if I smoke?" He turned towards Marty and then to me, waiting for permission.

Marty glared at him and I could tell that he was about to tell him that he did mind, but I cut him off before he could answer.

"Not at all, go ahead, Mr. Knox."

"Cameron," he corrected me, flashing that smile again.

"Cameron, sorry," I repeated. "From what I understand, what you told Officer Sullivan was not exactly the truth, was it? We have information to the contrary."

I looked right into his eyes, deliberately not blinking. I wanted to see if he would drop his composure and give me a hint of nervousness.

He pulled out a disposable lighter and lit the end of his cigarette.

He inhaled deeply, holding the smoke deep into his lungs, before he exhaled, making a conscious effort to blow the smoke away from us. "Bad habit, I know. But you got to have some vices." He looked at Marty and then turned his attention in my direction.

"I had nothing to do with that girl getting killed. I didn't even know she was coming up. Hey, I invited my stepsister and her friends to come up and party and the next thing I know, we are searching the woods for some girl who ran off. Believe me, it wasn't my plan, I just wanted to hang out it the hot tub and watch some movies." His voice remained steady, yet as he spoke, a slight smirk slowly formed on his face.

"Did you buy them alcohol, Cameron? Did you give them dope?" I asked him. This time he turned to Marty to answer.

"I swear, Marty, I didn't. They came with their own stash. My stepsister is quite resourceful when she wants to be. Katie and me weren't even really looking for the kid; we were having our own little party. Katie thought the girl was looking for attention from her boyfriend…says she does it all the time. Katie said the girl is a real bitch and a drama queen, so we just kind of stayed out of it. Next thing we know, we hear that girl Tiffany screaming." He took a long inhale of his cigarette and slowly let the smoke out.

"Why did you lie to Officer Sullivan, Cameron?" I questioned him, trying to avoid the carcinogens in the air while still keeping the conversation civil. Lord knows I wanted to smack the man.

He took another drag of his cigarette.

"Katie told me to. She just said to tell the cops I didn't hear anything—tell them that I was sleeping. She said she would come up with something. Katie is quite resourceful." He flicked the cigarette ashes onto the kitchen floor.

"So if Katie tells you to lie, you lie?" I wasn't sure if he was acting stupid or he just really was stupid. Suddenly he looked about as sexy as a bowl of oatmeal.

He smiled as if remembering something pleasant. "Have you seen that girl? If she tells me to bend over, I'm going to bend over. You know, we aren't related by blood, and she's seventeen years old. She's past the age of consent in this state. It's perfectly legal." Once again, he flashed a broad smile.

I shook my head in disgust. I thought Marty was probably right. This guy seemed too stupid to commit this type of heinous crime.

"What were Jamie and her boyfriend arguing about?" I asked him.

He shrugged his shoulders. "I really don't know. I do know that the guy was freaking out when they found her. Asshole came back to the house and started puking all over the place. It took me over an hour to get the floor cleaned up and the smell of puke out."

"I would like you to come down to the station and fill out a statement, Mr. Knox."

He started to correct me again; I beat him to it. "Cameron."

"Sure, no problem. Do I need an attorney?" He stubbed out his cigarette.

"I don't know, Cameron...do you?" I said, rising from my seat. Something got my attention. A few jars of caramel-colored substance sat on the windowsill above the sink. I walked over to it and lifted it up.

"Is this honey?" I asked him.

"Yes, I've got a few hives out back. I make my own. Would you like some? It's really good." He grabbed a jar and held it out to Marty offering it proudly.

I placed the jar I was holding back on the shelf.

"Cameron, did your guests know that you raise bees? I mean, have they been here before and know about your hobby?"

"Yeah, sure. I think they were cutting school one day when I was jarring some honey up. They seemed real interested in it," he replied. He held the small jar in his hands and he was admiring it, practically fondling it.

"How about Jamie?" Marty asked him. "Was she interested?"

"The girl that got killed? No, she wouldn't come near them. Said she was allergic. Wouldn't have nothing to do with it."

"Well, Cameron, we appreciate your candidness. I expect you to come down tomorrow and fill out a written statement," I informed him.

"Sure. Are you sure I don't need an attorney?" he asked, in almost childlike innocence.

"Not if you didn't do anything wrong, Cameron," I said, as we walked out the door. Do you mind if we take a quick look at your hives before we go?"

"No, help yourself. It's not much, but it keeps me bee-zy. Get it? Keeps me bee-zy." He was still laughing at his own joke as we pulled away and started back to town.

"You're right," I told Marty. "The guy is as dumb as a box of rocks. What a waste of good looks."

"You think he's good-looking?" Marty cajoled.

"Only until he opens his mouth to talk. Well I guess that answers the question about whether they were all aware of her allergy to bees."

I glanced down at my cell to see if I had gotten any messages. Nothing.

"Let's get back to the station. Maybe they will have picked up this Dylan kid and we can have a nice long talk with him."

I guess Marty heard something reflected in my voice, because he took his eyes off the road to look at me. He held the glance for an unusually long time.

"What?" I answered, sounding like my own teenage daughter. He was waiting to hear more.

"My daughter knows him," I elaborated. "She tutors him in science."

"And you're obviously concerned that she may be spending time with a murder suspect. It's not unreasonable, Jean. The kid is on my short list."

I sat back in the seat and started to explain my anxiety.

"It's just that she has been through so much these past few years. First Connie, then Annie, then Joe acting like a baboon. I never used to worry about her. She was my baby, my easy child. Cliff was the adventurer, the daredevil. I never had to worry about Bethany getting hurt or doing something stupid, like I did for years with her brother. I can't tell you how many times we ended up in the ER, needing stitches or X-rays with Cliff. Bethany is open and honest and naïve and was always so cautious. She would think things through before she did anything. My daughter hates to make mistakes, but she accepts them graciously."

"And now?" He looked at me sympathetically.

"I'm scared, Marty. It's very subtle, but it's there. My daughter is going through a personality change." I hesitated and then added. "And I don't think I like it."

"Why don't you give Hope a call? You know she thinks the world of you and Bethany. Better yet, how about you all come over one night for dinner?"

"I don't know. Maybe. There is so much going on right now. Let's see what happens with this Dylan person first. Why don't you drop me off at the station so I can pick up my ride? Let's hope they have him in custody and we can interview him. If not, I'll get some info on this kid so we know what we are dealing with. I'm just grateful tomorrow is Saturday, because that will give me a whole weekend to deal with the fallout of telling my daughter that I don't want her anywhere near this boy."

He pulled into the station's parking lot.

"She'll be fine, Jean. She's a smart kid. She's tough—like her mom."

I turned to look at him. "That's the problem, Marty, her mom isn't tough. Her mom is a fake. Her mom is feeling really vulnerable right now."

He gave my hand a squeeze. It was the one thing I really appreciated about Marty. He knew when to talk and when he didn't have to.

I shut the car door behind me, gave him a silent thank you and walked into the squad room. Dylan was not there, and he was nowhere to be found.

I spent a few minutes on my computer, trying to hunt up a few pieces of information on the boy. I got what I needed and headed for home.

Chapter Eight

MARTY
Friday Evening

Stepping through Hope's front door, Marty felt an immediate burst of energy. The last forty-eight hours he and Jean had been running all over town, conducting interviews and running down leads. He had been fighting fatigue all day long because of the lack of sleep and poor meal choices. The prospect of spending the evening with Hope had given him a fresh shot of adrenaline.

Although neither of them actually vocalized their position, it was mutually agreed upon that they considered their partnership exclusive. They had been together for two and a half years, and he still felt that every day with Hope was as exciting as the first few days of their relationship.

The moment he stepped over the threshold, he immediately recognized the impatience in the tone of her voice coming from the kitchen. The only person who could affect Hope that way, causing the familiar inflection in her speech, was her mother, Grace.

Hope was sitting at the kitchen table, the phone cradled between her neck and shoulder. The monitor of her laptop was opened and she was playing solitaire. With her right hand, she was using the wireless mouse to move the ace of spades to the open space on the left side of the screen. Her other hand held an empty glass. Her hair was tied back in a ponytail and it was swaying back and forth, as she made exaggerated movements with her head and neck. Her mouth was moving but no words were coming out. Whatever her mother was saying obviously annoyed Hope, so she was responding by mimicking the woman.

She looked up and smiled as he leaned in to give her a kiss. Her lips felt cool and tasted like wine. She handed him the glass and she used her eyes to ask him for a refill. He opened the refrigerator and pulled out the chilled bottle of wine and a glass for himself. He heard the sound of water boiling and was just a second too late in turning off the burner. Pasta and water spilled out of the stainless steel five-quart pot onto the stove. It sizzled and splattered as he tried unsuccessfully to keep the hot water from hitting his hand.

Standing up, with the phone still cradled between her neck and shoulder, and still listening to her mother ramble on, she mouthed a 'sorry' to him. Smiling, he grabbed a towel, wiped up the spill and picked up each of the escaped noodles and tossed them back into the pot.

After making sure the flame was low enough where the pasta would be safe, he got her attention and mouthed his intention that he was going to take a shower. Hope nodded. He took a last sip of his wine and made his way upstairs.

He showered, shaved, and got into a fresh pair of jeans that he had left hanging in her closet. He transferred the small jewelry box into his right front pocket and made his way downstairs, just in time to hear her say goodbye and hang up the phone.

"I'm sorry, baby, she was on a roll." She was scraping the pot. Macaroni lay burnt on the bottom.

He looked inside and just shook his head.

"How on earth do you manage to burn pasta?" He grabbed a piece of paper that a magnet held to the freezer section of the refrigerator. Reading the numbers off the paper, he punched them into the number pad on the wall phone.

As soon as the party answered on the other end, he gave his order.

"Large extra cheese, pepperoni, and sausage…" He looked at her sideways, waiting for her request. Smiling, he didn't have to hear her say it; he was able to read the expression on her face.

"And anchovies—on just half," he added, grimacing.

Marty didn't have to give the address; the caller ID identified the familiar customer for the pizza parlor employee.

"Sometimes I wonder, Hope, if you fake this not being able to cook. Nobody with your intelligence and talent can be so inefficient in the kitchen." He opened the refrigerator and poured himself another glass of wine.

When she smiled, the corners of her eyes became crinkled and her nose wiggled. He pulled out a chair and sat down. He grabbed her arm and pulled her down so she was sitting on his lap. He nuzzled her throat, taking note of how good she smelled. He could tell by the strength of the vanilla scent that it hadn't been that long since she'd had her favorite bubble bath.

She laid her head on his shoulder.

"Are you okay?" she asked. "You sound tired." Her fingers toyed with his hair.

"I am," he replied.

"Did you make an arrest?" When they last spoke, he had told her they had suspects in the young girl's death, but no one specific.

He shook his head. "No, but everyone we talk to seems suspect. I don't know how you do it every day, Hope…deal with crazy."

She gave him a look of disapproval. He knew that she didn't like when he used that word, but he couldn't help it.

"Mental illness is a disease, Marty, no one chooses it. You make it sound like people have a choice in the matter. They don't." Her hand dropped and she sat up abruptly.

"That's where we disagree, Hope, and we probably always will. People have choices, and they choose to act in certain ways. Somebody chose to turn that girl's face into ashes. There is mental illness, and then there is just plain evil. Whoever did this is just plain old evil."

She chose to take the conversation in another direction.

"How are the girls that found her? Do you think they are dealing with it? None of them showed up for counseling at the school today. Do you know if their parents arranged for them to get help?"

He took a sip of his wine.

"The girls have been lying. One of the girl's boyfriends drove them up there to party with Paul Knox's son, Cameron. They didn't hitchhike up there, like they first said. At least one of them, if not all of them, are culpable. We just have to find out who." He took another sip of the wine before he continued.

"Could we talk about something else? My head has been spinning with this crap and I could use a reprieve for a few hours. Let's just concentrate on you and me. No talk of murder and cra…sorry, mental illness."

She gently laid her lips on his forehead. "Sure."

"What did your mom want?" he asked her.

"I thought we weren't going to talk about murder and crazy?" She broke out in a broad grin.

"That bad?" He took her hand and raised it to his lips, tasting her fingers. He looked at her ring finger; it still exhibited a faint mark from the wedding ring she once wore.

"She's angry at her friend Bernice—who knows what for this time. The sun wouldn't rise if she wasn't griping about something." She followed his eyes; he was looking at her hands and she couldn't tell why.

"What?" she snapped.

She regretted it the minute it came out of her mouth. She knew she sounded curt and impatient. The few minutes spent on the phone with her mother had made her cranky. He let her rant on for about fifteen minutes about her mother's most recent transgressions. She was about to apologize when she realized he had been talking.

"Hope, I was wondering if you have ever thought about making this…" he stopped when a car horn blasted outside.

They heard a car pull into the driveway. The pizza man honked his horn again, announcing his arrival.

She jumped off his lap. "It's about time. I'm starving!" She grabbed her purse and pulled out her wallet. Marty grabbed the box and Hope gave the driver a twenty-dollar bill and told him to keep the change.

By the time the plates were put out and they began to devour the pizza, the conversation had turned once again to Hope's mother and her antics. Once again, Marty decided that the time just wasn't right for showing Hope the ring and asking her to marry him.

∽

JEAN

Friday Evening

By the time I made it home, darkness had fallen. I was sure my husband and daughter had already eaten dinner without me. I was a bit surprised when I realized that there was no one there to welcome me. Usually I got at least a four-pawed greeting from Roxy, but even she seemed to be unaccounted for this evening.

I dropped my purse on the kitchen table, took off my jacket and threw it over the chair.

The quiet in the house was disconcerting. My husband's car was in the garage, but he was nowhere to be seen. I grabbed a Diet Coke out of the refrigerator and started up the stairs to see if Bethany was in her room.

Bethany was lying belly-down on her bed, typing furiously on her laptop.

"Hey, baby, how you doing?" I walked over and found a seat on the corner of the bed.

She slammed the laptop shut.

Although I got a pang of uneasiness, I chose to ignore the obvious behavior. I always respected my children's privacy, probably because I trusted them implicitly. Neither of my children had ever given me any reason to feel otherwise.

"Where's Daddy?" I took a lock of her waist-long hair and let it glide through my fingers. It was the color of corn silk, a color I have been trying, and failing miserably, to replicate through bottles for years now. My hair color was a combination of mustard and sand, and remained so, no matter what the desired result portrayed on the front of the box.

She rolled over on her back, scrunching her pillow and placing it behind her head.

"He went for a run in the park. He took Roxy. Daddy thinks Roxy needs to go on a diet."

"Maybe you and Dad need to stop giving Roxy so many treats." I playfully slapped her on the thigh.

"How was school today, Honey?"

"Fine," she offered, with some reluctance. Her head dipped down and strands of her hair fell forward in front of her eyes, covering her face. I gently took the portion of her hair that was obstructing her view and placed it behind her left ear.

The terse reply was unusual for my daughter, who normally would go into a long monologue about her day. Once again, my gut felt a pang of uneasiness, but I chose to ignore it.

"How are the kids dealing with Jamie's death? I heard that Dr. Rubin was at the school for grief counseling. Did you get to see her?"

"What do you mean?" she asked me, in a tone that sounded defensive. "Are you asking if I went to see her for professional reasons? Isn't that a little intrusive?"

I was startled at her reaction, but I didn't want to make too much of it.

"Bethany, no, I—what's wrong? Lately you act as if you're angry with me. Is there something that I've done that has upset you?"

I was in brand new real estate here with my daughter, and I didn't like the piece of property I was standing on.

She shook her head. "No, Mom, sorry, I'm just in a bad mood."

"What is it, baby? Is it what happened? I know some really bad things have happened to people you know and love, and it's not easy to understand why, but you need to be able to express them. That's what I'm here for."

"I know...I'm sorry, Mom. I have a lot of homework to do—I really should get back to it."

I rubbed her knee and gave it a slight squeeze.

"I would like to ask you something first, okay? Then you can get back to your schoolwork."

"What is it?" I heard impatience in her voice. As she sat up, her cell phone buzzed, signaling that a text had come in. She glanced down at it.

She looked up at me, her eyes conveying that she wanted to give the person a reply. She must have read me right, because she quickly typed the letters 'TTYL' and then turned her attention back to me.

"I'd like to know a little bit about the boy you tutor. Dylan Silver."

A look of pure panic crossed her face.

"Dylan? Why do you want to know about Dylan? He had nothing to do with Jamie getting killed."

"I heard that Jamie and Dylan were seeing each other, is that true?" It was obvious to me that I was encroaching on sensitive territory where this Silver boy was concerned. I needed to tread lightly if I was going to avoid her shutting down on me.

The possibility crossed my mind that she was more invested in this kid than just being his tutor. That gave me a sick feeling in my stomach.

She didn't answer me, but I could almost see the gears in her mind turning as she was trying to formulate an answer that would satisfy me without betraying anyone else.

"Bethany?" Once again, her face was hidden by fallen hair.

"Dylan had nothing to do with Jamie getting murdered," she insisted defiantly, lifting her head so she was looking at me now.

"How do you know that, Bethany? The girls lied about getting a ride from a hitchhiker. It was Dylan who drove the girls up to the woods that night. Dylan was there when they found Jamie, and then he took off. Dylan and Jamie had an argument that night; it's why she ran off by herself. That makes him the number one suspect on my list."

"I just do," she blurted out. "Dylan wouldn't hurt anyone. He's really very sweet." She turned away so she wasn't looking at me now. She had found a small thread on her blouse and she was trying to tie it into a knot with just the one hand.

"Look, Bethany, until I get a chance to interview him and find out what he knows and what they argued about that night, I would prefer he get another tutor."

"No!" She glared at me. "Anybody at my school could have killed her!" she shouted. "Maybe I shouldn't go to school, 'cause everyone could be a suspect."

I held my temper, but I wasn't happy at all about her raising her voice, and I certainly didn't want to drop the conversation.

"What does that mean, everyone?" I asked, the volume of my words rising as well.

"Jamie was a class "A" bitch. She thought she was the prettiest girl in the whole school and she was stuck-up. She would make fun of everyone, no matter what. Do you know that blind boy Matthew in my class? He's smart, and he's in my Advanced Science Class. Do you know that when he first got there, Jamie thought it would be funny to send him into the girl's locker room, instead of the boys'? He was so humiliated. She did so many mean things to everyone, even people she considered her friends. No one is crying that Jamie Camp got herself killed. I know it isn't right, but I saw a few kids doing a victory dance when they heard."

I was mortified; it wasn't what my daughter was telling me, but how she was telling it. I had always been so proud of my daughter's ability to empathize with others. I just assumed that she would have felt bad for Jamie Camp, feel compassion for her family, and want the perpetrator to be arrested and brought to justice. It was as if she was sympathetic to the murderer, which made me question her relationship with Dylan Silver even more.

"Bethany, even if Jamie wasn't a nice person..."

"Bitch," she said under her breath,

"Okay, bitch. However she acted, no one deserves to die the way she did. Someone hurt not only that young girl, but has broken the hearts of her family who loved her. Think about it, Honey, there is a four-year-old little boy who will never get to see his big sister again."

I heard the downstairs door slam and the sound of Roxy's four paws trying to get traction as she flew up the wooden staircase. Seconds later, she was jumping up on the bed, her tongue hanging out. She lifted her left paw, tapping me on the shoulder, requesting a rub. I accommodated her for a brief moment and stood up.

"Finish your homework, Bethany. We'll talk about this later."

She turned her back without answering.

I walked downstairs and was greeted by Glenn, sweaty and guzzling down a container of iced tea from the fridge.

He put the container back in the fridge and leaned over to kiss my cheek. Lord knows he smelled like he ran five miles. I pulled back.

"That bad?" He lifted his armpit and took in his own scent. "Yeah I guess it is. Bethany and I ate yesterday's leftovers for dinner. I left you a plate. Do you want me to heat it up?" He stood there, his right bicep slightly twitching, the sweat glistening on the few graying chest hairs he possessed.

"No, actually, I need to go out," I said. "Can you hold down the fort for a while?"

"Jean, come on. You just got home; we haven't seen you in two days. Can't it wait?" He sounded slightly annoyed with me.

"No," I said, moving so I was downwind of him. "I really need to do this now. Go take a shower, I promise I won't be long."

He said okay, but I could tell he was a little more than ticked off at me. Holding my breath, I leaned in and gave him a kiss on his lips. "Please go take a shower...I'll be back shortly."

I grabbed my purse, grateful that I never bothered to change out of my work clothes. Normally, I would have taken off my holster and put my Glock in my lockbox, but for some reason I hadn't. I grabbed my cell phone as I was pulling out of the driveway and punched in Marty's number.

"Keal," he answered, as if he was trying to swallow something.

"Marty, it's Jean. Can you meet me at 1399 Pine Avenue?"

"That's Silver's residence, I thought you wanted to do that first thing in the morning?"

"Change of plans...are you game? Where are you? If you want, I can run by and pick you up."

I heard him tell someone he had to go out. "Yeah, sure. I'm at Hope's. Swing by, I can be ready in ten minutes. What's this about, Jean? You find out anything else?"

"Not really. I'll explain when I see you. I hope I'm not interrupting anything."

I heard him chuckle at the other end.

"No," he answered.

"Okay, I'll be there in ten minutes." I hung up and threw the cell phone onto my console. I hoped that my daughter was right and that Dylan Silver wasn't a cold-blooded killer. I didn't want to have to shatter her world and arrest someone she apparently had developed feelings for.

I had to pass my partner Joe's house on the way to Marty's girlfriend. The house sat in total darkness. When Joe and Connie were home, the first thing they did when night came was turn on the floodlights that hung on the corner of the house.

Not long after Connie died, Joe added a timer, so the lights would go on automatically. He was afraid that he would forget to turn them on every night, because it had been Connie who made a ritual of making sure they were turned on before they went to bed.

It was one of the small ways he tried to keep his wife's presence in the home they had shared for so many years. All the things that Connie had nagged him about getting done and he had blown off suddenly became a priority for him. He had made himself a list and, as if he was possessed, he spent hours and sleepless nights completing all the things he had accused her of nagging him about.

He never got to the end of the list, because every time he finished one task, he remembered something else she had asked him to do.

I wondered if he just forgot to set the timer for the light when he left, or if it had burned out.

I wanted so bad to talk to him about Bethany. I wanted to finally show him that she was not perfect, and she was just as normal as any other teenage girl. He would tease me relentlessly about how my children weren't normal…that they were too perfect, and were probably conceived in a lab.

I was so compelled to talk to him right now that I actually ached inside. I missed him terribly.

~

I pulled up in front of Hope's house and waved to her as she stood on her tiptoes and kissed Marty goodbye. These two looked so good together. Even though he was at least a foot taller, they seemed to fit like two pieces of a puzzle.

Marty pushed the seat all the way back to accommodate his long legs as he got in the car.

"What's up?" he asked me as he locked the clip on his seat belt.

"I just want to find and interview this kid Dylan before he gets a chance to lawyer up or take off."

He looked at me as if he knew I had another agenda, but chose not to say anything.

"Did I interrupt anything? I'm sorry."

He laughed. A massive dimple appeared on his right cheek.

He reached into his front pocket and pulled out a small jewelry box. He jiggled it around in his right hand.

"Is that what I think it is? Congratulations! Did I interrupt you proposing? Oh, Marty, I am so sorry. I'll bring you back." I started to turn the car around, but he put his hand over mine.

"No, it's okay. Tonight didn't seem to be the night, anyway." He opened it up and just stared at the diamond that sat in the center of the box.

I thought it was the most gorgeous piece of jewelry I ever saw. It must have set him back six months' salary

"It's beautiful," I told him, taking my eyes of the road for a split second to admire it.

"Her friend Diane helped me pick it out. She's on pins and needles, waiting for Hope to call her with the news. There just never seems to be the right moment. Besides, what if she says "no"?" He looked at the ring for the last time before closing the box and putting it back in his pocket.

"Don't be ridiculous, Marty. Why would she say "no"? That girl is so in love with you, and it's obvious how you feel about her. You're made for each other. Besides, you'll make incredibly beautiful children."

"It's not that I don't think she loves me, it's just she seems so content the way things are. She had a bad marriage and she never once has even hinted that she wants to walk down an aisle and do the whole white dress thing again." He sounded deflated.

"Marty, I think your worries are unfounded. Hope knows that you are not remotely, in any way, anything like her ex-husband. I don't think you have anything to worry about. She may not be the type that needs the whole ritual wedding thing, but that doesn't mean she doesn't want to be totally committed. Maybe she's afraid that talking about it will scare you off."

"Maybe," he said, stretching his legs out again. "It's just that she seems real comfortable the way things are, me spending a few nights and weekends with her and living with my father the rest of the time."

He turned his eyes downward before continuing. "Actually, that is a dilemma for me, as well. I don't like the thought of the Captain living by himself again, even though he keeps telling me to take the plunge and move in with Hope."

I took my hand off the wheel and gently punched his shoulder with my fist. "The Captain is quite capable of tending to his own self, Marty. He's a grown man. Besides, it's not like you would be that far apart. How long does it take you to get to the Captain's from Hope's? Fifteen, twenty minutes?"

He made a face, pretending that my punch was painful. "I know, but I've worried ever since that fall he had, when he lay there all day with a broken hip. That wouldn't have happened if I was living at home."

I couldn't tell if he was trying to convince himself or me.

We reached our destination and pulled into the driveway of a run-down red brick ranch house. The front bay window had black tar smeared across the top where there must have been a leak. The wooden white frame windows desperately needed painting. A street light lit up the area like it was daylight and everything was visible, even though night had fallen. A red tricycle lay on its side next to a broken-down push mower. The lawn was in desperate need of mowing.

I turned to him as I shut off the motor. "Marty, life happens. You need to live your life and stop worrying about your father. I know that's what he wants for you."

I exited the car and met him on the other side. We walked a narrow red brick pathway that matched the exterior of the house. The glow of a television flashing dark and then light could be seen through the bay window.

As we got closer, I could hear the sound of children playing inside the house. I recalled the file I had gotten on Dylan. Dylan and his two siblings, a two-year-old girl and ten-year-old boy, lived with their widowed mother and grandmother. Dylan's father, a decorated Marine, had been killed in action the day his two-year-old daughter was born.

I rang the doorbell and immediately recognized the sound of a young child running to the door as if in a race. "I'll get it!" a boy's voice hollered out.

I heard a voice of authority yell for him not to open the door, but the kid either didn't hear or chose not to heed the warning.

When the door opened, a wide-eyed boy stood there with his mouth agape. From the expression on his face, I assumed he was expecting someone else.

"What did I tell you, Griffin? Didn't I tell you to never answer the door without asking who it was?" The woman, who I guessed was the grandmother, grabbed the boy by his arm and gave it a tug. "Now go get ready for bed, and brush your teeth!"

The boy took one more good look at Marty and me, and with an abundance of reluctance, walked away."

The woman turned her attention back to us.

"Can I help you?" she looked at us with suspicion.

Faceless: A Mystery ~ Dawn Kopman Whidden

"I'm sorry to bother you, but we would like to have a word with Dylan. Is he home?" I told her, as I tried to scan the room behind her.

"And you are?" her hand remained on the door as if she would be ready to slam it shut.

"I'm sorry, I'm Detective Whitley, and this is Detective Keal. May we come in?"

She looked us both over carefully. I took out my badge and showed it to her. She examined it and seemed satisfied. She took her hand off the door and backed up so we could enter.

"Are you Dylan's mother?" I asked her.

"No, I am his grandmother. The police were already here, asking for Dylan. What's this about? This about that girl that got killed?" She sounded more suspicious than curious.

Another voice came from inside the house.

"Mama, what is it? Who's here?"

A very pretty woman with short, dark hair, a younger version of the older one, came rolling out in a wheelchair. A toddler lay across her lap, in the beginning of slumber, eye half closed, her mouth making slow sucking motions from a bottle. Her little fingers were wrapped around a blanket that hung from her mother's shoulder.

She rolled to a stop right behind the grandmother and looked up at Marty and me, her face contorted in a state of complete panic.

"Mama? What is it? Is it Dylan, Mama?"

"I'm sorry, Mrs. Silver, I apologize if our visit has caused you any concern. We came here to talk to Dylan. I understand he isn't home?"

"No, Dylan didn't come home," the older woman answered. "It's really not like him. He knows we worry about him. He's a good boy, but sometimes he goes off and wants to be by himself. He's got a lot on his plate." She spoke affectionately of her grandson.

"How long has it been since he was home, Mrs. Silver?" I looked down to the boy's mother.

"What do you want with Dylan? Why are you here?" The lady maneuvered the wheelchair so she could see us better.

"Can you tell us the last time you saw Dylan, Mrs. Silver?" I asked again.

Faceless: A Mystery ~ Dawn Kopman Whidden

"Look, what is this about? My grandson is a good boy," the older woman interjected. She was practically jeering at me until the baby, who was becoming jittery and started to cry in her mother's arms, took her attention away.

The older woman immediately took the baby from her daughter's arms. She rocked the little girl and turned away as if dismissing us. She left the room with the baby, leaving Dylan's mother to deal with us.

"Please, can you tell me what this is about? Dylan hasn't been home in two days. It just isn't like him to stay away this long. He did call me this morning, told me he was fine, and that I shouldn't worry." It was obvious she wasn't paying her son's words any attention. Worry was written all over the woman's face.

"Does this have something to do with the girl that got murdered?" Her voice took on some urgency.

"Why do you ask that, Mrs. Silver?" I questioned her.

"I know they went to the same school, and I think I recognized her name. I asked Dylan and he said that he knew her, that they were friends. He sounded very upset that she had died."

"Did Dylan tell you he was the one who drove the girls up to the woods that night, Mrs. Silver? Did he tell you he was one of the kids that found her body?" Marty asked her.

I noticed her hands were turning white as she gripped the metal frame of her wheelchair tires.

"Look, I don't know what you're thinking, but I know my son and he wouldn't hurt anyone." She stopped and thought about it for a few seconds and then qualified her answer. "Well, he certainly wouldn't hurt a girl."

"Well, we would like to be able to talk to him Mrs. Silver, so Dylan can tell us himself what happened. Right now, it isn't looking so good for him, so he needs to come into the police station and talk to us."

"Detective, my Dylan would not hurt that girl or any other girl," the woman insisted. "I can promise you that. If my son Dylan has gone off, it's because he needed to think. He has always done that, ever since he was a little boy. He has a tendency to take off, and I guess you can call it 'meditate.' When he was too little to leave the house, he would climb up on the roof and just stare at the stars and daydream. I can promise you that Dylan isn't trying to avoid you, detective, he is just off somewhere trying to figure things out." She spoke defensively.

I handed her my card.

"Please have him come in or call me as soon as you hear from him, Mrs. Silver. Like I said before, this is not the time for him to pull a disappearing act to think." I put an emphasis on the word "think."

"It's doesn't look good for him. A young girl is dead, and your son may be able to give us information we need. I'm going to give him till tomorrow morning to show up or call me, or I'm going to have the judge sign a warrant for his arrest. Do you understand?"

She nodded a reply and didn't say anything more. She maneuvered the wheelchair again so she was able to shut the door when Marty and I turned and walked out of the house.

CHAPTER NINE

I was just pulling up to Hope's driveway to drop Marty off when the call came in. I knew that he must have overheard the dispatcher, because he grabbed the blue globe, positioned it on the dash, and hit the siren.

"What the hell?"

I just shook my head in disbelief. There was no way that this was happening. A couple of men stopping at the side of the road to take a leak stumbled across a Jane Doe in the woods, not far from the Forester house. She was barely alive, her face badly burnt. She was being transported to St Katherine's Hospital. I backed the car out of the driveway and the tires squealed. I took off in the direction of the hospital.

I pushed the speed-dial on my cell and it rang twice before Glenn answered.

"I thought you would be home by now, Jean." I sensed a bit of attitude.

"I know—me too. Where's Bethany?" I tried not to sound anxious.

"She's holed up in her room, why?"

"Are you sure? Go check!" I demanded.

"Yes, I'm sure. What's going on, Jean?" Now he was sounding a bit anxious himself.

"We're on our way to St. Katherine's. Another girl's been hurt. Can you just go upstairs and check on her? Please. I'll be home as soon as I can. I'm sorry, Glenn."

"Do you know who it is? Someone from Bethany's school?" he asked.

"No, right now it's a Jane Doe; that's why I need you to just pacify me and make sure she's in her room."

The traffic light ahead was amber. I hit the accelerator, causing Marty's head to snap back. I threw him a look of apology.

I heard silence for a few seconds, and then he said something that caused all my anxiety and fears to leave my body.

"I can hear her stomping around upstairs, she's there, unless Roxy is wearing boots." I could tell that even with the slight humor in his answer, he sounded relieved.

I pulled into St. Katherine's and parked in a No Parking Zone behind an empty ambulance. I quickly got off the phone with Glenn, and Marty and I marched into the ER.

Doctors and nurses were running around like someone had stepped on a fire-ant mound. Off to the side, with his back towards us, a familiar looking uniformed officer, was standing by the nurse's desk, doing some paperwork.

"You want to fill us in?" Marty asked when he caught his friend Justin's attention.

Justin pointed to a couple of gentlemen who appeared to be in their early thirties.

"They had a few beers and needed to take a leak, so they pulled over to the side of the road. The taller one claims that he tripped over her and fell into some brush. Claims that's how he got those scratches on him. She was just lying there, half-naked like the other one, her face badly burnt, barely alive. They called 911, and Beck and I got there about the same time as the ambulance."

I was about to go talk to the two gentlemen who made the call when one of the attending physicians walked over to us.

"Do we know who she is yet? I need to have her transported to the Burn Unit at Cornell. We're just not equipped to treat her here," he said, more frustrated than apologetic. "She's unconscious and in critical condition, but those burns require immediate attention. We would like to have parental authorization if possible."

Justin walked over, his cell phone in hand. "See if she has a scar on her abdomen from an appendectomy. We got a call earlier about a missing teenager…Kimberly Weston, age sixteen."

He handed me the phone. Displayed in the window was the image of a beautiful raven-haired teenage girl. I recognized the girl immediately. She was one of the girls in Father Murphy's youth group at the church. The doctor walked back to the room the girl occupied, quickly pulling the drape that enclosed the cubicle. He spoke to one of the nurses, who was in the process of applying some sort of salve to the girl's skin. He didn't say anything when he turned back around, he just nodded. We now had a name for our Jane Doe.

Marty and Justin took off in Justin's patrol car to inform the girl's parents. I was left to interview the two men with the bladder problems. Their story seemed to hold water and left me satisfied that they weren't culpable for the girl's condition, but I had them give all their information to one of the other uniformed officers that had responded to the call.

I was just finishing up with them when the attending physician came back out. I stopped him and asked the doctor whether Kimberly had any other injuries.

"Nothing that stands out," he informed me. "Her pupils are dilated, and I'm concerned that she may have been under the influence of something. I need to know if she has anything in her system so I ordered up a blood work and a tox screen. I haven't gotten the preliminary results back yet, but I would make an educated guess that she has some sort of drug in her system. There doesn't appear to be any other obvious injuries, no."

A familiar voice called out my name. Father Murphy was racing over to me.

"Jean, how is she? Marty called and told me to get down here. He's on his way with her parents." The priest could barely catch his breath. Apparently, he had run from the parking lot, and he wasn't as in good a shape as he looked.

I pulled him aside to allow medical personal to get in and out of Kimberly's room.

"She's alive, Father, and they are going to airlift her to Cornell as soon as her parents arrive. They don't have the facilities to care for her injuries here."

"What in the good Lord's name is going on here, Jean? Why would someone do this?" He ran his hand through his hair as he took a deep breath.

"How well do you know her, Father? Do you know if she was friends with that other girl, Jamie?" I led him out of the ER and into a small waiting area. There were a few people seated, waiting for medical attention or with others that required attention.

I walked the padre over to a small bench that was unoccupied and we sat down.

He shook his head in disbelief. "I don't remember, I'm not sure. Maybe. Oh sweet, Jesus." He sat back, leaning his head against the wooden bench and stretching out his legs. He rubbed his thighs as if massaging out a cramp.

"We have a few different groups, sometimes they overlap. I think the girls must have known each other, but I don't recall if they were friends." His hands patted his pockets as if he was looking for something. He pulled out a pack of Marlboro Lights. "I need a cigarette," he said, continuing to pat his jacket. "I seem to have misplaced my lighter." His voice was brittle and sober. "Maybe it's a sign it's time to give it up."

He looked up when he heard the clatter of multiple feet rushing toward us.

Kimberly's mother, an older version of the photograph I was shown of Kimberly, was approaching us, a look of pure panic on her face. Quickly following behind her was her husband, who was holding a small child dressed in pajamas and wrapped in a pink cotton blanket. The little girl was sucking hard on her thumb, her index finger bent over her nose. Her father's hand was holding the child against him so his movement would not cause the little girl's head to bang relentlessly against his shoulder. Behind him, another child, a boy about twelve years old, fought to catch up.

"My daughter…someone said my daughter was brought in. Please, can someone help me?" The woman had stopped in the middle of the room, not knowing in which direction she should go, and was shouting aimlessly.

Her eyes darted from each individual in the room until her eyes rested on Father Murphy. Recognizing him immediately, she covered her mouth and let out a muffled scream.

He immediately got up and walked over to her.

"No, no, she's alive, Rita, she's still alive." He grabbed her hand and rubbed it. The woman looked at him, stone-faced, not knowing where to go, what to do.

It was her husband who spoke next.

"What happened? Can we see her?" He handed the little girl to her brother. The girl did not resist the changing of caretakers in the least. I flashed back on memories stored in my head of all the times I handed

Bethany to her older brother Cliff, and how comfortable she felt in her big brother's arms.

Someone must have notified the doctor that Kimberly's parents had arrived, because he came out and pulled them off to the side. He explained what was happening and obtained their authorization for additional treatment. Before he left the room, he gave them a stark warning of how horribly she had been hurt and what to expect.

Father Murphy made his way over to the boy, who now was shifting the little girl's weight from one arm to the other. He didn't say a word to him, he just put his hand on the boy's shoulder in a sign of support.

It wasn't long before the victim's parents were brought back into the waiting room. Someone obviously pointed me out, because the girl's mother marched immediately over to me.

"Who did this? Who did this to my beautiful baby girl? Did you see what they did to my baby?"

She spoke through gritted teeth, her nostrils flaring.

"I'm sorry, Mrs. Weston, at the moment we don't know who did this. Our best hope is that when (and I emphasized the word when) Kimberly regains consciousness she can identify the perpetrator. Believe me, I want to put away this bastard just as much as you do."

"Is this the same person that killed Jamie Camp?" Kimberly's father asked me.

He had taken the little girl from her brother and was holding on to the child, as if to protect her from this unknown danger that was still lurking. I knew that if this were my husband, Glenn, he would be consumed with guilt, feeling that he had failed to protect his daughter. I guessed that it was the same emotion that Mr. Weston was now feeling.

Marty walked over to us and turned to Mr. Weston.

"Mr. Weston, Officer Beck has the weekend off," he told the girl's father as he pointed to the petite female officer. "She has offered to drive you and your family up to Cornell so you can be with your daughter. She can stay as long as you like, and then, when Kimberly regains consciousness, she can be there to interview her. Would that be all right?"

The attending doctor came out and informed us that preliminary tests showed that Kimberly did have an unknown substance in her blood system that was yet to be determined, but he hoped that she would overcome the unconscious state she was now in. However, he wasn't willing to make a prognosis this early.

After a few minutes of deliberation and coordination, the family decided to take Officer Beck up on her kind offer. Just as they were walking out the automatic glass doors, I called out her name. "Wait, Officer Beck!"

The group stopped.

I ran over to Kimberly's mom. Her husband continued into the parking lot.

"Mrs. Weston, was your daughter a friend of Jamie Camp?"

The woman was trembling. It took a moment to gather her thoughts and get the words out. I waited patiently as I held one of the glass doors so it wouldn't shut.

"She was, at one time. They went to school together and Girl Scouts and I believe they both belonged to the youth group at the church." She looked over at Father Murphy for corroboration. "Jamie and Kim were very competitive. They are both up for …" She stopped and broke down crying. Her son reached up and took his mother's hand. Shaking her head she just turned, letting go of her son's hand and continuing to join the rest of her family in the parking area.

It was the boy who stopped to finish his mother's sentence.

"Kimmy and Jamie were both running for prom queen. My sister was going to win." He spoke defiantly as he turned and walked rapidly away, trying to catch up with the other family members.

"Mrs. Weston, please," I yelled after her, now running myself. The glass doors shut behind me. "Does your daughter know Dylan Silver?"

She stopped immediately in the middle of the parking lot.

"Yes, of course, Dylan and Kimberly dated on and off since grade school. Why?" It was a demand, not a question her voice was raw with emotion. She was jittery and she wanted to go. I was holding her up and I could feel the resentment.

I gently took her arm in an effort to lend her some support.

"I'm just trying to find out what happened Mrs. Weston, and I need as much information as you can give me. I know that you're anxious to get to the hospital and be with your daughter. I know, trust me, I have a daughter of my own. Did your daughter and Dylan get along?" I probed gently.

She turned back to see her husband settling his little girl in the back seat of Officer's Beck's patrol car.

"Do you think Dylan did this, Detective? Do you think Dylan did this to my baby?" It came out in a moan, her voice catching in her throat.

"I don't know, Mrs. Weston, we have been trying to find him, to talk to him. He is just a person of interest at this time."

She shook her head as if she was trying to picture something in her mind.

"I don't know too much about Dylan anymore, detective. Kimmy stayed in touch with him, but she had said that ever since his mother was diagnosed with MS, he has changed. She was pretty concerned about him. They were best friends for years. They would go steady and then have a fight and break up. It was pretty tame stuff. Dylan spent a lot of time at my house and I liked him, but when his father was killed, he changed. When his mother got sick, Dylan became very aloof and stopped coming around. Kimmy said he became angry and bitter." She turned back to see her family waiting for her.

"I have to go, I have to go be with my baby. I can't do this right now." She shook her head. "Please find out who did this to my girl." She turned and walked away as I let go of her arm.

As a cop, I wanted to detain her and continue the interview. As a mother, I just had to let her go and be with her daughter. My questions would just have to wait.

CHAPTER TEN

Sunday Morning

Weekends for Marty usually meant hanging out with family and friends. Although finding whoever was responsible for the heinous acts was a top priority, the investigation had stalled.

Numerous samples and possible DNA were processed at both crime scenes and sent to the lab, but results took time, and sometimes the waiting was excruciating.

They did establish that the can of lighter fluid found at the first scene was in fact the incendiary that caused the burns to the first victim, Jamie Camp. Unfortunately, there were no distinguishable fingerprints on the can, and the footprint casts that were made at the scene were inconclusive. They had yet to uncover any evidence of what had caused the burns to Kimberly's face, and she had yet to regain consciousness.

Marty had slept most of Saturday, but Sunday he was alert and raring to go. He decided this would be the day he'd finally pop the question.

Hope and Marty were spending the day with the Captain and his friends, Justin and Diane, and their new baby.

They had been watching the Yankee game when Marty offered to get the refreshments. He walked into the kitchen and opened the freezer to get ice for their drinks. He had scooped up a dozen or so cubes when he saw the wallet sitting on top of a carton of Birds Eye frozen peas.

His father had mentioned the evening before in a phone call that it was missing and he thought it might have been stolen. Marty picked it up and dried it off. He opened it to find two hundred dollars in cash.

He walked back into the living room a with a Cheshire grin on his face.

"You looking for this, Captain?" He held out the wallet like a trophy.

The Captain's face expressed relief.

"Where did you find it? I just called and cancelled all my credit cards and was going to make an appointment to get a new driver's license." He took the wallet from his son's grip. The feel of the cold leather puzzled him.

"It was hiding between the frozen sausages and green peas. I've heard of 'cold cash,' Captain, but isn't this going too far?"

"Very funny. Maybe you should change careers and try comedy," he answered, skimming through the folds of the wallet, making sure everything was in place.

"Unless you think that the French fries or cauliflower have a background in petty larceny, I think you can rest assured that the contents are all there." Marty told him, a wide smirk on his face.

"How the hell did it end up in there?" his father cried out in disbelief.

Justin, overhearing the conversation, couldn't resist butting in. "Maybe the IRS is freezing your assets, Captain."

"Very funny, Justin, maybe you should go on the road with your friend here," he hollered back to his son's friend, placing the wallet in the back pocket of his pants.

Hope and Diane walked back downstairs, the baby cooing in Hope's arms. Now in a fresh diaper and smelling like baby powder, the infant drooled happily into a clean cloth thrown over Hope's shoulder.

A patch of the white baby powder had found a home on the hip area of Hope's slacks. Marty gently brushed it off.

Not knowing exactly what was going on, but taking notice of the look on the Captain's face and noticing the smirk on Marty's, she immediately came to the older man's defense.

"Captain, is he giving you a hard time? We can retaliate by me taking over the preparation for dinner. Marty is probably just salivating for my meatloaf." She grabbed a spoon with her free hand, brought it to her lips, and playfully licked it.

A look of pure panic crossed Marty's face. He had been looking forward to his dad's ribs the whole week. He loved this woman to death, but the fact remained, the woman could not cook if her life depended on it.

"Not fair. That would be considered cruel and unusual

punishment, and there's no reason for Diane and Justin to be collateral damage." Marty gently took the baby from her and lifted him in the air. A stream of drool landed on Marty's face.

Hope admired the fact that Marty took it in stride. The carrot-top infant looked so natural in Marty's arms. She envied him that. She, on the other hand, felt totally inept and inadequate. No matter how many times Diane told her that the fears she was experiencing were absurd and that she had the makings of a wonderful mother, Hope wasn't convinced.

The fact that she was a successful and well-respected child psychiatrist had no influence on her fears. She felt insecure and knew that, although intellectually she wasn't like her mother, it didn't keep her from fearing that she would eventually end up emulating the woman. That thought scared her immensely.

Her thought process was interrupted when she suddenly became aware of Marty calling her name.

"Hope…hello! Marty to Hope…"

"I'm sorry, I was daydreaming." She looked at him and took the corner of the rag that was on her shoulder. Standing on her tiptoes, she wiped the baby's drool from Marty's cheek.

"More like you were on another planet," Marty informed her.

"I'm sorry." Hope turned her attention to Marty's dad.

"Captain, can I help you with anything?" She then turned to Marty. "Why don't you take the baby and keep Justin busy and out of trouble? Diane and I will help the Captain with dinner."

"No, no, Hope. This chef works better solo," the older Keal told her, almost in a panic, as he shooed her away from the entrance to the kitchen. "Why don't you and Mary just settle back and relax. I'll take care of everything."

"Diane," Hope corrected him.

"Right, sorry. Diane, Mary…whatever…Go. I'll call you in when dinner's ready."

Reluctantly, she grabbed Marty's hand and joined their friends in the den.

"See Hope? Even Mr. Magoo knows what a disaster you are in the kitchen," Marty told her as they walked into the living room.

"What's with the Mr. Magoo? What was going on when we walked in?" Hope asked.

Justin filled her in.

"Marty found the Captain's wallet in the icebox. He mistook it for a safe." Justin said, laughing as he took possession of the baby, who had been passed around and now was finally lying across his father's knees.

Suddenly something the Captain had said just seconds before took on a new meaning, but her attention was diverted when she noticed that Diane was giving Marty a verbal spanking and was curious to know what they were talking about. She put her concerns about the Captain on hold and sat down next to Marty. Diane mysteriously shut up.

"Am I interrupting something?" she asked, as she helped herself to a Wheat Thin from a bowl on the coffee table.

Giving Marty a sharp look, Diane answered her, redirecting the conversation.

"No, Marty was just telling me about Mayor Knox's son. I think I remember him. He was a little weird. Do you remember him, Hope?" Not waiting for an answer, she continued. "Didn't he go to the sleep-away camp with us? I think they caught him stealing the girls' counselors' underwear one year. Remember?"

"Was that him? Creepy Cam?" she coughed, trying not to choke on the cracker.

"Probably," Marty replied. "He's a bit strange."

"Do you think he killed that girl, Marty?" Diane quizzed him curiously, as she handed Hope a glass of water.

"Honestly Diane, I don't know. So far, we can't find any evidence showing that he was anywhere near the body. We are trying to track down this Dylan Silver kid. Right now, he's our number one suspect, because he seems to be missing. We have an APB out on him now."

"How's the other girl doing? Has she regained consciousness?" Hope responded after taking a sip of the water.

He shook his head.

Justin spoke up.

"You should have seen this girl...she was beautiful—'was' being the operative word. So was Camp. Word from everyone we spoke to was that they were both a couple of Class "A" bitches. Beautiful but bitchy." He took a long gulp of his drink.

Hope turned to face Marty.

"Do you think that is the reason the girls were attacked, Marty? Could it be someone jealous of the girls' attractiveness? It would explain the burns to the face."

He took hold of her hand, massaging it. He looked over at Diane, who was glaring at him. Hope caught the tension in the air.

"What's going on with you two?" Hope asked, turning from Marty to Diane.

The baby grabbed onto a strand of Diane's long red hair, and she fought to get him to release his sticky fingers. Using that as an excuse, she smiled and ignored Hope's question. Getting up, she grabbed Justin's hand.

"Let's go take the baby for a quick stroll, maybe he'll fall asleep," she suggested.

Justin was about to protest when he read the stern look he was getting from his wife. He knew that look and knew he was sunk. He put down his glass and reluctantly followed his wife and new baby out the front door.

Marty was just about to get down on one knee when they heard the commotion coming from the kitchen. Drawers were being slammed and the Captain was saying words he normally didn't say.

They both got up and walked into the kitchen. Silverware was strewn all about. Pots and pans were on top of the counter. The kitchen, which the Captain normally kept in such immaculate condition and organized with what Freud would call anal retentiveness, was in disarray.

"What the heck is going on?" Marty asked his father, who was now red in the face.

"I can't find the damn can opener!" he said, frustrated, throwing a towel at the sink.

Marty turned toward the counter where the electric can opener sat. Where it always sat. He looked over at Hope. There was a look of concern on her face.

"It's right here, Pop, right where it always is."

Marty walked over to the machine and moved it toward the front of the counter. "It's right here," he repeated it. "It's right here."

His father was standing in the middle of the room, looking confused. The man Marty perceived as brave and courageous…the man who survived a knife attack at the high-security prison he worked at for twenty-five years until he retired…the man who raised nine children as a single father after his wife died of cancer when Marty was only nine years old. Suddenly, the man Marty often thought of as some sort of superman looked vulnerable and tired. Marty was perplexed and didn't know what to do.

Hope walked over to the Captain and put her arm over his. She walked him to the long wooden table sitting in the center of the room…the same elongated oak table that served as a centerpiece for evening meals for the large family…the very same one that he often found himself sitting alone at, now that all but one of his children were married and had families of their own.

The past few years, it had just been him and Marty, but even Marty was spending less and less time at home.

"What's going on, Captain?" Hope asked him, gently brushing some crumbs off the man's sleeve.

"Nothing, forget it. I'm just having a bad day. I'm sorry." He rubbed his eyes trying to avoid Hope's.

"Captain, please, something is going on. You need to tell me how long these episodes have been happening."

The gray-haired man turned to his son.

"Marty, don't you have something to do?" he bellowed angrily.

Marty didn't answer; the expression on his face was obvious enough.

The older man turned toward Hope, his eyes almost pleading for her not to ask any more questions.

It didn't work.

"Captain, answer me, how long?" she demanded forcefully.

He shook his head, and shrugged his shoulders at the same time.

"It's nothing." He went to get up, but Hope's arm, as thin and petite as she was, held him down as if she had the strength of a pro wrestler.

"I don't know. A while," he answered her, with a bit of reluctance.

Hope looked over at Marty. "We need to get him scheduled for a CAT scan. I want you to make an appointment first thing Monday for him to see a neurologist."

"Hey, let's not get ahead of ourselves. I don't need a CAT scan, Dr. Rubin. It's just a bit of old age. When you get to be my age, young lady, you'll see!" He broke into a slight smile, the skin at the corner of his blue eyes folded into tiny creases.

Hope looked over at Marty, letting him know it was time for him to intervene.

"I'll call his primary Monday, get a referral," Marty said.

"I can do it myself," the Captain said in protest. "I'm still quite capable of making my own appointments!"

"Oh, old man, I didn't say you weren't, but I don't trust you to do it," Marty answered abruptly.

The Captain stood up. "Fine, suit yourself. Make the damn appointment. You'll see, it's just my old age. Now, can I go back and get dinner ready?" He didn't wait for an answer.

"Clear off the counter, so I can open the beans and get dinner on the table. Hope, you call Justin and Diane in, let's get you people fed."

It was as if nothing had gone wrong. The Captain was back to shouting orders, just like normal, and the ring stayed put in Marty's pocket.

~

Saturday I slept in and just hung around the house. Saturday evening, Bethany had a birthday party and sleepover, so Glenn and I had the evening to ourselves, but I was so exhausted I had fallen asleep by eight p.m. and didn't wake up until seven o'clock Sunday morning. I was looking forward to a leisurely day at home, and just doing some chores.

Later that morning, I entered Bethany's room with a bundle of clean, folded clothes and I dropped them on her bed. I was so proud of the way my daughter kept her room, whereas her brother was a slob. More often than not, his clothes would lie in piles, resembling cow patties in a pasture.

Faceless: A Mystery ~ Dawn Kopman Whidden

Bethany was more like her dad, who was teetering on OCD. Her dad was a neat freak, and everything had its place. Bethany's bed was made up with her mauve-and-white bedspread tight and neat—not a wrinkle in sight. Her white Formica dresser and desk were dust free and each item on it sat perfectly in its own spot.

I was about to put her clothes in the dresser when I had this overwhelming urge to open the laptop that sat in the middle of her desk.

That just wasn't like me; I never intruded on my children's privacy. Never. My daughter had kept a journal since she was able to read and write, and unless she chose to read me something out of it, I never felt the need to intrude.

I don't know what it was—maybe a mother's intuition—but something compelled me to open the lid on that laptop.

The lid was covered with a plastic protective cover stamped with a 1960s-styled tie-dyed design. It had been in sleep mode and immediately went to her Facebook page. I saw that there was a notation that she received a message, so I pointed the mouse and clicked on it. A list of 'to' and 'from' messages came up.

I was in a state of panic and was about to hyperventilate when I read whom the messages were from.

Dylan Silver had been conversing with Bethany since the day that Jamie's body had been discovered. I knew that my daughter's smart phone was had a Facebook app, so she received the same messages on her cell phone that I was now reading on her laptop. The last one that came in made my heart pound. It had come in at eleven p.m. last night.

"Meet me at our spot," was all that was it said.

I tried to scream Glenn's name, but no sound came out. My throat felt like someone had stuffed a dry rag in it.

Finally, my vocal chords began to work and my scream was so loud that Glenn came running up the steps in a pure panic.

"My God, Jean, what's wrong?" He was standing in the doorway, trying to catch his breath.

I dialed my daughter's cell phone number. It went straight to voice mail.

I started to frantically look for my daughter's phone book. I found it in the top drawer of her desk and immediately flipped through the pages until I came to the letter M. Bethany listed her friends by first names, and my fingers traced the names down until I came to her friend Melanie's name.

I pointed to the laptop as I dialed Melanie's number. As my husband read the messages that Bethany and Dylan were sending back and forth, I waited impatiently as the phone rang and rang. No one was picking up. I was just about to hang up when Melanie's mother came on the line.

"Denise, it's Jean, Bethany's mom. Can I speak to my daughter?" I tried to remain calm. Silence was what I got for the first few seconds.

"Jean? I'm sorry, Jean," she sounded bewildered. "Bethany isn't here. Is everything all right?"

"Did Melanie have a sleepover last night?" I asked, praying to myself that she just meant that my daughter wasn't there at that moment.

Again, for a second there was a pause before she answered.

"Oh, no, Jean, I'm sorry. Bethany wasn't here last night. Let me call Melanie and ask her if she knows where she is."

I nodded my head as if she could see me. Then I remembered we were on the phone. "Yes, please, can you do that, Denise? Can you get back to me as soon as you can?"

I apologized for being blunt, hung up quickly, and turned to my husband.

"She's not there, Glenn, she lied to us. There was no sleepover. Where the hell is she?" I was frantic.

"Hold on, you sure it was Melanie's house she was going to? Maybe you got it wrong, you've been so preoccupied lately."

I looked at him as if he was crazy.

"Of course she said Melanie, I'm positive she said Melanie." I began to question myself, hoping that maybe he was right. I pictured the conversation I had had with her the day before. It came back to me loud and clear.

"No, she said Melanie. I'm positive, she said Melanie got that new mare for her birthday and she wanted to go riding with her."

The phone rang and we both jumped. I grabbed it.

"Bethany!" I practically screamed into the phone.

"No, Jean, I'm sorry, it's Denise. Melanie hasn't spoken to Bethany. She doesn't know where she is. I am so sorry. Is there something we can do?"

I knew as a mother she was feeling my fear and panic, especially because of what had happened to those two young girls in the last few days.

"Yes, Denise, please have Melanie call everyone she knows. See if she can find out where Bethany is. I need to go!"

I hung up the phone and turned to my husband. "You stay here, just in case she comes home. And keep calling her cell phone. Go through her messages and see if you can figure out where they were meeting."

I grabbed my purse and ran out of the house. I hadn't even closed the door of the car as I took off down the street. I had to pull it shut fighting a force of wind as I drove down the road.

I dialed Marty's phone, asked where he was, and told him that I needed him to come with me. I knew I was driving erratically as I punched in the numbers on the phone, but I didn't care. I called my partner Joe's phone number next, quietly praying to myself that he had returned home.

That call also went straight to voice mail. I left him a message. I was crying now and I'm not even sure if he would be able to make out a word I said, but I knew he would call me back.

I couldn't believe that this was happening to me. I was a cop and I should have more control over my family. My daughter had lied to me, she was not where she said she was going to be, and she was probably with the prime suspect in a murder and attempted murder.

I was scared to death.

I pulled up to the Captain's house and Marty, the Captain and Hope, Justin and his wife were waiting outside for me. I briefly informed them of my dilemma as they tried to figure out a way to help.

Hope and Diane decided to go to my house and help Glenn make phone calls to see if they could find someone who knew where my daughter may have met up with Dylan. The Captain offered to stay and watch the baby while Justin went back to the station and organized some sort of search.

My first stop was Dylan's mother's house. When I got to the

house, I banged on the door like a madwoman.

"Jean, you have to calm down," Marty said, grabbing my arm.

I took a deep breath. Intellectually, I knew he was right, I knew acting like a crazy woman wouldn't help me find my daughter. I needed to take a deep breath, stop and regain some composure.

We heard someone coming to the door. When it opened Dylan's mother was in her wheelchair, this time without a child on her lap.

I blew right past her and entered the living room.

"Where's Dylan? Where's your son?" I looked around the room frantically.

"What are you doing? He's not here. What do you want?" She kept spinning her chair in each direction I went.

"I want to know where your son is." I leaned over her, my arms on each side of her chair.

"I...I don't' know. He called me and told me not to worry; he said he was okay." She cowered as I hovered over her.

"Jean." Marty gently pulled me away.

"Mrs. Silver, my partner's daughter is missing and the last person her daughter communicated with is your son Dylan. So you can understand her concern," he informed her. He was stern but soft.

She looked at me, I thought I saw pity in her eyes, but it was probably just confusion.

"Dylan called. He was very upset about someone getting hurt. He said he just needed to be by himself. I gave him your number; he promised he would call you."

"Well he didn't!" I yelled at her. "If you hear from him, you tell him to have my daughter call me. You find out where he is and you call me. Do you understand?"

She nodded.

"Detective, I know my son and he would never, never hurt anyone. If your daughter is with my son, she's fine, I know my son," she insisted.

I didn't say anything; I just wanted to slap her. No one knows his or her children, I thought now. I thought I knew my daughter, I now knew I didn't. My partner Joe didn't know that his daughter would try and take her life. *No, I thought, we may think we know our children, but we really don't.*

I couldn't figure out where to go next, so we headed over to the rectory to Father Murphy. It was getting late, and I knew that Mass was over and he would probably be with Sunday's youth group in the gymnasium, where on a normal day, my daughter should be. Now I was thinking that normal was an elusive thought.

Chapter Eleven

The Roman Catholic Church at St. Mary's was a large, gothic-style building that had two towers on either side of the front of the building, which was constructed of Belleville stone in 1890. The building featured various sized stained-glass windows and large, exquisitely carved wooden doors.

Behind the main building stood a much larger and more modern redbrick structure, which contained the school and the business offices. Behind that building was a less-elaborate building, which housed the living quarters of several of the clerical staff.

To the north of that building was the new gymnasium donated by several philanthropists whose families had been members of the church for generations since the church's inception. Although the majority of the population in this area of the Catskill Mountains was of Jewish descent, the church's youth group was non-denominational and served the entire community.

The floor of the gymnasium was a bustle of noise, with teenagers hanging out, playing Ping-Pong and bumper pool. It looked like a scene from my youth with not an electronic game in sight. I scanned the room for Bethany, but whatever false hope I envisioned was dashed when I couldn't find her face in the crowd. My hopes were dashed when I realized she wasn't there.

"Jean?" Father Murphy came up behind me.

"Father, have you seen Bethany?" I blurted out.

His brows turned inward.

"No, I haven't. I thought she would come to the group today."

I looked around again; I recognized Katie Hepburn and her friend Lisa Padilla. I bee lined it straight over to them.

"Where is he?" I grabbed Katie's arm.

Father followed Marty and me, and attempted to quickly defuse the situation by gently taking hold of my forearm.

"Where's who?" Katie cried out as she pulled her arm away and rubbed it, as if I really had hurt her. Perhaps I did.

"Dylan! Where is Dylan Silver?" I spoke in almost a hiss as I became more and more agitated.

She threw back her hair as if she was a model posing for the camera.

One of the other girls who had started to crowd around us shouted out her resentment. "Hey!"

It took a moment to put the name to the face. It was Tiffany, the girl that had found Jamie's body, the one with nervous tic. I hadn't noticed before, but her face was covered in freckles. I felt like ripping each one off her face one by one.

"Jean, please!" It was Father Murphy interceding, as he tried to calm me down. "Please, tell me what's wrong," he urged, making an effort to defuse the situation.

Marty was the one that spoke to him; I was too incensed to speak.

"Bethany is missing, Father, we think she's with Dylan Silver, and we can't locate either of them."

"Please, come into my office," said Father Murphy. He looked at the girls. "You too, all of you."

The girls paraded behind us, Marty taking up the rear. We walked into a small office that was sparsely furnished. A metal desk with a couple of beat-up vinyl covered chairs sat in the center of the room. Soccer balls and pool sticks were sitting in a cardboard carton in the corner. On the wall behind the desk stood a flimsy bookcase that looked like it was made of particleboard.

"Girls, do you know where Dylan is?" The priest positioned himself on the corner of the desk as we all crowded into the small room.

It was Lisa who spoke first. "Honestly, Father Murphy, we don't. We haven't seen Dylan since that night." She turned and looked at me. "Honestly, Mrs. Whitley, we haven't seen him."

I don't know why, but I thought that I believed her.

"Do you know where he would go, Lisa? Do you have any idea where Dylan might go? To think? To get away?" I used the terminology that his mother had used to describe the disappearing act. I pleaded with her. She shook her head.

"Lisa, I need you to answer me honestly. I need to know, did Dylan kill Jamie?" I knew I sounded like I was begging her for an answer.

"No, ma'am, I don't think he would, really. Dylan was just mad at Jamie because she was being mean to Tiff and me. Dylan didn't like when she acted like that, but he wouldn't hurt her. Or Kimberly," she added.

I looked at the other girls. "Do either of you know where I could find him?" It came out more sharply than I intended. I knew I had to play them like they were playing me.

It was Katie that answered.

"Dylan likes to hang out at the lake. There is a kind of old shack down there that he used to go to."

At that moment, my phone rang. I grabbed it. I could barely get out a "hello."

"Mom?" It was my daughter. My heart skipped two beats.

"Damn it, Bethany, where are you?" I screamed into the phone.

"Mom, listen to me. Please!"

I looked up. Everyone was staring at me. I walked out of the room and found a quiet corner.

"Okay, I'm listening. Where are you?" I said, willing myself to calm down.

"I'm with Dylan. Mom, please don't be mad. I can explain. Please...you have to listen."

I swallowed the spit that I had been unconsciously holding in my throat. "Okay, Bethany," I said exasperated. "Come home and we'll talk."

"Mom, promise me you won't arrest Dylan. Promise me," she pleaded.

"Bethany, I can't promise that, he is a suspect in the murder of Jamie Camp and an attempted murder of another."

"Mom, I swear, he didn't do it, please—you have to promise me."

Marty had come out of the room and was waiting for me. "Okay, Honey, I promise. Where are you? I'll come get you."

I heard her whisper to her accomplice. She came back to the phone. "We're at the old ice cream shack by the lake. Mom, remember— you promised."

"I'm on my way. Don't you dare move!" I motioned to Marty that a crisis was averted. I turned to look at Father Murphy and the three girls. Only Lisa looked like she was even remotely concerned about what was going on. I wondered if the other two girls were void of emotion.

I was hurrying to the car to get my daughter when I caught something out of the corner of my eye. Father Murphy had stepped outside to smoke a cigarette. I could swear he had one of those old-fashioned lighters, the kind of lighter that uses lighter fluid…the same type of flammable liquid that caused the burns on Jamie Camp's face, and maybe Kimberly's, as well.

But, I thought, the hell with everything else. My main concern right now was getting my daughter back safely, and giving her a piece of my mind and then grounding her for the rest of her life.

~

There were four different directions from which to enter the lake area. The route that Marty chose to drive came from the east, which would bring them directly to the shack that Bethany had mentioned in her phone call to her mother.

He drove down a bumpy dirt road canopied with oak trees. It was once the site where teenagers and young families spent their days swimming and playing Frisbee on this area of the lakefront. But times had changed, and what was once an active and populated area of the lake in the 1950s through the 1970s was now desolate and unused.

Bungalow colonies had once dominated the area. Mothers and children would spend the summers in the small cottages while their husbands stayed home in one of the cities crowded boroughs during the week and worked. Weekends would mean long commutes for the fathers, who would drive upstate on Friday after work to spend the weekend with their families, and then head back home to the city on Sundays so they could be back to work Monday. Those days were long gone because it took two incomes to sustain a decent lifestyle and mothers were also in the work force. The Catskills and a summer vacation were no longer an option for young families of the twenty-first century.

Jean was out of the vehicle before Marty came to a full stop. In one hand, she held her cell phone, relaying her position to her husband

Glenn, telling him that she had the shack in her sights where Bethany evidently had spent the night.

The small, white, wooden building that once served as an ice cream and candy dispensary for the visitors to the lake was now dilapidated and barely still standing. The door was hanging off the hinge, and the sliding window that once brought pure delight to children's faces was just shards of broken glass.

Where Marty carefully watched every step he made, Jean marched on like a woman on a mission. Disconnecting her phone call, she hollered out her daughter's name.

Marty didn't recognize Bethany at first. It seemed that she had changed dramatically in a matter of months.

It hadn't been that long since he had seen her. *Wasn't it just weeks ago that she was still in that awkward stage?* He thought to himself. The girl had been all spidery legs attached to a long, thin torso, with not much evidence of budding maturity.

Yet here she was, standing in front of him. Gone was the boyish-looking figure, and she was way past the cusp of blossoming into a woman. He suddenly understood Jean's fear and anxiety.

Bethany was standing in the doorway, against the shack, half facing the direction they were coming from and at the same time watching over someone in the shadows, consciously protecting her friend from their view.

It was obvious to Marty that Bethany was reluctant to move from her position, as if she didn't trust her mother not to betray her.

Jean's pace became more vigorous and her facial expression more animated as she reached her daughter. Marty could see that as she got closer to her daughter, she was uncertain about how she should react or which way to proceed. She didn't really have to make a decision, because Bethany raised her hand up in an attempt to stop her mother from getting any closer.

Jean stopped in her tracks and Marty stayed a few feet back, still unable to see if it was definitely Dylan hiding in the small building.

"Mom," Bethany said, with caution in her voice. She looked over in Marty's direction, trying to calculate whether or not he presented a threat.

"You promised. You said you would listen, you said you weren't going to arrest him," she stammered.

Then, suddenly, she stood up straighter, making herself taller, as if she was standing in defiance. She was taking a stance in an effort to protect her friend, even if the approaching enemy was her own mother.

"Bethany, what the hell were you thinking?" was the only thing that Jean managed to vocalize, her anger now overcoming her fears. Her anxiety had vanished, now that she knew her daughter was not in any immediate danger.

"What the hell is wrong with you? Damn it, Bethany! Where is he?" Marty watched the transformation in amazement. Jean was now morphing back into cop mode, shedding her maternal persona like a snake sheds its skin. The minute that Jean had concluded that Bethany was safe and unharmed, she no longer was the child's mother, but a cop on the job.

Slowly and cautiously, Dylan emerged from the building, bending slightly in order to protect his head from a piece of wood that had hung from the entranceway. He placed himself between Bethany and her mother, as if suddenly his sole purpose was to protect the girl, and not the other way around.

He was not at all what Marty expected.

Extremely thin and tall, although not nearly as tall as Marty, he had an abundance of dark, wavy black hair and piercing blue eyes. His jaw was strong, his complexion soft, with patches of peach fuzz above his top lip, causing his baby face to emerge into a more mature look. There was nothing about him that appeared to Marty to perceive him as a teenage Lothario. In fact, he sort of reminded Marty of himself at that age.

Dylan stood there for a second before he broke his silence.

"I'm sorry, Mrs. Whitley, I didn't want Bethany to get into any trouble. She just wanted to help."

As Dylan spoke, he turned to face Bethany, who was a few inches shorter than him. He took her hand in his, his fingers interlocking with Jean's daughters'.

At that moment, Marty turned to see Jean's expression. She was mortified and he feared what would happen next if he didn't intervene.

He wasn't fast enough. In a catlike move, the veteran detective got close enough to grab the boy's wrist and pull it behind him, thrusting her knee into his back. In one quick motion, she pushed him up against the wall of the shack, taking out her handcuffs out and snapping them closed around the boy's wrists.

Bethany screamed in protest. Dylan remained silent and an expression of surrender and daze appeared on his face.

"Mom, you promised! Stop it, you're hurting him!" her daughter cried out as she reached out for Dylan, trying to get between her mother and her friend. Jean pushed her daughter's arm away.

"Dylan Silver," she looked at the boy, pure hatred in her eyes. "You are under arrest for the murder of Jamie Camp and attempted murder of Kimberly Weston. You have the right to an attorney…"

Marty knew she was overreacting. He looked over at Bethany. She was pleading with her mother to stop, but Jean was deaf to her pleas.

"Whoa, Jean, hang on." Marty walked over to her. "Jean, listen to me!"

He grabbed her arm and was able to break her focus and concentration on the boy. He knew she was acting on pure adrenaline, and if she had a moment to step back, she would realize how much of an effect this was having on her daughter. She wasn't thinking and he understood why, but he knew for her sake, and her daughter's, he needed to intervene.

As if she was coming out of a trance, she suddenly let go of her grip on Dylan's wrists that were now securely cuffed behind his back.

Marty turned to Dylan and gently walked him over to the side of the building, motioning for him to sit on the ground. Bethany was staring at her mother with an intensity that made him afraid for his partner. Bethany's expression changed and the look in her eyes softened as she turned away from her mother and sat next to the boy seated on the floor.

"Don't move," Marty told them, as he walked back to Jean. She stood motionless, just staring at her daughter as if she didn't recognize her. In all fairness, Marty thought her daughter's expression was a mirror image of her mother's. This girl no longer was recognizing her mother.

"Jean," Marty put his arm on her shoulder. He could feel the tension in her muscles.

"She's just a baby, Marty, she's only fourteen years old." She turned and looked over Marty's shoulder, where she was able to view her daughter. Her eyes burned as she tried to hold back her tears.

"She may look sixteen because she's tall and she's so damn smart and savvy, but she's only a baby!" The back of her hand quickly wiped away the tears from below her eyes.

Then it hit him, the real reason that Jean was so emotional. Jean was upset and angry because Dylan and Bethany had spent the night together.

He turned back to look at the two teenagers. It appeared that Bethany was trying to console the boy. Jean was going to be walking a thin tightrope. It was obvious that the girl cared about Dylan, and her mother could destroy the bond she had with her daughter if she wasn't careful how she handled the situation.

"Look Jean, there's not enough evidence to arrest this kid for murder. You're jumping the gun here." He looked directly in her eyes. "Let's hear what he has to say. Your daughter is a pretty perceptive kid. I don't think a pretty face would hoodwink her. Give her a chance to explain."

She didn't get a chance to answer him. Her cell phone rang and she glanced down at the caller ID. She walked away from Marty to answer her husband's call. She knew he was frantic and needed to let him know that Bethany was safe.

⁓

I was still shaking when I disconnected the call from Glenn. He was insisting on coming to the lake and picking up Bethany, but I wanted to try and handle the situation myself. I wanted to believe that he would stay away, but I also knew if the situation were reversed, there would be nothing he could say or do to keep me from seeing for myself that our daughter was unharmed.

I was consciously aware that my relationship with my daughter was on the verge of imploding, and if I didn't calm myself down, I was going to risk causing irreversible damage.

I walked back to where the three were huddled. As I got closer, I could hear my daughter begging Marty to remove Dylan's handcuffs. I was afraid to look at Bethany, afraid that I would just blow up, so I consciously made an effort to train my eyes on Dylan.

It was the first good look I had gotten of him. I began taking a visual inventory of him. Bethany was talking to him, but he wasn't replying, just looking down at the ground, his hands bound behind his back. He looked up when he realized I had approached.

His eyes were so blue that I actually felt a chill looking at them. They stood out even more in contrast to his hair, which was so black it gave off a purple hue, like feathers of a raven. I could see why the girls were so drawn to him. Although he was still just a young boy, he emitted the sexuality of a grown man. He was probably at least six feet tall, but because he was seated, his present posture made him appear shorter. His back was rounded and his shoulders turned in, as if he felt ashamed.

I wanted so bad to just take my boot and slam it into his square, hairless jaw.

I looked over at Marty.

"You know we may not have enough evidence yet to charge him for the murder of Jamie, but I sure as hell can arrest him on the charge of statutory rape."

"Mom!" my daughter yelled out in protest.

"Don't! Don't you dare try to make excuses for this bastard! You are fourteen years old. He took advantage of you." I grabbed a hold of the kid's arm and lifted him up from the ground.

"Mom, we didn't…he…we didn't have sex. Dylan didn't touch me! Let him go!"

Bethany grabbed his other arm and Dylan became the object of a tug of war. I finally turned to look at her. Was she telling me the truth? Or, was she just trying to save this kid's ass?

"You mean to tell me you two spent the entire night out here, and he didn't touch you?" I peered into the opening of the shack and saw a small mattress on lying on the dirt floor. "Do you think I was born yesterday?" I kept looking at her; I thought my eyes were going to burn a hole through her forehead. Each second that we stood there felt like an eternity to me.

Dylan started to talk but my daughter cut him off.

"Dylan didn't do anything wrong. You promised me you wouldn't do this. You promised! You're a f***ing liar. I hate you!" She screamed her words, startling me.

I didn't think. I just reacted.

I slapped her so hard her head snapped back. I was mortified at what I had just done. I stood there, motionless, wanting to say I was sorry, but the words weren't coming out.

Her hand flew up to her cheek and I could see nothing but pure hatred in her eyes. My attention was averted when I heard a vehicle pull up. My daughter suddenly turned away and ran toward the car, crying.

"Daddy!" she hollered out, as if she was in physical pain. She ran into her father's arms as soon as he exited the car.

I could see the confusion on his face as he was tried to comprehend what the hell he had just walked into.

Glenn took a good look at his daughter; my handprint had left a vivid red mark on her face. He turned to look at me. Disappointment was written all over his face. I could tell that he just joined the list of people—myself included—who were questioning my ability to handle the situation.

He took a few seconds to console her and convinced her to get into his car.

"What the hell is going on, Jean?" he turned to look at the boy on sitting on the ground.

"I'm sorry Mr. Whitley, I didn't want Bethany to get into any trouble. I just needed someone to talk to, and she's been a good friend. I wouldn't hurt her…never." He voice wavered as he spoke.

Glenn just looked at him. For the first time since I have been married to this man, I couldn't tell what he was thinking.

I was afraid that I was starting to believe Dylan, too. The kid sounded so damn sincere, yet sociopaths were usually smooth talkers. I was so conflicted with wanting to believe that my daughter was still innocent and hadn't been molested, and knowing what my gut was telling me. I wanted desperately to believe that the kid was telling me the truth, even though I was convinced that this piece of crap was responsible for the death of one child and the critical condition of the other one. I just had to prove it.

"I'm going to take Bethany home, Jean," Glenn said as he turned and walked away. "You do what you have to do. We'll talk about this when you get home, whenever you manage to get home."

It was a dig. It was finally surfacing. I had been getting the feeling that something had been bothering him for days now, but I just couldn't put my finger on it. He was apparently bothered by the significant time I had being spending at work, and he finally was voicing his displeasure.

The man who had been my biggest supporter, the most understanding husband in the world, was starting to make noises like a cave man.

I didn't know what to say. I watched him drive off and I just stood there staring into an empty vacuum, until Marty broke my concentration.

"Jean, let's go. Why don't we take Dylan back to the station and talk to him there? We're not going to accomplish anything here."

The voice of reason had spoken. I just nodded and walked away, letting him place Dylan in the back of the unmarked car.

I couldn't look at him. I just stared straight ahead, watching the roads curve before me as Marty drove. I knew that I had to get my emotions under control if I was going to interview this suspect effectively. I closed my eyes and all I could see was the look on my daughter's face after I slapped her. All I could hear was the sound of my hand connecting with the flesh of her cheek and what happened just before that— my sweet little girl yelling an obscenity at me.

I was torn between the arguments that were going on in my own head. *Was I justified in hitting her? Did I overstep my responsibilities as her mother? Was I as evil as she obviously was portraying me in her fourteen-year old mind? I didn't know.*

~

When we arrived at the station, Marty removed the cuffs from Dylan's wrists and sat him in a chair in front of his metal desk.

The boy rubbed his hands trying to get circulation back; the cuffs had left indentations and red marks.

"Please, Mrs. Whitley, I swear to you, nothing happened," he declared, in a voice hoarse with fatigue. "I really like Bethany, she's been a good friend." His eyes cast downward, but he continued to try and convince me of his innocence. "I didn't hurt Jamie or Kim. I wouldn't do that."

I turned to get a good look at him. For some reason in this lighting, he looked much younger. Maybe it was the lighting, maybe it was because he looked so vulnerable right now, but then the vision of the two girls burned faces flashed before my eyes and I could feel my blood pressure rising again. My anger was intensifying.

I grabbed a chair and pulled it over to face him, I leaned over so I was within a hair of his nose. I was in his personal space, and reveling in every second.

"Do you want to tell me, Dylan, why you took off? Why did you run away after you found you dead friend's badly burned, faceless dead body lying in the woods? That doesn't sound like a very caring friend."

He shook his head. With his hands now free, he cupped one over each ear, as if warding off a headache.

"I was scared. Katie said that the police would think I did it, because we were fighting. She said that if I wasn't there when the cops came, no one would know we had a fight and I wouldn't even be on the radar. Katie said the girls would just say they hitchhiked up there and no one would have to know I was even there. I know, it was stupid."

I sat back a little to give him some space.

"What were you fighting about, Dylan? What did you fight about before you killed her?" I accused him, my voice softer then before.

I took a different approach, hoping his fatigue would cross him up.

He lifted his head suddenly looking directly in my eyes. "No, no...I didn't hurt her. I slowed up to stop the car and she jumped out of the car. She took off, and the next time I saw her, she was dead."

He rubbed his eyes, and then with his right hand, he covered his face and began to sob quietly.

"What were you fighting about?" I asked again, this time leaving out the accusation.

"Can I have a glass of water?" he asked me, when he composed himself. I could tell he was having trouble swallowing.

Marty left to get the kid a drink. He came back a second later with a Coke and handed it to him.

"Thanks."

"Go on, Dylan, now that your mouth is nice and moisturized, you should be able to talk." I threw in some sarcasm, realizing I was sounding less like me and more like my missing partner, Joe. I knew if he were here, he would be just as outraged as I was about how this boy had dragged Bethany into this mess.

Dylan looked up at me. Once again, his brilliant blue eyes caused me some discomfort. I felt a chill going down my spine. I wondered if my daughter experienced the same feeling.

He took a long gulp of his soda.

"She was being a real bitch."

"Who's 'she,' Dylan?" I pressed him.

"Jamie—she was being a real jerk."

"How? What did she do that got you so angry?"

"Jamie was making fun of…"

"Hold it! Don't say another word, Dylan." A female voice with a hint of Australian accent came from behind me.

I turned around, and a business card was shoved into my hand. A very attractive young blonde with a dynamic smile stood before me. I looked at the card.

It read in bold, black letters— Alexis Marciano, Attorney at Law.

"Have you been read your Miranda rights, Dylan?" She immediately walked over and put her hand on Dylan's shoulder.

Dylan looked just as surprised as Marty and me. The boy looked at me, almost as if he was asking my permission, and then at the attorney.

"I think so," he told the lady, not quite understanding what was happening, or where this woman had appeared from, seemingly out of the blue.

"Okay, Dylan, you are not to say another word, understood?" Ms. Marciano turned back to me.

"I am being retained to represent Mr. Silver. Is my client under arrest, detective?" She was wearing stilettos, which gave her the appearance of being taller than she actually was.

I looked at Marty and then back to Dylan.

"No," I said, resigned to the situation. "He is just being questioned as a material witness."

"I would appreciate it if you give me a few minutes with my client…alone."

I kicked the desk out of frustration. Where the hell this lady had come from was beyond me. No one but Marty and me and my daughter knew that Dylan had been taken into custody.

"Yeah, sure."

I called one of the uniformed officers who was milling around the coffee station.

"Derrick, can you please show…" I glanced down at the card in my hand to read off her name. "Ms. Marciano and her client to a room where they can have some privacy?" It came out in a huff, and I didn't care.

When they walked away, I turned to Marty in utter disbelief.

"How the hell did she know the kid was here?"

He rolled his eyes just before he spoke.

"I guess it's better that she showed up now. The D.A. would have had our heads if we obtained a confession and it was thrown out on a technicality."

I knew he was right, and appreciated him using the word, we, but it didn't make me feel any better.

A half hour later, the attorney, Ms. Australia walked back in, with Dylan following a few steps behind her.

"My client will be glad to speak to you now, Detective. Of course, I will be advising him the entire time." Her face looked so familiar—I just couldn't place it.

"Yeah, no problem," I told her. I glanced toward a conference room behind us. I led the two of them into the room. We all took a seat at the long table. Marty was on the phone and hadn't joined us yet.

I decided to play this game with a different attitude. I put a smile on my face and turned to my guests.

"Can I get you a refreshment, Ms. Marciano?" I turned to Dylan. "How about you Dylan, do you want another Coke?"

Then it hit me who our Ms. Marciano reminded me of. She was the spitting image of that Australian actress, Tom Cruise's first wife.

They both turned in unison. I glanced over at Marty, who had just joined us, shutting the door behind him.

After we were all seated, I pulled out a small digital recorder. "Do you have any objections?"

Once again, both Dylan and Miss Nicole Kidman said "no" at the same time, as if it was rehearsed.

CHAPTER TWELVE

Marty felt a sense of relief when the attorney showed up. He understood why Jean was so angry, but he was afraid her emotions would affect her professional approach in the interview process.

By the time they were all seated, he felt comfortable enough with her change in attitude that he decided not to intervene and insist that he take over the interrogation.

He remained cautious, though, and was ready to take control if it became necessary, but Marty had a feeling that the pretty attorney was quite qualified to protect her client.

Jean waited until all the participants were settled in their chairs and a short period of eerie silence had passed before she began her questioning. He noted that she had placed a small digital recorder on the table and he knew then that she was going to play by the rulebook. She wasn't going to jeopardize the investigation because of her own emotional investment in the case.

"Dylan, you were about to tell us about the argument you had with Jamie before your counsel arrived. Do you wish to continue now?"

He nodded his head.

"Do you just want me to tell you what happened?" He sounded as if he was asking permission.

"Yeah, go ahead, I'll stop you if I need clarification, okay?" Jean told him. Marty noticed she was flexing her fingers under the table, as if she was just itching to wrap them around the boy's neck.

"Where do you want me to start?" His eyes turned down, as if he was embarrassed.

"Start from when you picked the girls up, Dylan. Whose idea was it to ride up to the Forester place?"

He didn't hesitate, and started to ramble. "It was Katie's. She wanted to go hang out with Cameron. I told her she needed to stay away from the guy, but they've got this sick relationship going, and when Katie gets an idea in her head, she can be pretty stubborn. She just wouldn't take no for an answer. She said we were going to party and hang out in the hot tub."

"I tried to get out of it by telling her that I had some chores to do for my mom and I couldn't go, but she wouldn't let up because I was the only one with a ride. Then Jamie called, and Katie put the phone on three-way and she said she wanted to go. She wouldn't let up. I finally gave in." He shook his head, reflecting on the consequences of what had followed.

"Go on," Jean prompted him to continue.

"I picked up Jamie first. She sneaked out of her house through the back door. She said her parents were in bed and kept saying how stupid they were. I think she had already smoked a joint, 'cause she was really giddy and acting really obnoxious."

"I picked up Katie and Lisa next, and then Jamie said we should just blow off Tiffany, but no one else wanted to do that, so I drove up to Tiffany's. She was waiting for us a few houses down from her house. The minute Tiffany got into the car, Jamie started on her."

He stopped and looked up at Jean. "Jamie could be really mean, and when she was high, she could be brutal."

"What do you mean, she started on Tiffany? How?" Marty prompted.

"She was making fun of her. Making fun of her freckles, and Tiffany's got this nervous tic." He pointed to his lip.

"I kept telling Jamie to shut up, but she kept getting worse. I told her if she didn't shut up, I was taking her back home. She stopped for a while and then she started on Lisa. Telling Lisa she was fat. Tiffany's a little tougher, and she just laughed it off, so I let it go, but Lisa started crying, so I got pissed and pulled over a little before we got to Cameron's place. That's when she opened the door and ran off. She told me I was a jerk and I needed to ..." His eyes turned away in what Marty felt might be shame.

"She said if I wanted Tiffany and Lisa so bad, I could have them. I was pissed at her, but I knew I wasn't about to let her go running around in the woods by herself, so Lisa and I went to look for her and Tiffany and Katie went to get Cameron."

He paused, his eyes definitely showing signs of fatigue.

"Lisa and I looked for her for at least an hour, maybe more, and then we heard Tiffany screaming. We ran over about the same time Katie and Cameron showed up. Jamie was just lying there. I think she was already dead and her face…" He stopped talking, tears started to fall. He wiped them as if he was trying to wipe away the memory. "Smoke was still coming from her face." The vivid memory was turning his complexion a pale shade of green.

"Was her shirt missing, Dylan?" Jean probed.

"Yes, she was lying there…her shirt was gone. We didn't know what to do. It was Katie who told us to all go back to Cameron's house. When I got there, I got sick—I started throwing up. I wanted to throw up when I saw her, but I didn't. But as soon as we got back to Cameron's, I started puking. I think Lisa did, too."

Jean shot a glance over at Marty. She wasn't sure she was buying the kid's story. She kept on with the interrogation.

"Did you have anything to drink, Dylan? Any alcohol?"

He nodded.

"Before or after you found Jamie lying there dead?"

"After, when we got back to Cameron's place. He gave us some wine to calm us down."

"Are you sure, Dylan? You weren't drinking before you got to the woods? Maybe you were already intoxicated before Jamie was found? Maybe you were drunk and just don't remember hurting her." His attorney began to object, but Dylan cut her off.

"I swear to you, I didn't hurt her."

"When did you pick up Kimberly, before or after Katie?"

He looked at Jean, his face a total blank.

"Kim wasn't there. She wasn't with us."

"Are you sure, Dylan? Maybe you just left out that part."

"No. Kim wasn't there." He was getting upset as Jean began to push.

"Did you smoke anything? Pot?" she asked him.

He denied using any illegal substances.

"No, I don't smoke dope, I really don't even drink, but I was so freaked out."

"Were you and Lisa together the whole time you went looking for Jamie, Dylan?" Jean persisted.

"I think so. The whole night has turned into a blur." He turned his eyes up and towards the ceiling. "I only had one flashlight, so we must have been together the whole time."

Jean flashed back to that evening and remembered that the moon was full and how well it had lit up the night sky.

"Whose idea was it for you to go home and leave the girls there?"

"Katie. She was afraid that I would get into trouble. Katie thought that because we were arguing, that people would think I did it, so she told me just to go home. Lisa was begging them to let her go home with me, but Tiffany and Katie talked her out of it. I didn't want to leave her, but they kept on insisting I go home."

"But you didn't go home, did you, Dylan?" Jean pushed back.

He shook his head. "No, I went to the shack. I was pretty shaken up. I called my mom and just let her know that she shouldn't worry about me."

"Did you have a fight with Kimberly, too, Dylan?" Jean leaned over, moving closer to him.

Dylan turned to look at his attorney. The woman nodded for him to answer.

"No, I didn't know what happened to Kim until Bethany told me."

Marty couldn't tell if anyone else in the room noticed it, but Jean's blood pressure must have skyrocketed the minute he mentioned her daughters' name. Her face became flushed, her knuckles white. Just the fact that boy spoke her daughter's name out loud had enraged her.

He felt he knew what Jean was wondering, and was pretty sure she was probably was too angry to ask, so he intervened.

"Why did you call Bethany, Dylan? Why bring her into this?" Marty asked in a sympathetic tone. The young detective knew he had to play good cop to Jean's angry one.

Dylan turned towards Marty, his eyes focused on the detective.

"Bethany texted me when we were out looking for Jamie. I told her what went down, about Jamie taking off and all. She called me to talk and she was on the cell with me when Tiffany started screaming. She was on the phone with me when we found Jamie's body."

Marty turned to look at Jean; he couldn't read her expression, he couldn't read what she was thinking now. Here was this kid, telling them that her daughter had known about Jamie's murder even before the police did. Bethany, her daughter, had been lying to her from the beginning. An APB was put out on this kid and her daughter had been aware of Dylan's whereabouts the entire time. In essence, she was withholding vital information and interfering with an investigation, putting her mother in a very precarious position.

Marty turned back to Dylan, whose head now was bowed as if he had betrayed a trust.

"Dylan." He waited until the kid looked up at him and he knew that the boy was paying close attention. "Who would want to hurt Jamie and Kimberly? Can you think of anyone that had something against them both?"

Dylan just shook his head. "I don't know, it was either you loved them or hated them. Both of them could be pretty brutal. They would say whatever they thought. They wouldn't care if they hurt someone's feelings or not." The last few words he spoke seemed to be with great effort. It was as if talking was becoming a great effort for him. Marty couldn't tell if it was just exhaustion, or the boy felt he was betraying the memory of his friends, one who was now dead and the other one fighting for her life.

"Are you trying to tell me they were bullies?" Marty asked him as he got up from his chair and walked to the opposite side of the room. He grabbed a pad and pen from the counter and threw it down on the table in front of Dylan.

Dylan looked at the pad and then turned his focus back to Marty. The expression on the kid's face was a mass of confusion.

"Did they bully you, Dylan?" Marty asked in an accusing tone, but Dylan just looked up at him as if he was crazy or totally off the wall.

"Can you give me examples of who they bullied and how?" The detective was reaching for a motive, yet he felt it was a reasonable conclusion. If Marty was right, the person who killed Jamie and was also responsible for Kimberly Weston's injuries may have been a victim of bullying, and probably one of the students at the St. Mary's High School or Father Murphy's youth group.

He glanced over at Jean and had the distinct feeling that she wasn't buying anything this kid was saying.

~

I was incensed. I knew my daughter, and there was no way I was taking in this crap that this kid was trying to throw at us. I didn't believe one frickin' word that was coming out of his mouth.

My heart was racing, and I had serious concerns that it was going to rupture in my chest and explode into a million particles. I envisioned the whole interview room splattered in blood, like one of those spin paintings my daughter used to bring home from the county fair.

Although it was killing me, I had no choice but to let Marty take over the interview. When Dylan tried to insinuate that Bethany was on the phone with him the moment they found Jamie's body, I was doing everything in my power to keep from jumping the table and putting my hands around his scrawny neck.

I wanted to call Bethany right then, put her on speakerphone, and have her denounce this boy's story and his accusations about her. On the other hand, there was a nagging feeling deep in my stomach. I was scared to death that he was telling the truth.

It got quiet in the room while Dylan compiled a list of names of both males and females who had been verbally victimized by both Kimberly and Jamie. The list seemed to go on forever, as if everyone who went to school with them was at one time or another a target of the girls' insensitive verbal and sometimes physical abuse.

As he was writing, I would casually look to see if he was going to add my daughter's name to the list. I could tell he was beginning to come to the end of the list because he seemed to be digging deeper into his memory and thinking longer before actually writing each name down on the page. Before he wrote down the last name, he looked up at me, those piercing blue eyes catching mine. He looked almost apologetic.

I was just about to pick up the paper when Detective Frank Robinson entered the room and handed me a report from the hospital.

"Jean, toxicology and blood work-up reports came in on Kimberly Weston." He was all serious and business until he took notice of the Nicole Kidman look-alike in the room. He broke out in a broad smile as he turned to acknowledge our Ms. Alexis Marciano, Esquire.

Frustrated, I grabbed the report from Robinson's hands. Another piece of the puzzle had been added to the equation. I handed the report to Marty, who looked over it and turned back to me, looking even more confused than I was.

They had found a small puncture mark on Kimberly's back, and the report had found that Kimberly Weston was injected with insulin. Considering her medical status, it very well may have been a lethal dose.

"Is Kimberly a diabetic?" I asked, as I flipped pages and looked through the reports. "It doesn't say anything about her being a diabetic." I tried to recall my conversation with her mother. I was pretty sure her parents never mentioned that their daughter was a diabetic or on insulin.

I looked back at Dylan. If they were such good friends, he would know if she was a diabetic. His face remained blank.

"Dylan, do you know if any of the people on this list are diabetic? Would any of them have access to insulin?"

He shook his head. I didn't want to admit it, but it was hard not to notice just how good-looking the kid was. I could almost understand why the girls were attracted to him. There was something about his persona that just emitted an abundance of charisma. He was the synthesis of sweet and tart. If you looked at him at one angle, his façade was that of the misunderstood bad boy. Look again, and you saw a sweet baby face, in need of nurturing and consoling.

I knew the second description was the one that must have attracted my daughter to him. She was always taking in strays, and Dylan Silver...he was her new project. Well, this was one project that my daughter would leave unfinished, if I had anything to say about it.

"Are you sure?" I asked him again.

He shook his head. His thick black hair showed signs of needing washing as it whipped back and forth across his forehead.

"The only person I know that is a diabetic is my grandmother, but she just watches what she eats. I don't think she takes insulin."

I noticed that his attorney put her hand on his arm, letting him know he had given us enough. She was determined to stop him from talking any further.

I knew that I had nothing to hold him on and it was only a matter of time before Nicole Kidman's look-alike insisted on us releasing her client.

"Get him out of here," I said, throwing down Kim's medical file.

"Are you releasing my client, detective?" the Australian attorney asked me as she started to pack up what looked like a brand-new briefcase, shoving papers in one of the leather side pockets. She was young, and I wondered whether it was all just a prop to make her look more mature and possibly more effective.

Again, that feeling of familiarity crossed through my mind. I turned my attention back to Dylan. I got close enough that our noses actually touched.

"Stay the hell away from my daughter. If you come within ten feet of her, I will have your ass behind bars and you will become someone's plaything! Do you understand?" I felt the heat coming from my own breath.

He started to protest, but Alexis Marciano squeezed his arm and gently pushed him toward door.

She was just about out of my line of vision when I threw out the next question.

"Hey, Marciano, how did you even know he was here? Who hired you?"

She turned back and looked at me. I didn't realize how petite she was until that moment.

"Mr. Whitley called me, Detective. Your husband hired me to represent Dylan."

She turned and walked away, her blond curls bouncing, leaving me with my mouth wide open and in a state of shock. Then it hit me why the woman looked so familiar to me.

It wasn't her resemblance to Nicole Kidman, I was mistaken. She didn't look like the actress at all. I had seen her at Glenn's office Christmas party last December. The little blond tart, Ms. Marciano, was the girlfriend of one of the engineers that worked at my husband's company.

~

Marty knew that nothing he could say was going to console his partner, so he remained silent. He let her do whatever she needed to do to calm down before she left to go home to confront her husband and daughter. In essence, that meant ducking as a Styrofoam cup half-filled with coffee flew across the room. Coffee splattered in every direction. The walls, the table, the floor, and when he glanced down, he realized that even his shirt had become a victim of Jean's sudden tantrum.

Marty looked at his watch. He had been so wrapped up in the search for Bethany and interrogating Dylan that he actually had forgotten the incident with his father. He didn't want to leave Jean, but as much as Jean was concerned for her family, he was beginning to have concerns about the Captain.

"Jean?"

She just raised her hand, the palm of her hand facing him. He gave her another few seconds to gain her composure and get her anger under control.

"I don't know which one, but one, if not all, of those kids killed Jamie Camp and then tried to kill Kimberly. I am willing to bet my career on it."

Still seated, she twisted her whole body around and grabbed her purse. "And I think that son of a bitch knows who it is."

Marty knew that if Jean believed that, she had to know she was implicating her own daughter. She got out of the chair and headed to the door. "Come on, I'll drop you off. I have some business to take care of at home, Marty. I'll meet you here at eight o'clock tomorrow morning. I am so done for today."

Marty just nodded. He followed closely behind, and shut the lights as he left the room. They drove in silence; neither of them spoke until Jean dropped him off at the Captain's house, where Hope had returned and was now patiently waiting for him.

Apparently, he interrupted a serious dialogue between Hope and his father, because the moment he entered the house, their conversation came to an abrupt halt.

Hope was sitting on the sofa, her legs folded like a pretzel beneath her buttocks. She had tied her hair back in a ponytail. The very sight of her caused a stirring in his groin and his eyes to well up with tears. Sometimes it scared him just how much he loved her, and how she made him feel so vulnerable. He wasn't used to needing someone as badly as he needed this lady.

Until he had met Hope, Marty really had no reference point to understand what his father meant when he would talk about his late wife,

Marty's mother, and how a piece of him died the day she passed away.

What scared him the most was that, if he felt this deep after only two years of being with her, what would happen if he ever had to go through the type of loss his father had endured? It made him question whether getting married was a good idea. The thought occurred to him that he might be better off if he ran as fast and as far away as possible, instead of taking the chance of getting hurt.

Marty was no coward, and he wasn't necessarily a gambler, yet he was putting all his chips on the table. He would rather risk having his heart broken in the future rather than miss a single moment with Hope now.

The Captain was the first to speak up.

"Did everything work out? Jean's kid…is she okay?" His words were filled with real concern.

Marty leaned over and gave Hope a kiss. She still smelled like baby powder, and because of that, he deliberately took another deep breath. Never before had the smell of Johnson and Johnson acted like an aphrodisiac for him.

Recovering from Hope's scent, he answered the question.

"Yes," was all he managed to get out.

Hope wasn't quite satisfied with his answer. She looked in his eyes and instinctively knew he was leaving something out. She asked him to elaborate.

The Captain stood up. "You must be starved. Let me fix you a plate, Marty. Here, sit down." He motioned for Marty to take his place on the couch and he headed to the kitchen. When he got out of eyesight and what he hoped was earshot, Marty turned his attention to Hope. She had unfolded her legs and he lifted them up in one swoop so they were positioned over his thighs.

With the Captain out of the room, the conversation went in a completely different direction. "How is he?" Marty asked her, turning toward the doorway his father had exited through. "What do you think is going on?"

"I don't know, Marty," she replied.

A bowl of snacks sat on the table. She leaned over, grabbed a fistful, and popped a combination of pretzels and chips into her mouth.

He was always amazed how this tiny woman could eat so much junk and never gain an ounce.

She finished chewing before she answered, her hand cupping her mouth so nothing came flying out.

"It could be nothing, he may just be stressed out and have a lot on his mind."

"But you don't think so?" Marty sounded fatigued as well as alarmed.

"Marty, let's wait and see what the doctor says. I'm not a neurologist. I don't want to make any guesses." She shifted her position and lay back so he was within reach of rubbing her feet. She didn't have to ask; he knew immediately what she wanted. He began to knead her toes between his fingers.

"What happened with Bethany? Is she all right?" Her concern was more than just a physician's for her patient. Hope had become very close to Jean's family two years ago when they had both been involved in the Madison double murder case.

"It's not good," he told her.

Hope immediately took her legs off Marty's lap and planted them on the ground. He saw the look of apprehension in her face.

"No, no, I'm sorry, she's okay, it's just that…well, Hope, it's a long story." He stopped when his father walked into the room with his dinner.

The Captain held a snack tray and a beer in one hand and a plate of ribs and baked beans and utensils in another. Marty started to get up and give him a hand, but his dad brushed him off. As he had done a million times before and with ease, he set up the tray while holding the plate in one hand and maneuvering the legs of the tray with his knee. He plopped the beer down on the table.

"Thanks, Pop," Marty told him as he picked up a rib and bit into it without hesitation. His father took a seat on the recliner opposite them.

"I overheard a part of what you were telling Hope. What's going on?"

Marty stopped and took a good look at his father. He hadn't noticed any change in the man's physical appearance. The man was rapidly approaching eighty years old, but was in reasonably good health and hadn't lost his good looks to aging. As Hope's mother would say, "He's a fine specimen of a man."

Yes, he had broken his hip a few years back, due to a fall, but he had remained physically active. He could still give his son a run for his money in racketball and arm wrestling. There was nothing different about his father's appearance leading him to believe that something was off. *Probably was nothing,* Marty thought regarding the recent episode *Maybe it was just a fluke. After all,* he silently reminded himself, *how many times had Marty himself misplaced his wallet or keys?*

He suddenly realized that he hadn't answered. He turned his attention back to his father and related what was going on with Jean and Bethany.

"Bethany spent the night by the lake with this kid, Dylan. Apparently they have developed a friendship of some sort."

His father, who had a daughter of his own, immediately wanted clarification. Hope, on the other hand, sat patiently waiting for Marty to finish the story.

"What kind of friendship? How old is this kid?" Unease and anger started to build up in the Captain's voice.

"According to the boy, it's just platonic, but it's more complicated than that," Marty told them.

Hope, being the more pragmatic of the two, asked the next question.

"What is the complication, Marty? What does this have to do with the murder?"

Taking a moment to swallow what he had in his mouth, he put down his fork. He meticulously wiped some sauce from his bottom lip. Hope sat back patiently.

The Captain, on the other hand, was jittery. He was screwing his face up with some very weird expressions. Marty was about to warn him to stop or his face was going to freeze that way, but he decided against it. Instead, he continued with his story.

"Bethany apparently knew about Jamie's murder before Jean did. She was on the phone with Dylan when they found the girl's body. Instead of letting her mother know what was going on, she chose to conceal the fact that she already knew a death had occurred and the kids were misleading us."

His hunger got the better of him, so he stopped and grabbed another rib and sucked the sauce off before gnawing into the meat. He waited until he had nothing left in his mouth before continuing.

"Jean is livid. To make matters worse, Glenn hired an attorney to represent this kid, Dylan Silver, without consulting her."

"Is this Dylan a suspect, Marty? Do you think he could have committed murder?" Hope quizzed him; although he knew her main question was left unasked. He knew what Hope was really thinking, because he was thinking along the same lines. Was Jean's daughter culpable of being an accessory to murder?

He shrugged his shoulders in response to her question, but gave her a verbal answer as well.

"Honestly, in my gut, I don't think this kid did it, but I do think that Jean is not off base when she says that one of those kids may be responsible. The question is which one?"

"Couldn't it be more than one, Marty?" Hope offered.

"Yeah, it could, but so far we haven't got any DNA evidence implicating anyone in particular. I mean, it could be Cameron, it could be some vagrant, but I highly doubt it, considering the second victim is also acquainted with this very same group of teens. We haven't found any connection between Kimberly Weston and Cameron Knox yet. My biggest concern right now is Jean. Maybe you should talk to her, Hope. She's like a ticking time bomb. Between Joe taking off and Bethany acting up, she's under a lot of stress."

"I'll offer, Marty, but Jean is the type of woman who needs to be the one to reach out. She's incredibly independent, and if I make too much of an issue of it, she may think that we are underestimating her ability to perform in Joe's absence."

The Captain interjected. "You know Marty, Hope may have something there. I vaguely remember a time when your mom died, and I went back to work. A lot of people thought they were helping, going out of their way to make things easier for me. I thought they were implying I wasn't ready to come back and that I wasn't capable of doing my job. People being kind, having good intentions…well it pissed me off, more than anything."

Marty smiled at the man. He could just picture his father trying to be polite, but just busting at the seams to pop someone in the side of the head.

Hope stood up. "Well, I should go. Captain, thanks for dinner. I'll cook next time." She leaned down and planted a kiss on his cheek.

"No. Please don't!" Both Marty and his dad spoke up simultaneously.

The Captain looked at Marty. "Go. Go with her. Give me a break and get out of here." His hands motioned, shooing them away.

"No, Pop, I think I'll stay here with you," Marty replied, trying not to let his father hear the worry in his voice.

"No, you won't," he countered, while giving his son a stern look.

"Are you sure?" Marty asked him. He was so conflicted. As much as he felt the need to stay with his father, just in case, he wanted desperately to go home with Hope and finally get on with the task of proposing to her.

"Yes, I'm sure. Now, get the hell out and stop hovering over me."

Marty turned to Hope, who nodded in agreement.

"Okay, Pop," he conceded, giving his father's shoulder a gentle squeeze.

"Love you, Pop."

"Yeah, I know. Now get out of here." He took the towel in his hand, and with a sudden motion, whacked it across Marty's buttocks. It made a loud snap as it made contact, causing Marty to jolt in complete surprise. He laughed at his father's action and just shook his head as he made his way out the door to join Hope.

Chapter Thirteen

Sunday, Late Afternoon

I originally intended to go straight home, but then instead I was compelled to do something I hadn't done in ages— I drove to St. Mary's Church seeking to find comfort in my faith.

The youth group and mass had dispersed and the parking lot was now deserted, except for the vehicles that belonged to a few employees and clergy, like Father Murphy's blue Lincoln.

I pulled on the brass handle of the intricately carved doors. A blast of Pine Sol cleaning fumes evaded my nasal passages as I walked into the large, empty sanctuary. Just a few hours ago, each pew had been filled with parishioners, but now an eerie quiet hung over the hallowed room.

I sat down in one of the pews and just put my forehead up against the bench in front of me. I didn't know what to pray for; I just knew that I needed help from something bigger than myself.

I sat there, reflecting, for a few minutes when I heard a familiar voice. I was hoping I would be able to run into Father Murphy, but instead found myself in the company of the other priest who was a permanent resident in the parish, Father Thomas.

The older cleric always reminded me of a snowman, his body arranged as if three completely different round compartments connected parts of him, with his thin legs not quite fitting into the equation. His head was as round as a bowling ball and it was covered with a good deal of thick, snow-white hair. His face was pale except for the area just below his eyes and on either side of his nose, which was a constant shade of pink. His eyes were a shade of ocean blue that twinkled whenever he spoke. I loved the tone of his voice whenever he spoke, his Irish brogue as strong today as it must have been when he left Ireland and landed on American soil sixty years ago.

"May I help you?" The tone of his voice was deeper than I remembered.

It was apparent he didn't recognize me. Well, I really couldn't blame him. I hadn't been a regular churchgoer since my kids were little. Time, work, and life seemed to take precedence.

"I was looking for Father Murphy—is he here?" I asked, as I stood up and made my way out of the narrow pew.

"Father Murphy wasn't feeling very well. Is there something I can help you with, young lady?" I was flattered that he was calling me young. I definitely wasn't feeling it at the moment.

"No, thank you. It's a legal matter. I needed to speak to him about an ongoing investigation."

Oh crap, I couldn't believe I was standing here lying to a priest. I was going to hell for sure. I wanted to talk to Father Murphy about me, about Bethany about Glenn, about life, not the case.

I handed him my business card. "If you speak to him, can you ask him to call me when he's feeling better?"

He took my business card and brought it about an inch from his face, looking it over carefully. A pair of bifocals sat atop of his head. He patted his jacket and pants, looking for them. He gave up and just nodded his head.

"Yes, I will, certainly," he agreed.

Before I turned to walk out, I pointed to the top of his head.

He looked confused at first, and then felt around and looked embarrassed when his hand came in contact with the glasses. He broke into a broad smile exposing a large gap between his front teeth, which made him look so much more endearing.

"Oh, Father, tell Father Murphy I hope he feels better," I added, as I pushed open the heavy door.

"Yes, I will. It's just his blood sugar. He needs to take better care of his body. You would think a man so concerned with working out and muscle building would take more notice of his food intake. Your body is a temple, you know?" He looked through the bifocals that now sat hugging his face.

I stopped short.

"Father Murphy is a diabetic?" I felt a slight tremor go through my body.

"Oh, yes. Since he was a child. Type one. He must take insulin daily." He took my card and placed it his pocket. "Have a blessed day," he told me before he turned and walked away.

I got back into my car and just sat there. My head was swirling with bits and pieces of conversations that had occurred from the moment that I realized my daughter was not home. It was like I was in a movie theater and the screen was 360 degrees and I was seated in the center. I was being assaulted by images and words coming at me from all directions but in no particular order or significance. My daughter's face and her hurtful words played over and over again in a continuous loop. I saw the horror she displayed as she held her hand to her face after I slapped her. I felt ashamed and embarrassed, not only by her behavior, but by mine, as well.

And now I was confronted with a new piece of the puzzle. Could Father Murphy be a suspect? No, I couldn't fathom it; I had known the man for years. He was a stand-up guy. Father Murphy was a well-loved and well-respected man of the cloth. It couldn't be, no…no, there was no way I was going to waste one ounce of energy on that prospect.

Yet Father Thomas's words echoed in my head "He must take insulin daily."

Could it be possible? I tried to rack my brain for a motive. Why on earth would Father Murphy want to harm either of these young girls? It just didn't hold any water for me. Or, could it be that there was some sort of perversion underneath that sweet and caring surface? Could he have an agenda that was irrational?" No, I refused to believe it.

I was so conflicted. I needed to go home and confront my family, and I needed to knock on Father Murphy's residence and ask him outright if he was a serial killer and responsible for the death of one girl and the mutilation of the other.

I chose the former. I turned the key in the ignition and was about to pull out of my parking spot when my cell rang. I immediately recognized the number that displayed on the screen.

It was my missing partner Joe. Finally.

I was just about to blast him. I had every intention of screaming and hollering and giving him a piece of my mind, but the moment I heard his voice, I broke down in hysterics.

He waited patiently until I was able to get my emotions in check.

"I'm sorry, Jean. I got your messages, but I've been so wrapped up and busy..." he apologized.

"Forget it," I told him, anger still lurking in my voice.

"I spoke to Glenn, he told me that Bethany was safe. Jean, I'll be home in a couple of days. Look, we need to talk." He sounded calm and less tense then he had been in a long time.

I could hear crackling on the line. I didn't know if it was coming from my phone or his. I repositioned myself to see if I could get better reception.

"How's Annie?" I wiped my tears and took a glimpse of myself in the rear view mirror. I looked like crap. My mascara had run, giving me a resemblance to a raccoon on a bender. "Is she going to be all right?"

"I think so, Jean, it's been a rough ride, but I think she's doing better. I'll fill you in when I get home. Can you fill me in on what's going on with this case? I have access to a fax machine. Send me what you have and I'll take a look at it. Maybe I can give you a fresh perspective."

I sat there for fifteen minutes, giving him a rundown of everything we had so far. It felt good when he would throw a question at me, like old times. I would wait until he got all the words out and I would let them resonate in my mind, turning them over like pancakes on a skillet before I answered.

Joe had a way of making me think. He pushed my mind to the brink, like I was a contestant on a game show. I missed that. I realized that I needed to do that to Marty. I needed to push him, to challenge him.

I was exhausted and my voice was tiring by the time we hung up. I knew that I had to get myself together before I went home. I needed to approach my family in a constructive way. I felt better after I spoke to Joe, but there was one more person's voice I needed to hear before I headed for home. I went into the contact list on my phone and tapped my son's name.

The sound of his voice lifted my spirits more than I could have conceived.

"Hey Mom, what's up?" Loud music and a jumble of voices played in the background. As he talked, I could tell that he was walking around, attempting to find a quieter place to carry on the conversation.

"Nothing, baby, I just wanted to hear your voice." I heard

someone calling his name. It was unmistakably female.

"Are you sure? You sound down. Mom, are you okay?" The last word became muffled, like he put his hand over the phone to mute something out.

"Yes, Cliff, I'm good. What's going on? Sounds like a party." I suddenly felt like an intruder in my own son's life.

"Yeah, it's my roommate's birthday. We're just throwing him a little pizza party." He stopped and yelled out to someone in the distance. "I'll be right there." He turned his attention back to me.

"Are you sure you're okay? Is everything all right up there? Dad okay?" He must have found a quieter spot, because his voice sounded clear and sharp.

"Yes, Honey, he's fine. Look, go back to your friends. I just wanted to say hi, hear your voice. I miss my baby." I looked at the mirror again. Where had all the years gone?

He laughed at the expression. He was six foot two—hardly a baby.

"Okay, I'll call you during the week. Tell Dad and Bethany I love them."

"I will, Cliff. Behave yourself. I love you," I told him, glad that I was perceptive enough not to Skype him. If he actually saw what I looked like, I know he would be upset and wouldn't be willing to say goodbye so easily.

"Love you too, Mom," I heard him say just before I hit the disconnect button.

I leaned back in the seat and took a deep breath. I was ready to go home to try and repair the damage. I just prayed one more time that I could find the right tools to mend the broken pieces.

∽

Marty was pretty quiet on the ride to Hope's house. He knew Hope well enough to know that she was waiting for him to gather his thoughts before she interjected her own. He knew her silence was her way of sitting back, patiently waiting for him to start the conversation, even though being quiet was not one of her strongest virtues.

Marty was a nurturer. It was the one thing about him that Hope told him that she loved and respected, even if it drove her crazy at times.

Hope admired the fact that he wanted to take care of everyone, but sometimes he acted like a mother hen, which was hard for her to accept. She often remarked that she had spent her entire lifetime fighting off her mother's constant micromanaging and her ex-husband's control issues.

Hope was intellectually aware of the fact that, in Marty's case, it wasn't a control issue, but his deep compassion, strong attachment and honest attempt to want to protect those he loved. He knew that is where her own insecurities caused her so much trouble. Hope was not easily accepting of the fact that anyone, much less Marty, could care so much about her. So when Marty blurted out what he did, he knew he caught her off guard.

She wasn't quite sure she'd heard right.

"I'm sorry, what did you just say?" she asked him.

He turned into her driveway, killed the headlights, and shut off the ignition.

"I said," he turned to her, took her hand, and raised it to his face. "Will you marry me? It's not exactly how I wanted to ask you, but every time I start to ask you by reciting this long, drawn-out speech, something happens, so I'm not wasting any more time. I want to know if you'll marry me?"

When silence took the place of the "yes" he had hoped for, and the imagined hug, and the tears she would shed, he opened his hand, letting her hand drop.

She sat there, dumbstruck. He could tell that she wasn't expecting this at all.

She raised her eyes to meet his and looked at him as if she was trying to grasp what had just happened.

"I guess not," he said turning his eyes from her. He reached into his pocket and after a bit of maneuvering he was able to take out the small blue velvet jewelry box. He placed it on the console.

He pushed down on the chrome door handle and opened the driver's side door. "The jeweler said there was a fourteen day return policy. I almost didn't make it."

"You've had that for two weeks?" She glanced down at the closed box. "I…Marty…I…"

She didn't know what to say. Her heart was beating so hard she was afraid he could hear it.

"Yeah, Diane helped me pick it out."

"Diane knew?" She looked bewildered that her friend had kept mum for two weeks. It wasn't like Diane to keep a secret. Hope was going to kill her.

Now, it was Marty who was surprised. Hope was never this short with her words. He sometimes would tease her unmercifully about how she had a tendency to chatter away like a cockatiel on speed.

"Come on," he said. He felt his keys dig into the palm of his hand. Enough time had passed that it made an indentation before he felt the pain and relaxed his fist.

He started to get out of the car, taking great effort to keep her from seeing his face. He knew he didn't have a poker face, and was trying not to let her see how embarrassed he was feeling.

Hope grabbed hold of his shirtsleeve.

"Marty, wait," she said to him.

"Look, Hope, I understand. Forget it, it's okay. We can pretend this never even happened." He turned back to her, trying to hide his embarrassment.

"I just don't understand," she faltered. "You never mentioned getting married before. Why have you changed your mind?" Her top teeth bit down on her bottom lip.

He raised his eyebrows. He looked at her, astonished, as if she was thinking that his proposal had come out of nowhere.

"Changed my mind? I never changed my mind Hope. I always wanted to marry you. I love you so much it hurts sometimes. I want to spend the rest of my life with you. I want to have little Hopes and little Martys running around with dirty diapers needing to be changed and keeping us up nights driving us crazy. I've wanted to start a family with you since the first day I laid eyes on you, Hope. It's not as if we have plenty of time to do that.

I haven't changed my mind, Hope. I was just always so afraid to bring up the subject, because I knew in my gut that this would be the answer I would get."

He knew he sounded annoyed and angry. He didn't care.

Now she was getting angry at his assumption that he knew how she would react.

"First of all I haven't given you an answer, so don't get all smug and testy with me." She lifted the small box, her finger rubbing gently on the velvet cover. She closed her eyes and willed herself to open it.

The moment it came into her view, she let out a loud gasp. The beauty of it struck her, and she knew that he had put a lot of thought into what she would want. A two-karat princess diamond set in white gold stared back at her. On either side of the diamond sat a stone in a rich, deep ruby color. Her birthstone.

She turned and looked back at him. He was watching her now; unsure of what was going on. He couldn't tell what she was thinking.

"Marty…" she stopped as the headlights of a neighbor's car passed by and lit up the inside of their car. She suddenly noticed a five o'clock shadow on his face. She softly passed the back of her hand across his cheek and felt the rough stubble.

"Marty, it's beautiful." Her eyes started to well up with tears.

"A lot of good that does me," he grumbled.

"Marty, you know I love you. There is nobody in this world that I love more than you." She paused for a second. "Well, maybe the Captain takes a close second." She smiled, trying to get him to loosen up.

"I hear a 'but' in there," he responded, voice turning slightly bitter.

"There is no 'but,' Marty, I'm just being practical. It's just a very big step. I mean, where would we live? Do you move in with me? Are you really ready to fully move out of your father's house? Especially now?" Her eyes were brimming with tears now, and she was afraid to move. If she turned in the slightest, she knew a dam would break and she wouldn't be able to control the tears that would fall.

Marty flashed back on the episode in his father's house in earlier in the day. He was half in and half out of the car. His fingers tapped nervously on the steering wheel.

"I was hoping that you weren't worried about that. Tell me you aren't worried about that." Suddenly, he was no longer concerned about her answer about getting married. He had been trying all day to put his concerns about the Captain in the back of his mind. He wondered now if subconsciously that was the reason he blurted out his proposal.

Hope closed the jewelry box and palmed it.

"Come on, let's go inside." She leaned over and gave him a soft kiss on his lips. "Let's continue this conversation inside, Marty." She wiped her eyes with cuff of her sleeve. She had managed to keep the tears where they belonged.

He tossed the keys up in the air and grabbed them mid-air as they made their way down. He didn't say another word, just followed her into the house and secretly wished he could have a do-over of the entire day.

Chapter Fourteen

Sunday Evening

I thought I had it all figured out in my mind. I knew exactly what I was going to say and do when I got home. I had rehearsed my words over and over again on the way to my house.

The minute I pulled into the driveway and parked the car, my well thought out and organized thoughts turned to mush.

I could see into the living room through the front window, and was able to make out the shadow of Glenn, sitting in his favorite chair. The old plush leather lounge chair was a hand-me-down from his father. I had begged Glenn to get rid of it, or at least have it reupholstered, but he refused to even consider it, and was adamant that the chair would remain untouched. Because he was so attached to it, I let it go and no longer made an issue of it. I did insist that we cover it with a small blanket that had a design that blended nicely into the decor of the rest of the room. For some reason, the moment my eyes fell upon that piece of furniture, I became overwhelmed with resentment about it.

In my head, I could hear the voice of my psychiatrist friend, Hope, telling me that I was transferring my anger at my husband to the chair. I didn't care, I was so irate!

I knew he heard my car pull up. My temper soared even further at the fact that he hadn't made a move. I slammed the car door and stomped into the house through the garage like a bull in a rodeo arena.

I slammed the door behind me so hard that it caused Roxy to back up instead of giving me her usual enthusiastic welcome. The dog whined and looked at me, her big brown eyes trying to get a feel of whether or not she had done something wrong. I imagined a thought bubble over her furry head as she tried to remember if she had dug a hole or got into the paper towels and shredded them. I immediately felt remorseful and rubbed the back of her ears, apologizing to my best—and maybe only— friend residing in this house.

Glenn knew what was coming, so he just sat there, waiting for me to make the first move. We very rarely argued, but we had developed a pattern, and I knew exactly how he was going to handle my outburst. He was going to let me rant and rave for however long it took.

"What the hell were you thinking?" I yelled at him, knowing he would remain silent.

I was totally blown away when he yelled back at me without raising his voice.

"Keep your voice down. I finally got your daughter to stop crying and go to sleep." He stood up and threw down the remote control that he had been holding in his hand.

"Well, she needs to come down here and explain a few things to me. Do you realize the consequences of what she has done? Glenn? Do you even have a clue?"

"Yes, Jean, I have a clue. I know that your daughter is an emotional wreck. I know that she has been crying out for her mother's attention for months now, but you have been so busy being a cop and whining over Joe's behavior that you have been oblivious to your own daughter's needs."

I looked at him, stunned. I couldn't understand where this was coming from.

I shook my head.

"I don't believe this. Have you and I been living in the same house? Crap, the hell with that—have you and I been living on the same planet? How many times have I told you that, no matter what I do or say, she takes offense to it? Do you know what your answer always is? Do you?" He stood there, saying nothing.

"Well let me remind you, Glenn, your answer is, 'She's a teenager.' Does that ring a bell? That she's acting like a perfectly normal teenager, that I shouldn't take it so personally, that it's just my hormones overreacting. You have let her get away with murder."

The last word came way too close to the truth, and it came out in a choke. I prayed to God that I wasn't even remotely close to being correct and that I was speaking figuratively, not literally, when I spoke the word murder out loud.

"Do you not care that your fourteen-year-old daughter spent the night out with a seventeen-year-old murder suspect? Do you not care that she deceived us? Does it not bother you that our daughter knew that a young girl was lying on the cold ground, dead, and her beautiful face was so callously mutilated, and didn't bother to inform us so that she could protect some teenage Romeo?" I was shaking so hard that Roxie came up to me and rubbed her muzzle against my thigh in an effort, I suppose, to calm me down.

He sat back in his chair. His hands cupped his head.

"Of course I care, Jean, but I don't know how to make it better for her, or you. Our daughter has been walking a tightrope for way too long. I don't think either of us realizes just how fragile she is. We missed the signs, Jean, both of us missed the signs."

I sat down on the floor at the foot of his chair. Roxy lied down and put her chin on my lap. We both sat there in silence for a few moments. All we could hear were the soft sounds coming from Roxy's snout as she lay there breathing.

"Why did she do this, Glenn? What possessed her to keep silent? That's not how she was raised. That's not who she is." I was beginning to calm down, but I was still wary of how this was going.

"She thought she was helping a friend, Jean," he told me. "She said that Dylan was distraught and scared and that she was going to tell you, but he needed her help. Bethany believes in him, Jean. I need to trust her instincts. I don't think she was trying to deceive you as much as she was trying to protect and help a friend. She made a mistake."

I shook my head.

"No, Glenn, she didn't make a mistake, it's not that simple. She broke the law. She aided and abetted a suspect in a homicide investigation. She interfered with on ongoing criminal investigation. That is a crime, Glenn. Our daughter could be charged with obstruction of justice as an accessory to murder!" I was actually admitting it to myself for the first time as I was saying it to him.

And then it hit me.

"That's why you hired Alexis Marciano. You didn't really do it for Dylan, you hired her for Bethany." I suddenly had a flashback of my daughter as a toddler. A little girl with a skinned knee and drool running down her chin, her daddy blowing raspberries on her belly. If I had the slightest hint that my little girl would be convicted of a crime, my first instinct would have been to take her and run. My husband, the practical one, hired an attorney.

I folded my legs, Roxy's head dropped to the floor. I put my two knees together, and wrapped my arms around them, clasping my hands together and rocked back and forth.

My cell phone buzzed and Glenn gave me a look that said, "Are you really going to answer that now?"

I pulled it out of my purse and recognized the number immediately. It was from the Chief. I looked up at Glenn and apologized to him without saying a word.

I sat silently and just listened to my superior on the other end as he relayed the information I needed to hear. It was short and sweet. I turned to my husband.

"Kimberly Weston just died." I told him as I stood up and started walking in the direction of my daughter's room.

"Maybe you need to come with me, Glenn. I don't want to do this alone. We need to find out exactly what she knows, and why she didn't tell us."

He didn't say anything, but he did stand up and followed me up the staircase. I reached behind me and opened my palm to take his hand. He accepted it by entwining his fingers with mine.

∽

Marty and Hope had barely walked in the front door when his cell phone buzzed.

He didn't want to answer it, afraid that it would mean he would once again have to go out on a call. It was late, and he was tired, and although he was wary about continuing the conversation he and Hope had started in the car, he wanted to get it over with.

He recognized the number displayed on the screen. The call was coming from his friend Justin. He looked at the time and realized that Justin was probably just starting his shift for the evening.

"Yeah, what's up Justin?" He tried to sound cheerful, so as not to let his friend get an inkling of his mood.

Justin was anxious to hear if Marty finally asked Hope to marry him. He was looking forward to having Marty join the ranks of the indentured like himself. But he immediately let him know that the phone call was work-related.

"Marty, we just got word that the Weston girl died. I thought you would want to know," he said.

Marty held the phone away from his ear for a moment and then thanked Justin for informing him.

Justin started to get into the personal matter of proposals, but Marty cut him off and promised to give him a call the following morning. He disconnected his call and turned to Hope who was standing in the kitchen, waiting patiently.

"Do you have to go back to work?"

"No, that was Justin. Kimberly Weston didn't make it. Now we have a double homicide. Maybe Paul Knox wasn't that far off base. This is starting to smell like a serial killer. I wonder if Jean is going to want to bring in the state police or feds."

He took off his jacket and removed his side holster, taking out his weapon and carefully laying the gun on the kitchen table. He gently began to tap his fingers on the slide of the Glock like he was playing a piano.

Hope pulled out one of the kitchen chairs and sat down.

"Those poor families," she said. "It's bad enough to lose a child, some people never recover from that type of loss. But to lose them in such a senseless and horrible way, I can't even begin to imagine."

She looked at him, trying to get an idea of what he was thinking. That was the one thing that she really loved about the man.—you didn't have to ponder or guess with Marty. She never had to ask him if he liked what she was wearing or what she had cooked. Marty wore his emotions on his sleeve. It was all there, right out in the open.

"What is it?" she asked. "Something have you baffled?"

There were times that he was grateful that Hope was a psychiatrist, and this was one of them. He had a question that would easily be answered by an expert in her field, and here was one sitting right in front of him.

"You know, I was leaning toward the mayor's daughter on this, Hope. She seems so…what's the word, when someone is so into themselves and doesn't care about anyone else?"

"Narcissistic?"

"Yeah, Katie Hepburn, the mayor's stepdaughter, seems so disconnected from it all. I mean, she finds her friend's body in that condition and it was like, 'Oh well. No big deal'."

He got up and grabbed the jug of milk from the refrigerator. He lifted it to his mouth and chugged a good deal of the white liquid down in one gulp. He gave her a sheepish grin, his left dimple making a brief appearance, after noticing her disapproval of his unsanitary habit, and then continued to speak.

"You know, she is a beautiful...no, she's past beautiful, the girl is stunning. You would think that she would be scared to death that she would be next. This whole thing doesn't seem to faze her."

"I don't understand, Marty. Are you not considering her as a suspect anymore?"

He sat back down, tilting the chair back and letting it balance on the back legs.

"Isn't it unusual for a serial killer to be female?" he asked. "I mean, aren't they all white males, between thirty and fifty years old, or am I stereotyping?"

Hope took the jug of milk from him, wiped off the lid with a paper towel, and put it back in the fridge. She turned around and took inventory of the kitchen. Everything was in its place. She made a few last minute attempts to straighten up so she could go to bed without thinking she had left the kitchen untidy.

"There have been women, Marty, that have been labeled serial killers," she told him. "They normally tend to use methods such as what is happening in this particular case. Poisoning is a very popular method for females to use to commit murder, and from what you have told me so far; this is very personal, this is up close and personal. Whoever is doing this is dealing with some very strong anger issues. It could be they don't know the girls at all, and are just using transference."

She noticed a look of confusion on his face, so she began to explain it using layman's terms "The killer can be looking at the victims as someone that has caused them emotional pain in the past. It's not impossible at all that the person who has committed these murders is female. It is unusual, though, for a girl Katie's age to engage in this type of crime, but I have seen a lot of anger, in even younger girls than her. If Katie is suffering from some sort of psychotic disorder, she could be responsible. Pretty girls can kill just as easily as not-so-pretty ones."

She carefully placed a towel on the oven door handle and shut off the kitchen light. He got the hint, picked up his holster and gun, and followed her to the bedroom.

They undressed as the conversation continued. Hope walked into the bathroom and started to brush her teeth. With a mouth full of foam, she asked for more information.

"What do you know about her family life? Do you think she was abused or is being abused? I mean, it probably would have to be a female that she is having a problem with, or has had a problem with. Whoever is doing this is most likely directing their anger toward a female."

"I didn't have the feeling that there was any kind of problem with her mother," Marty replied. "They seemed comfortable with each other. Something weird may be going on with her stepfather, our esteemed mayor, and certainly something weird is going on with her stepbrother."

He sat on the bed after stripping down to his jockey shorts and leaned up against the pillow. Hope was watching his reflection in the mirror. She was admiring the fact that not one roll of fat accumulated over the waistband. Jealous, yet proud, Hope rinsed, spat and then joined him on the bed.

"Do you think she could consider these girls as competition? I mean, you said that the two girls who were killed were very pretty. Is it possible that there was some sort of jealously involved?" Hope slid under the top sheet and turned off the bedside lamp, which was the last remaining light in the room. It took her awhile to adjust her eyes so she was able to see him in the darkness.

He turned his head to look at her.

"I don't think Katie Hepburn considers anyone a threat. I don't know, maybe I am totally off base. Maybe there is some freak out there somewhere. I just hope whoever it is quits now, or takes their deviant behavior somewhere else."

He turned his back and rolled over on his side so he was no longer facing her. "I've got to get some sleep, Hope."

She was wide-awake and really didn't want to leave their earlier conversation up in the air, but she knew him too well. This wasn't the time to push him, or even try and explain her position on the proposal. So she turned off the lamp and cozied up to him, her arms around his waist and her belly up against the small of his back. She felt his muscles stiffen but she chose to ignore it. Her eyes closed and within seconds, they both fell into a deep slumber.

~

I held my breath and my head was spinning as I turned the doorknob leading to a room full of angry hormones bursting out of the developing body of my fourteen-year old child. Bethany was somewhere in that empty void between a girl and woman. I had absolutely no idea how I was going to handle this confrontation with her, so I just jumped into it blind and unscripted.

She was not asleep, as Glenn had thought, but prone on her bed, typing away furiously on her laptop.

The minute she heard us enter, she slammed the lid down. That immediately got the hairs on the back of my neck standing at attention and ignited an anger that had actually started to subside. To me, that was a simple act of conspiracy and evasiveness, and I wasn't exactly thrilled about it.

I was about to grab the laptop from her hands when she turned toward me and I saw the residual redness from my hand on her right cheek. I didn't think I'd hit her that hard. Seeing it now made my stomach turn.

Worse than that, though, was the look in her eyes. Those beautiful big brown eyes were puffy and swollen from crying. I couldn't tell if it was fear or hate looking at back at me, because my own vision became blurred as my own eyes started fill with tears.

Bethany turned away from me and focused on her father. She looked at him as if she was pleading for him to come to her rescue. I had seen that look many times before, but it was usually reserved for me. I used to be her best friend and confidant. I wondered whether I would ever have her look at me like that again.

"Bethany, look at me." I got no response so I repeated it this time with a little more directive.

"Bethany, look at me!" I don't know whether it was my tone or the fact that her father gave her a non-verbal command, but she did turn her face toward me. She was making a conscious effort to keep from looking at me directly. Her eyes still avoiding mine.

"Why?" I asked. "Can you please tell me why you didn't come to me and tell me what you knew? What would possess you to keep something so critically important from me?"

I could tell she was about to break down. Her shoulders gave a slight shudder and she shook her head. Blonde curls swayed in front of her face.

"Bethany, look at me!" I tried to be gentle in my tone, but I was losing the battle. I was trying so hard to contain my anger and it was slipping away from me. Here I was, still able to look at my beautiful daughter's face, into those beautiful eyes, when there were two grieving mothers out there that would never have that same privilege ever again.

I reached out and put my hand under her chin. She gave a short jerk to pull away, but must have changed her mind and stopped when I spoke.

"Kimberly Weston died a few minutes ago." I informed her.

"It wasn't Dylan, he didn't hurt her." She was adamant.

"You know Bethany, right now I don't give a damn whether it was Dylan or not. What I care about is the fact that you didn't come to me the minute you knew that someone was in trouble; why you felt the need to conceal that fact that you knew someone was brutally murdered. Do you realize you could be considered an accessory to murder and face prosecution? Do you have any idea of what the consequences of your actions could be?"

She didn't respond. I could tell though that it was all finally coming into focus for her. I could still read my daughter's facial expressions and I knew that look. I had seen it before many times while she was diligently doing her schoolwork. Math was her weakness, and there were times she would ponder an equation for what would seem like hours and suddenly it would click and she would get the answer. When she was happy, her face would light up like a Christmas tree. When something was puzzling her or she was sad, it would become dim, as if someone had flipped a switch.

"He needed my help, Mom. You don't understand. He knew everyone would think it was him, and he didn't do anything wrong. Dylan needed my help. We were going to tell you, but he just needed some time. He was so upset about seeing her like that, and he was crying so hard, and I had to help him. We were going to tell you. I called you. You promised me!" Tears flowed forming a wet streak down both sides of her cheeks.

It hit me hard just then. All this time, I thought my daughter was so mature, so responsible. I never really treated her like a child, but spoke to her as a peer and expected her to act and behave like one. Maybe all the times that Joe would tease me about my children being perfect was just a façade that I had created in my own mind. She suddenly looked so young and vulnerable to me, yet now she was becoming a woman. It was too late to for me to treat her like a baby and expect her to be the little girl I never really let her be.

"Did you have sex with him, Bethany? Did you sleep with Dylan?" My hand was still in the vicinity of her chin and I held onto her jaw and forced her to look at me. I realized that her father was in the room and I had often imagined what this moment would be like, but I never pictured myself asking my daughter this question with her father in the room.

Now, it was her dad's eyes she was avoiding. She replied at first by shaking her head no. After a few seconds passed she found her voice. It was timid and soft.

"No, we didn't have sex. No, I swear." She looked up at her father and it was then I knew she was telling the truth. She would never be able to look Glenn in the eyes if she was lying to us.

"He was so upset. You don't understand what he's been through. First, his father dies, and then his mom got sick. He was working at the supermarket after school to help his mom with her bills, but he got laid off last week. His whole world has been coming apart, and he got behind in his classes because he had to take care of his brother and baby sister because his grandma had to go to work."

"That's all very noble of him, Bethany, but that's no excuse for what he did, or what you did. He left the scene of a crime, and you helped him conceal information that was pertinent to a criminal investigation."

I picked up her laptop. She started to protest, but her father was giving her a piercing, grave look. It was so intense I was afraid her forehead would start to smoke from the burning stare.

"Until I have more information and I can rule Dylan out completely as a suspect, you are not to have any contact with him. Do you understand?"

I handed the computer to Glenn as I stood up.

She began to protest. "Dylan didn't even know that Kimberly was hurt. I was the one that told him. That's when we called you."

"Honey, we don't know yet exactly when Kimberly was attacked. You weren't with him the whole time. We still cannot rule him out. This isn't up for discussion. Dylan Silver had a relationship with both these girls and now they are dead. I don't want you to be the third."

"Mom, please! That's not fair! If I don't help him with his science, he'll fail and they'll throw him out of St. Mary's," she protested angrily.

"No, I am sorry, Bethany. This isn't a minor infraction; we are talking about two homicides—two very grisly homicides. There is some very sick individual out there targeting pretty girls and mutilating their bodies. Until that person is caught, you are not to go anywhere with anyone but your father or me. I will take you to school and pick you up, and then you will stay in this house until your father or I come home. Is that understood?"

She reluctantly nodded her head. I held out my hand. She knew exactly what I wanted and she didn't want to, but pulled out her cell phone from under her pillow and handed it me.

"You know I love you, Bethany, but I am so disappointed right now in how you have handled this. I think you really need to spend some time thinking about those girl's families and what they have lost. If you would have come to me immediately, it is very possible that Kimberly Weston might be alive right now. You do understand that, don't you?"

She nodded, but I wondered if she really was capable of understanding her role in the chain of events that had occurred. I made a mental note to ask Hope if I had miscalculated the conscience level or thought process that my fourteen-year-old actually was capable of. Maybe I had expected way too much of my daughter and now I was getting a reality check.

As I walked out of the room, I felt the soft touch of my husband's hand on my back.

∼

Monday Morning

When Marty got to work the next morning, the first one he ran into was Detective Frank Robinson.

"Meeting in the break room. Who Done It Board is up and Jean's in a foul mood and wants everyone in there ASAP." A habitual gum-chewer, Frank pushed out a thin membrane of Bazooka and slowly turned it into a bubble that was just short of baseball size. With expertise and years of experience, he allowed it to pop without leaving any residue on any part of his face.

Walking into the room together, Marty nodded to Jean, who was deep in conversation with Chief Bergman.

Justin was sitting on one of the desks, showing pictures of his son to the young rookie, Patricia Beck. It just blew Marty's mind how Justin Thyme had changed from Casanova and confirmed bachelor to doting father and husband in such a short period of time. He would have bet that he himself would have walked down an aisle and started a family long before Justin took that stroll. Now, although he had surpassed Justin in the professional world, his friend was leaving him in the dust when it came to personal life achievements.

Marty grabbed a folded metal chair that was leaning up against a defunct steam radiator beneath a row of windows that were in desperate need of washing. Dusty streaks allowed a hazy sun to slip through the window, leaving shadows of Marty's legs on the tile floor. A black chalkboard on wheels was standing behind a wooden podium. Across the board was a list of names, some with check marks next to it, some circled.

He could see the tension in Jean's face.

He wasn't sure how much the other occupants in the room knew about Bethany's involvement in this case, but he wasn't about to be the one to bring up the subject. If Jean wanted the other investigators and officers to know about it, it was clearly her decision to make, not his.

A few more men and women entered the room and grabbed chairs. The room was filled with chatter until they became aware of the police chief clearing his throat, trying to get their attention. Chief Bergman, at six foot five and two hundred and seventy-five pounds of pure, raw, power, towered over most of his men and women. It didn't take long for the room to quiet down.

As soon as everyone was paying attention, he surrendered his position behind the podium to Jean, who had added a name on the board before turning back to her audience.

"I just want to thank everyone so far for putting in all the hours you have. I know you have been working above and beyond the call of duty, but obviously, we are not even close to catching this bastard. So let's see what we have so far." She turned her back toward her coworkers and faced the board.

"We have two victims, Jamie Camp and Kimberly Weston, both female, seventeen and sixteen years old, respectively, both from St. Mary's High School. Both girls were very attractive and popular among their peers, but not very well liked. I have been getting reports from everyone that has interviewed the kids at the school that both girls have often been accused of being bullies, or for a lack of better word, bitches."

It was the veteran Sully that threw out the "C" word loud enough for all to hear.

"Bitches' is being kind, detective, from what I've been told," he remarked as he broke off a piece of a chocolate bar and shoved it into his mouth.

Jean rolled her eyes in frustration, but made sure everyone in the room knew exactly how she felt.

"I don't care if they were neo-Nazis or puppy abusers. These girls had families that loved them. They were just kids, and they deserve justice. There is no one who deserves to die the way they did. There are two grieving mothers are out there today who will never be able kiss their daughters goodnight."

She let that settle in before she went on by pointing to a group of four names on the board.

"The first victim, Jamie Camp, was found by four fellow students from St. Mary's High School and one adult male who is not a student."

She called out their names. "Tiffany Bennett, Lisa Padilla, Kate Hepburn, Dylan Silver, and the adult male, whose name is Cameron Knox."

The last few names started tongues wagging. It was obvious that everyone now knew that the mayor's stepdaughter and son were part of the equation. When she said Dylan's name aloud, she thought she heard some chatter. For those in the dark and unaware of the most recent episode, she explained.

"Dylan Silver was at the scene, but was convinced to leave by his friends, so he wouldn't be considered a suspect. Dylan Silver was intimate with both girls and had an argument with Jamie Camp a few minutes before she disappeared." She waited until it got quiet before she continued.

"The second victim, who succumbed to her injuries yesterday, Kimberly Weston, was found by two people passing by who were relieving themselves on the side of the highway. These two men have been cleared and are not suspects in either homicide."

She grabbed a bottle of water from the desk and took a sip, then continued.

"Jamie Camp was intentionally stung with bee venom, to which she was allergic. Kimberly Weston was given an injection that turned out to be a fatal dosage of insulin. She was not a diabetic. Both girls had their faces burned. The accelerant, determined to be lighter fluid, that caused Jamie's facial burns was recovered at the scene. We have not found any substances that resulted in Kimberly's burns at that crime scene. Both girls' tops were removed, in what we believe may be some sort of calling card of the killer. There is no evidence of actual sexual assault."

"So we do have a serial killer with a flaccid dick running around?" Sully blurted out. A few of the women moaned in annoyance and several of the men laughed nervously.

She ignored the remark but made sure she addressed the serial killer remark.

"It's too early to make that kind of determination, Sullivan. Let's hope that this is something specific to these two girls, and the killer is done."

She reiterated. "We hope the killer is done. Just keep your eyes and ears open out there. Talk to the kids; listen to what they are saying. So far, we have nothing to prove that any one of these five people is responsible, but I am not crossing any of them off this board until I can positively eliminate any of them."

Frank Robinson spoke up.

"What about this Cameron character? Do you think we should lean on him? I would be more than willing to do that," the detective offered freely.

Jean finally loosened up and gave a chuckle.

"Go for it, Frank, just don't get his daddy the Mayor Paul Knox's tail feathers up. I really don't need that imbecile crawling up our asses." She put down the bottle of water and placed the chalk on the top of the podium. It started to roll down, but she caught it before it fell off the edge. She placed it in an indentation on the stand so it would stay in place.

"Well that's about it. Does anyone have questions?" She waited a few seconds, but no one had any.

"All right, that's about it. Let's get this son of a bitch." She turned and started to walk toward Marty.

She grabbed his arm and quietly pulled him aside.

"We need to take a ride to St. Mary's and see Father Murphy," she said.

He looked down at her, confused.

Without looking up at him, she continued walking, her pace becoming more rapid and her stride wider. She wasn't at all surprised when he got to the exit before her. He held the door open and she walked through. When they were both outside the building, she told him what she had learned.

"Father Murphy is a diabetic. He takes insulin daily."

Marty didn't ask for any explanation he just pulled out his car keys and held them up. She nodded compliance, knowing it meant he intended to drive.

Chapter Fifteen

The best thing about working with Marty is that he knows when to initiate conversation and when to let me sit and sulk.

I think Joe had given him plenty of tips on the best way to survive working with me when I was *on the cotton pony*, as Joe so often colorfully described my period. I guess Marty decided to take that advice to heart and apply it to my current situation. I might as well have been suffering from PMS or DMS or AMS (During Menstrual Syndrome or After Menstrual Syndrome), because I had been on an emotional roller coaster for days now.

I was overthinking everything, and my thoughts were becoming obsessive and repetitive about the events that had occurred with Bethany. My brain was on overdrive. I was rehashing what had been said and what I wished I would have said, and I was accomplishing nothing productive.

I knew that somehow I had to find a way to stick my personal issues somewhere out of reach so I could get back to the business of concentrating on the case. I was overcome with guilt and remorse and was feeling so inadequate now as a mother, and maybe even as a wife.

Had I let my family down? Why now, fourteen years after my daughter's arrival into this world, did I suddenly feel like I didn't know her? I never once had questioned my parenting skills with my son, who I thought was the much more complicated child. Cliff was a good, well-mannered boy, but he was a boy, and broken bones and gashes were a constant occurrence. Not once did he ever raise his voice or tell me that he hated me.

I was so engrossed in my own thoughts that I didn't realize we had arrived at our destination when Marty pulled into the church's parking lot.

"Hey, are you okay? Do you want to just chill here for a few minutes before we go in?" He had shut off the engine and turned, shifting his long legs sideways as he leaned his torso against the driver's side door.

Faceless: A Mystery ~ Dawn Kopman Whidden

"No, I don't think I am all right," I told him, suddenly craving a cigarette, something I had given up several years ago. "I just don't know what to make of it anymore. I feel like I woke up last week and everything around me is off somehow. Everyone I came in contact with looked the same, sounded the same, but they weren't the same. It's as if I've entered a totally different dimension. I feel like I am in an episode of *The Twilight Zone*. A really bad episode."

Marty's fingers tapped the console as if he was playing an instrument. I noticed that he would do that when he took the time to carefully formulate his thoughts before speaking them aloud.

"You know, Jean, the world has changed so much, even since I was a teenager. The kids today don't have the same coping skills that my dad's generation or your generation or even my generation had. They have too many choices. My dad swears that the trouble with the world today is just that simple. Think about it— when he was a kid, he had no TV, just radio. So you didn't have to decide between three hundred channels to watch. You had AM or FM radio. And what, maybe three or four stations? You had the choice between black and white film and color.

Today, you can watch a movie on Netflix or on your iPad or your computer, Windows or Mac, or your iPhone or your Android. You had Pepsi or Coke, not a zillion different flavors, and it was either a large or a small, not a zillion different sizes to choose from. You can't just have water anymore, you have to decide if you want it to be flavored or enhanced with vitamins. You bought a Chevy or a Ford or a Dodge, now you have a million different styles and colors to choose from in just one vehicle.

"I don't know how their brains function anymore, being bombarded with all the choices they have to make. When was the last time you walked into the electronics department of Wal-Mart and had to pick out a game as a gift? Xboxes and Wii's and PlayStations. It's hard enough to decide which product to buy, without having to choose a game to play on it. I think we would be all better off if we could roll back technology and go back to playing Monopoly or Chutes and Ladders, and get rid of all these electronic gadgets."

He had a valuable argument there. Now we knew why the world was so screwed up; what we could do about it was another dilemma altogether.

I nodded and opened my door. He exited his side. I waited until he was on my side of the car before I responded.

"Right now, the only choice I'm concentrating on is which one of these suspects is a cold-blooded killer, and whether Father Murphy's medical condition has any bearing on this case."

"Well," he said, as he took a long stride towards the building. He glanced down at his watch. "If memory serves me right, Father Murphy should be overseeing basketball practice in the gymnasium around this time of day. Let's head toward the gym."

"You know, Marty, it's not just the insulin, there's also the lighter fluid. I don't know if you noticed, but Father Murphy partakes in the bad habit of smoking tobacco, and he uses a one of those old-style lighter fluid lighters to light those cigarettes."

From the look on his face, I could tell he was greatly troubled by what I said.

He immediately stopped walking.

"Jean, you're not actually contemplating the idea that Father Murphy is remotely responsible for the deaths of those girls. Please tell me that is not what you are insinuating here. There is no way. I've known the man for years. I was one of his students; he was a great teacher, a warm, caring guy. No, there is no way..." He shook his head in disgust.

"I don't know what I am saying yet, Marty, I'm just putting two and two together. Father Murphy knows the victims. Father Murphy has access to insulin. Father Murphy has a cigarette lighter that uses the type of lighter fluid that was found at the scene, which was positively identified as the substance that caused the burns on Jamie Camp's face."

I knew what I said was troubling him, but it had to be considered.

"Right now, Marty, I just want to find out if he has an alibi for the night the girls were killed. I just want to rule him out. Then I want to have a long chat with each of the girls, and then I want to pick up Cameron Knox and have another talk with him."

He started to walk again, shaking his head. "No way. There is no way that Father Murphy has anything to do with this. I am willing to bet my firstborn child on that. If I'm ever to have a firstborn."

I had totally forgotten about the fact that he was planning to propose to Hope. I was just about to ask him how that worked out when we reached the building.

FACELESS: A MYSTERY ~ DAWN KOPMAN WHIDDEN

I could hear the echo of the basketballs pounding the gymnasium floor. We pushed through a pair of double heavy wooden doors and the smell of sweaty bodies permeated the air, assaulting my senses. I suddenly got a flashback of my son's room before he left for college.

The Ping-Pong and other tables were folded up and placed off to the side, but thirty or so students of various sizes and ages were actively engaged in a vigorous game of basketball.

Off to the side was a female coach, giving instructions to a group of scantily dressed cheerleaders. Although a few heads turned when we entered the building, I was convinced that the girls were more interested in admiring my partner's exceeding good looks than the fact that two strangers had just entered the room. The fact that two of their fellow students were recently murdered seemed to have little effect on the current population. Maybe I was wrong. Maybe I was way too cynical and I just wasn't looking deep enough.

~

Father Murphy was off to the side, near a small section of bleachers. He was talking with his hands to three tall boys resembling beanpoles in blue silk gym shorts. He was animatedly pointing to the goal zone when he noticed us. He threw us a smile and quickly finished his instructions before he walked over to us. He tried to make conversation, but the noise level became so intrusive he signaled for us to follow him. He led us to the same office that we had been in the other day. As soon as he shut the door behind us, the noise evaporated. It was obvious the room was soundproofed.

He looked relieved that he had a chance for some quiet, and it didn't appear that he was worried about our visit. I took that as a good sign. Or maybe, he was just a real sociopath and a great actor to boot.

He walked around the desk, pulled out the chair, and practically fell into it. I hadn't noticed it the other day, but I took note of the thin folds of skin and other signs of age that had recently taken up residence on Father Murphy's face and hair. I don't know whether it was the sudden recent events that took a toll on the still very handsome priest, or I had just never really studied him this closely.

"I heard about Kimberly's passing, this is such a tragedy." His hand rubbed his jaw and throat before it settled down on a stack of papers on his desk. "We were just making arrangements for Jamie's services when we were notified. What's going on, Jean? Is this insanity going to stop?"

"I don't know, Father, I hope so. How are you feeling?" I asked, leaning back against the wall.

He looked up at me, slightly bewildered.

I explained. "I stopped by last evening on my way home. Father Thomas said you weren't feeling well."

"Oh it was nothing, Father Thomas tends to be a little dramatic. My blood sugar was a little high, so I turned in early." He swiveled the chair around a 90-degree turn and I noticed a small refrigerator behind his desk. He leaned over and grabbed a bottle of water from a row on the top shelf.

I was able to see into the small refrigerator. There were three small shelves, and on one shelf, I saw several cardboard boxes. On the side of them were pharmaceutical labels. On one of the lower shelves, I thought I saw a small plastic bag with some words in big red letters that read CAUTION: MEDICAL WASTE and that it contained some loose hypodermic needles. On another shelf, there were more needles.

"Can I get you anything?" He held up the plastic bottle of water.

Marty said no and I just shook my head. I was about to ask him about his insulin when there was a knock at the door.

He looked apologetic as he called out, "Come in."

Tiffany Bennett was flushed from physical exertion when she entered the room. Her freckled face was beet red and her hair was plastered to her face from sweat.

"I'm sorry, Father, but Ms. Nelson told me to come in and get a bottle of water and a couple of Band-Aids." She lifted her left hand to show him a small stream of blood coming from a cut.

He nodded to her and she walked over to a small metal closet that contained some first aid materials and clean folded towels. After a little bit of shuffling things around, she seemed to find what she was looking for. She smiled meekly as she turned and was making her way out of the room when Father Murphy called out to her.

"Tiffany, could you tell your mother that I said thank you? I found the check that she left on my desk the other day, but with all that has been going on, I haven't had a chance to thank her personally. Please tell her that I will give her a call and thank her myself. In the meantime, please tell her that I'm sorry I missed her, and thank her for the generous donation. It is very well appreciated."

The girl stood there, staring at him for a moment as if she didn't understand what he was talking about, but then nodded her head and turned to walk out.

I was blocking the door and I was close enough to smell her sweat.

"Tiffany, will you be going directly home after school today?" I asked.

Her face was starting to regain its normal color, and even seemed to pale in comparison to what it had been just moments ago. I noticed she was making an effort to cover the slight, uncontrollable movement of the left side of her mouth with her hand. It obviously made her self-conscious.

"Um, sorry?" she replied.

"Tiffany, Detective Keal and I would like to sit down and talk to you in depth about Jamie and that night she was killed. It would help a great deal if we can gather as much information as we can about both of the girls. You may have knowledge that can help us find their killers, you might not even be aware of what you know."

"I really don't know any more than I already told you." Her eyes darted from me to Marty and then to the now-opened door. I glanced out beyond the opening and I immediately recognized her friend Lisa was staring in our direction.

"Well, how about you tell your parents that we will be coming by later this afternoon for an interview. Would that be all right with you, Tiffany?" I asked.

"Yeah, sure, excuse me, I have to go." She briskly walked out of the room and my eyes followed as she bee lined her way to her friend.

Father Murphy got up and made sure the door was closed tightly and then made his way back to his seat.

"What's going on, Jean? Is something going on I should know about?"

"Father, Kimberly Weston died of an overdose of insulin."

I saw the color drain from his face. He looked at Marty and then closed his eyes and shook his head. His hand covered his mouth in utter disbelief.

"Kim was a diabetic? I wasn't aware."

"No, Father, she wasn't. Whoever killed Kimberly injected her with insulin. Intentionally. They had access to the drug."

It took him a few seconds, but he started to put two and two together. He turned back and looked at the small appliance that was storing his medicine.

"Am I a suspect, Jean? I..." If he was acting, he was a damn good actor. He seemed to be stunned.

"Father, I'm sorry, but I have to ask. Can you account for your whereabouts the night Jamie was murdered?" We still hadn't established an exact time that Kimberly was attacked, so I intentionally left her out of the equation.

"Jean, you called me at the rectory. You have to know that I would never..." As he shook his head, a lock of thick brown hair covered his forehead. "I'm sorry, I know you're doing your job. It's just so bizarre. I was in bed asleep when you called. We had a budget meeting that ran rather late, and we retired about midnight. I can have you speak to Father Thomas, he can vouch for me." He lifted the handset from the phone that sat on the desk.

"No Father, that's not necessary right now," I told him. "It's just that there are a few things that are troubling."

I picked up a gold lighter that was sitting on his desk. "Father, what kind of lighter fluid do you use for this? Do you keep it here?"

"Oh my God, Jean. The burns?" His eyes got watery and he immediately opened the bottom drawer in his desk. He furiously tossed things around before turning and looking back at me, a look of shock and alarm on his face.

"My lighter fluid—it's gone," he said, his hand still rummaging through the drawer.

"What brand of fluid do you use Father?" I asked. "By any chance, is it...?"

We said it at exactly the same time.

"Zippo."

"Father, do the students have access to your office, or do you lock it when you aren't here?"

"Oh, dear God," was all he was able to say when he realized that whoever killed those two girls was someone that he knew, and probably knew well.

"Father," I asked. "Is any of your medication missing?"

He shifted his chair and leaned down to open the small refrigerator. He pulled out the box that was labeled Injectable Insulin Pens, 3.0 ml (Five per Box). He lifted the thin cardboard lid. I could tell he was calculating his prior usage with the contents of the box.

It was apparent from my view that three remained, and for a moment, he looked relieved. That is, until he shifted a few more things in the small refrigerator and pulled out another box that, for all intents and purposes, looked unopened. He shook it gently and looked perplexed. He carefully lifted a curved see-through adhesive tape that sealed the box. The label on this box also indicated it should hold five pens, but when he lifted the lid, there were only three.

Father Murphy's face drained of all color. He now knew without a doubt there was a murderer in close proximity, and the place he had always considered sacred and safe had been compromised.

Chapter Sixteen

After the priest emptied the contents of the cardboard box onto his desk, Marty stepped out to the car to retrieve some latex gloves from the trunk. Father Murphy and I sat silently as we waited for Marty to return.

It wasn't long before Marty came back and slipped on the latex gloves. He carefully took possession of the now-empty carton. He slipped the cardboard box and remaining insulin pens into a plastic bag and sealed it by sliding the red plastic zipper across the top. I hoped that whoever had gotten into the priest's medication was careless enough to leave behind some fingerprints.

As we walked out of the office, Marty and I noticed that neither Tiffany Bennett nor Lisa Padilla were anywhere in sight. Marty started to walk toward the parking lot when he must have realized that I was headed in another direction.

"Hey!" he hollered out, as he turned and increased his pace to catch up with me. "Where are we going?"

"I want to have a chat with Father Thomas and make sure that Father Murphy was exactly where he said he was the night Jamie Camp was murdered." I pulled open the heavy wooden door and headed down a wide hallway that led to the older cleric's office.

"You don't actually think he would lie to you, Jean, he's a priest, for heaven's sake. They don't lie."

His naiveté astonished me.

"Tell that to all those boys that sued the church because they were molested," I retorted.

"We are talking about Father Murphy, Jean. I have known him most of my life. You have known him for years. He has never been accused of any inappropriate behavior, much less homicide," Marty insisted. "I think you're reaching here."

"Maybe. I just want to rule him out," I maintained. "Can't hurt to cross him off my suspect list, Marty. Believe me, I don't like even the slightest thought of him being responsible for this, but we need to be sure."

We reached Father Thomas's office and I was about to knock when the door opened and the elderly priest walked out. He looked up, startled at his visitors.

Suddenly a bell rang, announcing a change of classes, and the building rocked with noise as a herd of adolescents emptied into the hallway. As if he had done it a million times before, he grabbed my arm and pulled me to the wall, preventing me from getting trampled by the students.

Taking off his spectacles, the priest wiped the lens with a folded cloth as he apologized for the near accident.

"They get out of hand sometimes," he said. "I wish we had more of a warning device for visitors."

I gave him a brief smile.

"What can I do for you, detective?" he asked as he put his glasses back on, returning the cloth to his pocket. "I think I've seen you more in the last few days than I have in the past ten years. You need to come visit more often, preferably under different circumstances."

"Yes, I know, Father," I replied. "I was just hoping you would be able to clear up something for me."

"Sure, if I can, what is it?" he inquired.

I was at least five inches taller than the man, but his presence made me feel like a child again. That started to make me feel a tad guilty about what I was about to ask him.

As fast as the halls filled with the students, they emptied out again. I waited till the last of the kids entered a nearby classroom and the noise dissipated before I asked my question.

"Father Murphy said that he attended a budget meeting on Wednesday night, and that it ran late. Can you verify that?"

He looked up at me suspiciously, but I could tell he was formulating a timeline in his mind. I wondered if I was the only one who thought he looked like a snowman.

"Yes, Wednesday evening we had a budget meeting with the board. We had quite a disagreement going on over the monies being allocated to the school band. They want the best, but they certainly don't seem to want to pay for it. It's such a shame that the children suffer because the adults can't seem to agree on anything. Yes, it ran rather late...um...I don't think I got to retire for the night until one a.m."

"Was Father Murphy there for the entire meeting, Father?" Marty asked. The aging priest nodded his head. A wisp of gray hair poked out from his black plastic eyeglass frames on either side. "Yes." He turned to me as if he was being deliberate. "I can guarantee that he was there. I can assure you, detective, that if Father Murphy said he was somewhere, you can take that to the bank."

He sounded as if he was lecturing us, especially me.

I could feel the "I told you so" that Marty was dying to say.

"Just making sure, Father—thank you for your time," I said, trying to let him know he wasn't intimidating me, even if he was.

I turned and headed for the door. Marty said goodbye to the priest and followed immediately after me. He didn't say another word until we were in the car and headed out of the parking lot.

"Where to?" he asked me.

I cleared my throat. It felt like I had been sucking on cotton balls.

"First, let's drop off this package at the lab, to see if they can pull up some prints or DNA. I think I want to have a little chat with Cameron Knox before we talk to the girls again. I know Frank said he wanted to do it, but I want to go over his story one more time to see if he left anything out, like whether there was one other person at this party of theirs."

I popped a mint into my mouth, hoping it would help with the dryness. I offered him one, but he declined.

"Are you thinking that Kimberly Weston was there? Don't you think one of them would have mentioned that when we first interviewed them?" He kept his eyes on the road, but his head turned slightly toward me as he asked.

I made a slight sucking sound as I inhaled the first taste of mint before I answered.

"First off, I don't know whether any of them can be trusted to tell us the truth. They had several hours to concoct a story and make it sound viable. Do we know where Kimberly was Wednesday night? How long was it before her parents called in a missing child report? Had Kimberly spent more than one night out of her house? Maybe Kimberly's parents were totally clueless about the teenager's whereabouts!" I told him.

Then I added, under my breath, "Like the rest of us."

Marty broke in. "Look, Jean, you need to give yourself a break," he told me. "Bethany has entered that mysterious black hole known as adolescence. She is a teenager, and a very bright one at that. Sometimes kids do stupid things, no matter what their IQ. If you add a good-looking, popular teenage boy to the equation, you have what the Captain calls 'scrambled judgment on hormones.'"

I let out a deep sigh. I knew he was right, but I wasn't easily convinced.

"Is that supposed to make me feel better?" I responded. "Damn, I wish I still smoked. I want a cigarette so bad right now. Why the hell did I stop, anyway?" I popped another mint into my mouth.

"Maybe because it's a nasty habit and it makes you smell bad and it costs way too much?" he offered. I knew he was about to break out in a smile because a large crevice appeared on his right cheek.

I again mumbled something under my breath.

We made a quick stop at the crime lab and Marty ran out to drop off the evidence bag. We were back on the road within minutes.

The rest of the drive was made in virtual silence until we arrived at the Forester mansion. The driveway was covered with grass cuttings and the smell of freshly cut lawn caused my nostrils to itch.

We could hear the sound of the lawn mower get louder as we got closer to the cottage where Cameron Knox was living. He was shirtless as he sat upon a small John Deere tractor that was pulling a finish mower, a set of headphones covering his ears. I could see his lips moving. It was as if he was singing along with whatever music he was listening to.

Marty stopped the car, got out, walked over to the passenger side, and joined me as I leaned against the door. Cameron seemed to be oblivious to his visitors as he continued singing and mowing. Getting impatient, I leaned into the vehicle, pressed down on the horn, and hit the siren. It took another four or five seconds, but it got his attention. He looked over and lifted the headphones off his head. He nodded and turned off the engine, climbed down and walked towards us.

As much as I had developed an immediate dislike of the man, I couldn't deny the fact that he was a sexy son of a gun. Sweat glistened on his chest, which was slick and hairless, looking like it had been waxed. His jeans were tight and hugged his lower body as if they were sewn on him. I wondered if the esteemed mayor ever had a DNA test run on this offspring. There was absolutely nothing about this man that resembled the short and stocky Paul Knox.

"Detectives, I'm sorry, I didn't hear you pull up." He wiped the sweat on his brow and around the back of his neck with what once had been a white handkerchief. Now it was gray with grime.

"What can I do you for?" he asked.

Marty pulled out a photograph of Kimberly Weston, obtained from her family.

"You know this girl, Cameron?"

Cameron took the picture from Marty and held it up between his thumb and other fingers.

"Come on, Marty, give me a break here. I already told your buddy, the only time I have seen that girl is when I saw her picture on TV."

He turned and flashed me a smile. I noticed one of his front teeth slightly overlapped the other one. If the man hadn't been such an idiot, I would have thought it charming.

Cameron waited for Marty to say something. When he didn't, he continued to talk.

"No, I didn't kill her, either. I never met that one. Pretty, though," he added. He touched the bottom quarter of the photograph as if he was studying it.

"You know, if you're lying, Cameron, we're going to find out," Marty advised him.

"Look Marty, I may be a lot of things, but I am not some psycho serial killer. As far as I'm concerned, whoever is doing this deserves to be boiled in hot oil. There aren't enough beautiful women in this world, and this jerk is eliminating them from the population." He turned and looked directly at me.

"Beautiful women are to be kept on a pedestal and admired and loved, not mutilated," he said. He glanced at his own reflection in the mirror, and seemed to admire what he saw. I was getting nauseated.

"Can you account for your whereabouts Wed, Thursday and Friday evenings, Cameron?" Marty asked him trying to cut through the bullshit...

"As a matter of fact, I can't. Thanks to all this, I have suddenly have become some sort of pariah. My girl isn't allowed to come near me."

"You mean your stepsister?" I asked him, my mouth spitting out sarcasm.

"We're not blood, and she isn't jail bait. No laws being broken." He turned and walked toward the tractor.

Before he started the engine, I yelled out. "Are you missing any of your empty honey jars, Cameron?"

He turned around, a puzzled look on his face. One foot had already started to climb the machine, but he stepped back down.

"What do you mean?" he asked me.

"Just what it sounds like," I continued. "Those jars you put your honey in—are any of them missing?"

He slowly walked back to where we were standing.

"What does that have to do with any of this?" Suddenly he was more interested in what we had to say.

"Just answer the lady's question, Cameron," Marty demanded.

"Not missing, but I did find one of my jars busted the other day. I can't figure out for the life of me how the hell it got out in the woods. What does my honey have to do with anything?"

"Where is it now?" Marty asked.

"What?" Cameron asked.

"The jar!" Marty was getting increasingly impatient.

"I threw it out in the garbage. It was broken in a dozen pieces. I picked up the pieces with some cardboard and tossed them out. I didn't want anyone to step on it. What gives?"

I suddenly got excited. If we had the jar, we might be able to salvage some prints.

"Where's your garbage, Cameron?" I asked, as I started to walk toward the cottage.

"They collected this morning," he informed us, causing me to stop in my tracks.

Once again, we hit a dead end. Totally frustrated, I got back in the car and waited for Marty to join me. I stuck my head out the window and called Cameron's name. I pointed at him.

"Just don't disappear, Knox…do you catch my meaning?" I told him, leaving my finger in midair.

"Yeah, I do, detective. I got no reason to leave, and every reason to stay. This crap is going to blow over, and Katie and I are going to be together. I can tell you this, lady, I didn't kill those girls, and neither did Katie," he said as he turned and walked away.

~

"What do you make of that?" I asked Marty. I wasn't quite sure I believed the guy, but I did think that the surprised look on his face when I brought up the honey jar was genuine. "Do you buy his story?"

Marty didn't answer, but I could tell he was pondering the question.

It had been unusually warm for early June. As we got back on the highway, I noticed in the distance the sky had darkened and a bolt of lightning lit up the horizon. It was as if summer had arrived, and spring never had a chance.

As we got closer to the darkened clouds, the sky opened up and large drops of rain suddenly pelted the windshield. He turned on the wipers. The sound of the wiper motor almost lulled me into something I hadn't felt in a while—relaxation.

I glanced down at the clock on the console. We had another hour and a half before I had to pick up Bethany at school, and then we were going to head over to Tiffany Bennett's for another interview.

"Hey, you feel like grabbing something to eat at the Lion's Den? I could go for their Shepherd's Pie."

He didn't answer me. I began to think the rain and the wipers were so loud he couldn't hear me. I repeated myself.

"Hey, Marty, do you want to grab something to eat? I'm famished."

Silence permeated the air. He had given me no answer.

"Hey, earth to Marty, you in there?" I asked, as I tapped him on the shoulder.

It seemed to bring him back from wherever he had gone.

"Oh, sorry Jean, what did you say? Yeah, food...Lion's Den is fine." He had heard me, but he had gone into another zone. He was there in body, but not in mind.

"Are you okay?" I asked. "You seem a bit off today."

He bit down on his lip. I got the distinct feeling he was contemplating whether or not he was going to confide in me.

"Hey, if it's none of my business, I'll butt out, but if it's something I can help you with..." I began.

He started to tap on the steering wheel as if he was typing on a keyboard. "I asked Hope to marry me last night..." He bit down on his lip a little harder now. I was afraid he was going to draw blood.

I was surprised by the expression on his face.

"She said no?" I asked, astonished. I never would have predicted that. I knew that Hope was very gun shy, but I knew without a doubt that she was deeply in love with him.

"Not really. It wasn't exactly a 'no,' but it certainly wasn't a 'yes.' Damn, I forgot. Do me a favor, there's a business card in the glove compartment, a Dr. Sears. Can you..." He pulled his cell phone out. "Can you dial that number for me? I need to make an appointment for a neurologist for the Captain."

I did what he asked and then waited until he completed his call before I asked him what was going on.

"He has to wait two weeks before he can get in. Whatever happened to the good old days, when you could call the doctor and get in the next day?" he complained.

"What's wrong with the Captain?" I asked. "What does he need to see a neurologist for?" Now I was concerned. I could tell that something had been bothering Marty all day, and now I wondered if it was more than his proposal to Hope.

The rain was coming down now in sheets and the visibility was near zero.

"We aren't sure. It's just that he's been a little off lately.

Misplacing things, forgetting things. Just off, that's all." He tried to shrug it off, but Marty would never be able to excel in the game of poker. His face was a road map to his emotions, and his eyes were definitely on the road to the town of worry.

He scratched his forehead before he elaborated.

"Something's just not right. He tore the kitchen apart the other day looking for the can opener, and it was right in front of him, where it always is. He thought his wallet was stolen the other day...canceled his credit cards and everything. The next day I found the wallet in the freezer, sitting right up front, atop of a box of peas."

He stopped as if he suddenly remembered something else. "He's been getting names mixed up. He called Justin's wife by my sister's name, which in itself would be no big deal, but...and the other day he called me Tommy. He never, ever, has called me by my twin brother's name. He has always been able to tell us apart. He has never once mixed us up."

It was as if he was trying to take inventory of all of the instances of confusion the Captain had displayed.

I didn't want to blow it off and make it sound like it was nothing to be concerned about, because I knew all too well it could be something. My own mother suffered from Alzheimer's and I had watched the woman that I loved and admired slowly turn into someone that I didn't recognize.

People tend to think that the tragedy of the illness is that the patient doesn't recognize the family, but there is another component to it as well. The family doesn't recognize the patient, either. It makes it hard to care for a person you don't even know, someone who has turned into a virtual stranger.

My children loved my mother, adored her even, but after a while, they became frightened of her. Even though I knew better, I became resentful of the woman that she had become.

I didn't know if Marty knew about my mother's disease, and I chose not to tell him about it at the moment.

"It could be just stress, Marty." I gave him the typical response, hoping it turned out to be the correct one, even though I knew that, more than likely, the symptoms the Captain was exhibiting were probably caused by a more sinister component than stress.

Faceless: A Mystery ~ Dawn Kopman Whidden

By his answer, I knew that Marty was well aware of that.

"Jean, that man has no stress. He is the happiest he has been in years. He has no money problems, his kids are grown and out of the house—well, most of them," he corrected himself. "He lives a stress-free life…soap operas during the day and poker with my uncles three nights a week." He unwrapped a stick of gum and offered me one. I turned him down.

"The Captain watches soap operas?" I asked him, flabbergasted at the thought.

"Don't ever tell him I told you that, he'll kill me."

I laughed out loud for the first time in days. It felt absolutely wonderful.

By the time we reached the pub, the rain was starting to slow down. I ran through several puddles before I got to the front door.

I was already starting to smell the Shepherd's Pie I was going to order when my cell rang. It was the dispatcher. The pie would have to wait.

The dispatcher explained in detail what the call was about, because she couldn't believe it herself.

"Call from woman at 129 Meadow Lane. A woman became curious when her two dogs kept barking incessantly in her back yard. After about an hour, she decided to investigate and noticed something behind her neighbor's flowerbed. It looked odd to her and it piqued her curiosity, so she grabbed her pool net and slid it though her chain-link fence and kept on poking at it, pulling it closer it until she was able to get a close enough look. When she got the suspicious item close enough, she realized it was a complete set of male genitals. She is now being treated by paramedics, and officers Hennessey and Stiskin are at the scene and are requesting your presence."

～

Ten minutes later, we were pulling up to the crime scene. The street was cordoned off and it seemed like the entire police force had shown up. Media trucks were setting up their equipment and neighbors were starting to congregate in small groups. We had to park quite a distance away and walk in order to get past the crime scene barricades.

We found Officer Hennessey interviewing the woman who made

the 911 call. A paramedic was taking her vitals. When Hennessey saw us, he excused himself. I saw him grab something out of his patrol car and then he headed our direction. He was holding up a plastic bag with what looked like some sort of sea creature.

"We found your husband's balls, detective, mystery solved," he said with an insane smirk on his face. He had been trying to get back at me ever since I took part in a practical joke that had the guy sweating bullets, thinking he was about to be a father, with eighteen years of child support on the horizon.

I took the bag from him and studied it carefully.

"Sorry, Hennessey, this couldn't be Glenn's. He would need a gallon-size bag. This quart-size bag would rule him out completely," I told him as I handed the bloodied genitals back to him.

"What's going on?" I asked as we started walking toward the fifties-style ranch home that was surrounded by our SWAT team.

"Suspect is inside, her name is Susan Goldman. She was just apprehended with the murder weapon, a machete, and the husband, Mr. Goldman, is now literally in pieces. Mrs. Goldman started to bury the body parts in the back yard, but the family pet, a really good-looking German Shepherd..." he paused. His train of thought seemed to get sidetracked as he reflected on the animal.

After a moment, he continued. "Anyway, the dog kept digging up whatever she would bury, so, she decided to cook up the rest of the remains instead. She said she got sick and tired of him sitting on his rear end watching TV and drinking beer, so she slipped him a couple of Ambien to knock him out and piece by piece dismembered him. She started with the family jewels," he said, as he lifted the bag and displayed the contents once again.

I rolled my eyes in disgust. It seemed like the world was going crazier with each call we got. The only thing good about this one was that it was an open-and-shut case. We had a confession and an overwhelming amount of profound evidence connecting the wife to the homicide.

∼

Two hours later, we were wrapping up when I realized the time.

"Crap. I forgot I had to pick up Bethany," I told Marty in a pure panic.

"Call her," he said. "She's probably outside waiting for you." He looked at his watch. "They just got out. She'll understand."

"I can't call her, I took her phone away. Damn it." I scrolled through my cell phone contact menu and found the school's telephone number. When the secretary picked up, I explained who I was and asked if she could find my daughter and let her know I was on my way. She agreed and I hung up.

Marty and I got into the car and headed toward the school. I didn't say a word when I noticed him exceeding the speed limit by twenty miles per hour.

A few small groups of students lingered in front of the church itself. It took a few seconds before I spotted her. She was leaning against the black wrought-iron fence that surrounded the perimeter of the church grounds. One leg was bent and the heel of her foot was tapping the railing.

I immediately recognized the two girls she was standing with and the hairs on my arms shot up. Lisa Padilla and Tiffany Bennett seemed to be lecturing my daughter about something.

I didn't bother to shut the door as I exited the vehicle. I raced to the spot where my daughter and the girls stood.

"What's going on here?" I asked, looking directly at my daughter, trying to determine whether her face showed any signs of stress or anxiety. I didn't notice any until she turned in my direction after recognizing the sound of my voice.

"Nothing," she answered coldly, and then turned to the two other girls. "See you later," she bid the girls goodbye as she walked toward Marty's car.

I turned to Tiffany and reminded her that I was going to pay her a visit later on in the day. She didn't answer, instead, she gave me a shrug of her shoulders. She said something as I walked away, but I couldn't make it out. Whatever it was, I was pretty sure it wasn't a warm and fuzzy goodbye.

Once Bethany was buckled in, she uttered her first words directed at me.

"You know, this is extremely embarrassing, having a police escort. No, it's worse than embarrassing, it's humiliating."

I ignored her. There was no way I was going to have this

conversation in front of Marty. I could tell by the look on his face that he already felt awkward.

We dropped her off at home and I reminded her that she was not to leave the house. She did say goodbye, but it was directed solely for Marty's benefit, not for mine.

Chapter Seventeen

Marty and I knew we had a few minutes to spare, since Tiffany would not be home yet, so we made our way back to the Lion's Den and ordered some dinner to go.

A half an hour later while Marty drove I devoured my Shepherd's Pie and it was working it's way through my digestive system while Marty's remained untouched, we reached the vicinity of the Bennett residence. While I was savoring each morsel of my Shepherd's Pie, Marty's stomach began to make gurgling noises.

When the GPS announced we had reached our destination, we found ourselves at the bottom of a steep hill and the beginning of a long asphalt driveway. A very expensive white vinyl horse fence surrounded the entire ten acres of the estate. I caught sight of at least five beautiful, dark-chocolate-and-white Appaloosas grazing in a pasture, which was manicured as if it doubled as a golf course.

A few moments later we reached the top of the hill, where we came upon a very large and exquisite three-story white mansion containing an obscene number of windows, many of which were adorned with cherry-red flower boxes covered in thick red-and-white geraniums.

Not too far off in the distance on the north side of the property, I noticed the horse's stable, which was painted in the same color scheme as the main house. It occurred to me that the horses resided in a building that looked bigger—and most likely cost more—than Marty's house and mine together.

"Nice pad," Marty said as he pulled up and parked in the circular driveway. He wasted no time in tearing open the bag that held his Meatball Hero. "I'm starving," he announced as his teeth ripped into the sandwich.

He barely got the first bite down when he noticed in the rear view mirror a pearl-white Lexus convertible pulling up. The now-familiar tall, slim, well-dressed woman of about forty got out, looking curiously at the strange vehicle in her driveway.

Tiffany's mother, once again attired in four-inch heels, made her way toward us. Marty frustrated that his hunger was not to be resolved he carelessly and quickly rewrapped his sandwich and got out to greet the lady as she approached his side.

"May I help you?" she asked him. I thought I heard a slight southern twang in her speech.

"Yes, Mrs. Bennett. We met the other day at the police station."

He introduced us. "My name is Detective Keal, and this is Detective Whitley. We would…"

"Yes, yes, I know who you are," she interrupted, as if she was in a hurry and wasn't too happy with the interruption. "Tiffany mentioned something about you wanting to talk to her." She glanced around, as if looking for someone. "Would you care to step inside? I have some groceries in the car and I need to have them refrigerated."

The words barely got out of her mouth when a short, Hispanic-looking woman in a white uniform came out from the main house.

"Miz Bennett, do you haff pakages?" the stocky woman asked in broken English.

"Yes, Maria, please…in the trunk." She handed the housekeeper her car keys and motioned for us to follow her into the house.

"Maria, is Tiffany home yet?" Mrs. Hoity-toity stopped momentarily and inquired of her housekeeper.

"Yes, Miz Bennett, she's in hur room," the stocky woman answered as she grabbed a handful of packages from the trunk of the car.

The housekeeper had left the front entrance open. We walked through the double-sized red front door and entered a wide foyer. The walls were decorated with a few fine—and what I guessed to be very expensive—paintings.

A gray-and-white marble floor led into an even more elaborate setting. We passed a large living room area that was furnished with what I believed to be French provincial furniture. The seating looked as if it had never made the acquaintance of a rear end.

Mrs. Bennett continued to walk, leading us further into the house, until she reached a room in which the entire outside wall was made up of nine-foot-tall windows, where the late afternoon sunlight beamed through.

FACELESS: A MYSTERY ~ DAWN KOPMAN WHIDDEN

The breathtaking view from this spot was so beautiful it almost seemed unreal. From where Marty and I stood, we could see the side of a mountain and the whitecaps of a waterfall coming off that mountain. In the distance, I spotted a very small cottage, again in the same color scheme. The cottage sat in a beautiful meadow at the bottom of the hill. I looked out in another direction and noticed two Appaloosas playing in the distance. I watched as they stopped to drink from a small pond about two hundred yards from the house.

The whole scene could have been mistaken for a landscape painting, except for the violent crashing movement of the waterfall on the rocks, and the subtle movement of the horses.

Two love-seat-sized and luxuriously deep-cushioned seats sat opposite each other with a Plexiglas coffee table separating them. A black slate fireplace took up an entire wall and a deep, thick, charcoal-gray carpet gave the room some added warmth.

"This is a beautiful room, Mrs. Bennett," I said, taking another glance out the window, still fascinated by the majestic view below.

"Thank you. We spend a lot of time in this room. I find it to be quite comfortable and relaxing. Let me go get my daughter. Can I get you some refreshments?" she asked as she walked to a spiral staircase that led to the upper floor. Mrs. Bennett barely got her daughter's name out when Tiffany appeared at the top of the steps.

"Tiffany, can you come down here? The police are here."

Tiffany didn't say a word; she just slowly walked down the stairs and stood in front of her mother, who carefully placed her hands on her daughter's shoulders. With her fingers, she tenderly toyed with her daughters' shoulder-length hair.

Mrs. Bennett was much taller and leaner than her daughter. There was quite a resemblance in the mother's and daughter's features, but the mother was definitely the much more attractive of the two. I wondered how uncomfortable that would be for the teenager.

I had reluctantly conceded to allow Marty to conduct the interview. This was the perfect scenario for him. Sometimes a pretty face like Marty's could be quite the advantage when interviewing a woman like Mrs. Bennett. I was well aware that he would appear much less intimidating, and the ladies were more apt to be forthcoming, with him asking the questions.

Mrs. Bennett was wearing a tight-fitting beige suit with a slit on the side. As she sat down, the skirt crept up just above her knees. I noticed that Marty was making a gallant effort to keep his eyes on the lady's face, but his eyes occasionally wandered and I could see that he was enjoying this other view as well. The woman's legs were shapely and seemed to go on forever. I also noticed what appeared to be some sort of makeup or spray-on tan as she crossed her ankles.

Once we were all seated, Marty explained the purpose of our visit.

"Tiffany, Detective Whitley and I would like you to go over the statement you made when you first came down to the police station."

He paused a second to watch her facial expression. There was none, it remained blank, so he continued to talk.

"Sometimes it takes a few days for someone to remember things with a little more clarity after witnessing such a brutal crime."

"I don't remember anything else…just what I told you that morning." She had placed her right hand over her mouth in order to hide what was now a very noticeable facial tic, making it hard to understand her muffled words. Her mother reached up and pulled her daughter's hand away and the two exchanged glances. Without missing a beat, Mrs. Bennett went back to playing with her daughter's hair.

"Well, let's try, Tiffany, okay?" Marty leaned forward a bit, his elbows leaning on his knees.

She gave a curt nod, shaking her head and rotating her shoulder in an effort to push her mother away. Mrs. Bennett immediately let loose, as if she had been stung.

"Can you be specific as to what was happening in the car before Jamie got out?" Marty asked her.

"What do you mean?" she asked. "Nothing special happened. She just got mad at Dylan, and when he stopped the car, she bolted. Took off into the woods. Probably met some crazy person in there. They had to be crazy, doing what they did, right?"

"Why did Jamie get mad at Dylan, Tiffany? What were they arguing about?" Marty asked as he tapped the pencil against his pad.

"Nothing special…same old stuff. Jamie was just being her usual self. I think she was making fun of Lisa. Jamie thought her crap didn't stink, and…"

Once again, her mother attempted to fix Tiffany's hair, and once again, Tiffany tilted her posture as if to push the woman away. This time, Mrs. Bennett didn't let go. It was if they were doing a dance that they had done a million times before. I wondered if the girl was being defiant, or was it just that her movements were uncontrollable, almost spasmodic, in nature?

"Did she make fun of you, too? Was she saying things that weren't nice about you?" Marty suggested.

"I don't know, I wasn't paying her any attention," she told him.

Her mother reached out her hand and grasped her daughter's hand in a gesture of support. This time, Tiffany accepted her mother's hand graciously.

It appeared to me that the two had a complicated relationship. I was beginning to empathize with the woman and wondered if this was the direction I was headed with my own child.

I realized that Tiffany had continued her description of that evening. I knew I needed to focus on what she was saying, and stop daydreaming about my problems with my own child.

"I was in the back seat with Katie, she was on the phone with Cameron, and…I don't know why Katie even invited her, except that Dylan probably wanted her to be there."

"Okay, so Jamie is making fun of Lisa. What kind of things was she saying?"

She shrugged her shoulders. "I don't remember. Just that she was getting fat and that she needed to stop stuffing her face. You know, things like that. Lisa started bawling, and Dylan got pissed, and then Jamie got pissed at Dylan for sticking up for Lisa. He stopped the car and she jumped out. We sat in the car for a few minutes, cussing her out and trying to decide what to do.

"Katie told Cameron where we were. He told us to come to the house and get some flashlights and we would go looking for her. Katie brought out some flashlights and me and Lisa and Dylan went off looking for her. Katie and Cameron just went back inside. They never did look for her; at least I don't think they did. They just did their own thing," she said with a grin.

"Did all three of you stay together?" Marty asked.

"At first, and then I went off on my own."

I looked up. "Weren't you scared, being out in the woods by yourself, Tiffany? I mean, it gets pretty spooky out there, all alone. I would be, that's for sure."

"Nope," she answered, with a note of pride. "I've gone to summer camp where we had to take courses for survival training. We would have to spend the nights alone out in the woods. I mean, the counselors were watching us, we just couldn't see them."

"My husband is a believer in giving our children every kind of advantage for every situation," her mother interceded. "He wants the kids, even the girls, to be able to handle themselves. Tiffany is a black belt in two martial arts, and takes kickboxing. My husband grew up on the streets in Chicago, and he doesn't want the kids to be soft," she told us proudly.

Marty turned his attention back to the teenager. "So that's why you went off by yourself?"

"Well, yeah, we thought we would cover more ground that way. We all tried calling her cell phone, but it went straight to voice mail. I didn't realize it then, but she had left her pocketbook in the car. Her phone was in it."

"And then what happened, Tiffany?" Marty prompted her.

"I'm not sure, I mean, I don't know how long I was looking, but I smelled something weird, and then I saw something lying in the woods. I went closer to get a look. At first, I thought it was just a burning log, like from a campsite. When I saw what it was, I just started screaming. That's when everyone else showed up."

"Do you remember who showed up first? Was it Dylan?" I asked.

Tiffany turned to face me. "I think so. Yeah, it was Dylan."

"Was he alone?" I continued to question her.

"No, I think he was with Lisa, yes, because she started screaming and Dylan was holding her. I think she got sick. I can't remember."

"Who showed up next, Tiffany?" Marty asked her.

"Cameron and Katie came, they were running. I remember because she almost fell and Cameron caught her." The memory made her laugh. I thought it was inappropriate, but it could have been her nerves.

I looked over at Mrs. Bennett. I couldn't tell by the woman's expression whether this was the first time she was hearing the story in detail. She was facing her daughter and looking at her adoringly. She seemed consumed by her daughter and the story she was telling.

"Then what did you do, Tiffany?" Marty pressed her to continue.

"We just stood there, not talking for a little while, and then we kind of ran back to Cameron's place. He gave us some drinks and I think Dylan and Lisa got sick and started puking. That's when we called 911."

"Did you get sick, Tiffany? I mean, no one would blame you." I tried sounding sympathetic.

"No, I didn't throw up. I mean, I got a little queasy, but I didn't get sick," she answered with a look of pride.

"Were you sad that this happened to Jamie? Or are you happy this happened to her, Tiffany?" I knew I sounded smug.

Tiffany was just about to answer when we were interrupted by the gruffness of a male voice.

"What's going on here?" I recognized the man immediately. Tiffany's father was a large man, with broad shoulders that looked like they were bursting out of the designer three-piece suit he was wearing. The man spent a lot of time in the gym when he wasn't defending some low-life in a courtroom. I had met the man on several occasions, and I never had developed a fondness for him.

Mrs. Bennett stood up to greet her husband.

"Dustin, this is Detective Keal and Detective Whit..."

"Whitley," Marty helped her out.

The man just stood there, staring at us both. His eyes were the color of cold steel.

"What's going on? Why are you here?" he blurted out with an air of superiority.

Marty stood up. The man was large, but Marty had at least an inch on him.

"We came to clarify a few things in Tiffany's statement, Mr. Bennett. We were just about to wrap..."

The man didn't let him finish.

"You're done now!" He turned to his wife, glaring at her. "You should know better."

He turned to the housekeeper, who was now standing in the doorway with an armful of freshly pressed laundry.

"Maria, show our guests out," Mr. Bennett directed her.

Marty spoke up.

"That's okay, we know our way." He turned to Mrs. Bennett. "Thank you." He then turned his attention to Tiffany.

"Tiffany, if you remember anything else..." He handed her a business card while he kept his eyes targeted on hers. He broke into a half-smile, exposing one lone dimple.

I glanced over at Mrs. Bennett, who suddenly looked as pale as a ghost. She said nothing; she just grabbed the laundry from the housekeeper and disappeared up the stairs.

∽

How cute, I thought to myself. A matching pearl-white Lexus now sat in the driveway, apparently belonging to Mr. Bennett. Their vehicles probably cost more than my house.

"Pompus jerk!" I snarled as I got into the unmarked car.

The minute he entered the vehicle, Marty started hitting buttons on a small laptop. The department's budget recently had allowed us to join the twenty-first century. I watched as he keyed in Mr. Bennett's name.

"What are you looking for?" I asked him

"Domestic abuse complaints. I wouldn't be surprised to find out that Mrs. Bennett gets her tail kicked on a regular basis," he answered as he scanned the screen, waiting for the page to download.

"I have a gut feeling that the lady's spray tan is for more than just fashion." He kept his eyes on the screen as he continued. "Looks like she was covering up some bruises on her legs."

I was impressed with his observations. And I had thought he was just ogling her legs. I was so intent on watching Tiffany's reactions that I totally dismissed the importance of her mother.

He looked disappointed as he shut down the page and put the laptop aside. "Nothing—no prior complaints, no arrests. Guy looks clean."

"That doesn't mean you're wrong, Marty, a lot of women don't report abuse, especially women in her income bracket. It's an embarrassment to them, and the husband usually controls the finances. She could be too afraid to file a complaint. You don't have the golden goose arrested and put in jail unless you have your own source of income."

"Doesn't seem right—a woman being afraid of her own husband. I just can't grasp how a woman can stay in a relationship with a man she deplores, or worse yet, is afraid of." He shook his head as if he was irritated and started the ignition.

"What's next?" he asked. "Or should I ask, 'who'?"

"Let's go speak to Kimberly's family," I said. "I want to see if we can get a better time frame as to how she spent her last hours. Did the crime scene techs find her cell phone?" I asked as I looked through the Weston file that now sat on my lap.

I was disappointed to see that, although the phone had been found, it revealed nothing more than the almost 100 unanswered incoming calls from a panicked mother. The calls started slowly at first, and then became more and more frequent as the woman realized something was terribly wrong and that something bad may have happened to her daughter.

All other history had been deleted, due to the smart phone's inability to hold that much data. We would have to subpoena the phone company for more detailed information if we wanted see who Kimberly had called or who called her prior to the time her family realized she was missing.

Although the days were getting longer as we got closer to the summer months, the sky was taking on an ominous color that made it feel like it was later in the evening than it was. I looked at my watch, it was barely six o'clock. It was obvious that another rainstorm was about to make another appearance. I was hoping we would reach the Weston's home before the sky opened up. It didn't happen.

We sat in front of the Weston home for five minutes while we waited for the rain to let up enough for us to get to their front door without looking like refugees from a water balloon fight. Lucky for me, Marty had a small umbrella that at least kept my hair from getting drenched. My pants cuffs and shoes got soaked as I maneuvered my way through a series of deep and muddy puddles.

Fortunately, Marty had the foresight to call the family and let them know we were coming, so as soon as I rang the bell, the door opened wide, letting us escape the now-cold rains.

Kimberly's younger brother, the boy I had met at the hospital, greeted us. He took the umbrella from my hands and placed it in an empty ceramic flowerpot that sat in the short foyer.

This home was so unlike the one we had just previously come from. The Bennett's house was like a museum, pristine and meticulous, compared to the quaintness and disarray of this small brick colonial. From the mudroom, almost the entire first floor was visible.

Unlike Jamie Camp's home, family photos were everywhere. Professional studio and amateur photos lined the walls, covering one wall completely. Children's toys lay scattered everywhere. The young boy made a futile attempt to make a path for us to walk through.

"I apologize for the mess, detectives." Kimberly's dad walked into the room. "We just got back from Cornell and the weather has kept the kids indoor most of the day."

"No apologies are needed, Mr. Weston." I interrupted. "I completely understand."

He cleared off a space on a well-worn green corduroy sofa and offered it us. He then took a spot on a worn-out chocolate vinyl-looking swivel rocker/lounge chair. He looked slightly embarrassed when he had to get up to remove a Cheese Doodle that was now sticking to the seat of his pants.

"Have you found out who did this? Have you found the man that killed my daughter?" His eyelids were drooping and he was unshaven. He looked like he had not had much sleep.

He was about to speak again when the doorbell rang. We overheard his son telling the neighbor that his mother was asleep and he would tell her about the visit when she awoke.

He walked back into the living room carrying a casserole dish.

"Ethan, can you put that in the refrigerator with the other ones?" his father asked. The young boy just nodded and walked past us, stepping over a pile of baby dolls and accessories. He disappeared into the kitchen.

"Ethan is taking this very hard. He was very close to his big sister. They're just..." he hesitated, his thoughts drifting, and then continued. "They were just a few years apart, and..."

His voice began to crack. I knew from experience that I had a very small window of opportunity to ask him questions before emotions inhibited a grieving parent's answers.

"I know this is a very difficult time for you, Mr. Weston, but if you can answer a few questions for us, perhaps we can find out who is responsible for your daughter's murder. The more information we can obtain, and the quicker, the better chance we have of nailing this person. Will that be all right?" I asked.

"Yes, of course. Whatever I can do. I just don't understand what kind of sick individual would do something like this." His eyes drifted back to the wall that was covered with photographs.

"You know, it hit me this morning that my two-year-old daughter will never remember her sister. She's too young to realize that something terrible has happened. To her, the world is the same. It's very hard for my wife. She doesn't want to show the baby how upset she is, but it's an impossible task. If you want, I can wake her, she went to take a nap with my daughter. She's trying to keep the routine normal."

He was rambling, and I let him. "No, that's fine, Mr. Weston. I hope you can answer our questions. If not, we can speak to your wife later, when she's feeling better."

"Oh, sure, no problem..." His eyes drifted over to the pictures again.

"Do you know if Kimberly was having any problems with anyone? Did she mention that anyone was making her feel uncomfortable?" I asked him.

He shook his head. He was tall and rather good-looking, in a rough sort of way. When I noticed a tiny diamond stud in his left ear, I imagined him riding a Harley.

"No, nothing specific. My daughter was very competitive, and she was very pretty. She complained at times that some girls gave her a hard time. My wife told her they were just jealous and that she should just ignore them."

"Did she mention any girls specifically, Mr. Weston?" Marty asked him.

Weston thought for a second before he answered.

"She was always in competition with the Camp girl. Kimmy was very excited about running against Jamie in the homecoming queen contest. They were competitive, but friendly, until this boy Dylan came into the picture."

My stomach did a somersault the moment he said Dylan's name.

"I wasn't privy to it, but my wife said that the girls would get into some pretty heated arguments about this kid. I think that's when their friendship ended."

Kimberly's brother came back into the room and put his hands on his dad's shoulders in a show of comfort. I hadn't noticed before how much he resembled his dead sister. He would be a constant reminder to his parents of the child they lost and the horror she endured before she died.

Mr. Weston put his hand up to his son's and laid it atop of the young boy's fingers, giving them a gentle squeeze. He lifted his head and looked at the boy.

"Ethan, did Kimmy ever mention that she was afraid of anyone? These people are trying to find the bas—." He stopped short, considering his language, and found a different word to describe our perpetrator.

"They are trying to find the person responsible for what happened. Do you remember if there is anything that Kimmy may have said that could help them?"

Ethan shook his head; his hazel eyes still red from crying.

"I don't know, Daddy, a lot of girls were jealous of Kimmy, but she wasn't afraid of anyone," he said, raising his voice in anger as he fought back the tears. It was futile, and he began to cry.

As a tear reached his dad's shoulder, the older man hugged the boy to his chest. Ethan could no longer control his emotions and sobbed quietly into his father's shoulder.

I got up, and Marty followed suit.

"I appreciate your help, Mr. Weston. If there is anything that you feel may be important, please—no matter how inconsequential you believe it may be—please don't hesitate to call."

I handed him my business card and I smiled at Kimberly's brother as he peeked up at me.

"When your wife is feeling better, please have her give me a call. I know how difficult this is for your family, but sometimes even the tiniest bit of information, or any uncomfortable feeling you may have about something, may be substantial in an investigation like this."

We left the house. I felt as though I had learned nothing of significance. I had two dead girls, both beautiful in physical appearance, but neither of them a candidate to win a Miss Congeniality award.

Was it their personalities that got them killed, or their looks? Or, was I totally off base, and was there some stranger lurking in the woods? Could they both simply have had the bad luck to be in the wrong place at the wrong time?

Somehow, I doubted it. I had a gut instinct that both these girls were lured to their deaths by someone they knew well.

The big question…who?

Chapter Eighteen

One Week Later

Marty didn't want to admit it to anyone, himself included, that he was still angry with Hope. As much as he anticipated her reaction to his proposal, he wasn't ready to accept her lack of a positive answer, much less no answer at all.

After the interview at the Weston's,' he dropped Jean off at home and headed to his father's place. He was still staying there several days later. He hadn't spoken to Hope or seen her since. She had tried to call him, but he always had an excuse as to why he couldn't talk or see her. He was busy with the case and didn't have any free time.

He knew he was being childish, but he didn't care. If Hope was so unsure of their relationship that she couldn't commit to him in marriage... *Well screw her,* he thought. *Let her see what life is like without me.*

The department set up a task force for the recent murders. Marty and Jean had spent the past few days following up phone tips and conducting interviews. They had learned nothing substantial, and he was wondering whether the killer was going to get away with murder.

After another day passed with the investigation at a complete standstill, Jean and Marty decided to call it an early day. He was able to get home early enough to have dinner with his father.

He smelled the sauce cooking on the stove before he set foot in the front room. His stomach began to gurgle, and he suddenly realized just how hungry he was. The cold meatball hero he'd had earlier hadn't made a dent in his appetite.

He headed in the direction of the spicy aroma, making his way into the kitchen as he called out for his father.

"Pop, smells good..." He stopped and stood in the center of the empty room as he got an overwhelming feeling that something was wrong. The small television that sat on the kitchen bar was on, but the volume was muted. The sauce was making a bubbling sound. Marty lifted the lid and immediately turned off the flame under the pot when he saw that the liquid was within seconds of boiling over.

The tiny hairs on the back of his neck stood at attention when he realized that the back door was wide open and his father was nowhere in sight.

"Pop?" he called out again as he made his way over to the open door. He looked out, his eyes focusing on the short path that led past the unfenced back yard and into the woods behind the house.

The sun was sinking into the horizon and daylight was rapidly coming to an end. Off to the northeast, storm clouds were starting to roll in again and the shadows coming from the spruce trees behind the house were making it hard to see very far into the woods.

Starting to get a little more anxious, he raised his voice, this time shouting his father's nickname.

"Captain!" and under his breath, "Where the hell are you, Pop?"

The landline telephone rang, startling him. Marty walked over to the ancient black phone that was hanging on the wall and lifted the receiver.

"Hello!" he barked anxiously into the phone.

"Marty, why are you yelling?" He immediately recognized his sister Mary's voice.

"Sorry, Mar," he apologized as he continued to scan the room, looking for clues to where his father may have gone. "I just got here and I don't see the Captain. The back door was open and..."

Although he didn't want to panic Mary, his eldest sibling, he knew the nervousness he was feeling was creeping into his voice.

"Let me call you back. No...call me back on my cell," he told her as he tried to stretch the black cord as far as he could. He couldn't get it long enough to be able to see out the back door and he didn't want to break the connection with her.

She hung up immediately and his cell phone barely got out a note of his ring tone before he answered it.

He walked back out the open doorway and tapped the speaker icon as he explained to Mary what he had found when he came home a few minutes earlier.

As he was explaining, he thought he heard sounds off in the distance.

"Shh," he told her, trying to get a feel for what it was he was hearing. His own footsteps sounded magnified as he stepped on small twigs and fallen tree branches.

"Marty, you're scaring me." He heard his sister's voice through the cell phone.

"Mary, ssh!" he told her once again as he walked deeper into the cluster of trees. "Pop!" he hollered out for a third time, again getting no answer. This time he realized the sound he'd heard was nothing more than a family of squirrels playfully chasing each other around one of the larger trunks.

He was about to tell Mary to hang up so he could call 911 when he heard his neighbor's familiar voice call out his name.

"Marty, it's Peri."

He kept the cell phone line open as he turned and walked back toward the house. Peri, the lady who had lived next door to his father for the last thirty years, was making her way through their yard.

"Your dad is at my house," she went on to explain. "Al found him walking down the road. He looked disoriented, so my husband convinced him to come into my house. He's okay now, but he is a little upset with himself."

Marty spoke into his cell phone. "Mary, it's okay, I'll call you back," he told his sister, breaking the connection without taking the time to say goodbye.

"Thanks, Mrs. Kolakowski," he said, letting out a sigh of relief. Suddenly, his thoughts went to Jean, as he realized exactly how she felt when she didn't know where her daughter was.

"Marty, he's okay, but..." She hesitated as she tried to find the right words.

Marty, being so tall, had to look down at the woman, for the top of her head barely reached his chest. Although the woman had no children of her own, she had become something of a surrogate mother to Marty and his family when his own mother passed away.

The now gray-haired Mrs. Kolakowski had fulfilled the feminine role that the family needed desperately at the time. It was especially a godsend for Mary, the only girl, who was still just a teenager living in a house full of testosterone.

Mrs. Kolakowski carefully gathered her thoughts before she continued.

"Marty, he was really angry there for a while. It was scary. What's going on? This isn't like your dad at all."

As he continued to walk with her toward the Kolakowski's house, Marty tried to find something to say.

"He has an appointment with the neurologist in a week. I'm going to try and move it up. I'm really sorry, Mrs. K…"

"Please, Marty, don't apologize. Your dad has been a saint to us. If it wasn't for him…" She stopped when she saw her husband and the Captain walking toward them.

Marty could tell by the expression on his dad's face that he was angry and humiliated. The Captain continued to walk past Marty, saying nothing, and made his way into his own home, leaving Marty to apologize once again and thank his neighbors for their help.

By the time Marty got back to the house, the sauce was back on the burner and his father was setting the table.

"Pop…"

"Look, I don't want to talk about it…just get cleaned up and get ready for dinner," the Captain said sharply as he opened and then slammed the refrigerator door.

"I have to call Mary back, she's worried," Marty said, glaring at him.

"Fine, call her back. Tell her I'm fine," he hissed.

"Dad, you're not fine. Something is definitely wrong." He turned and shut the back door that was still wide open.

Marty walked over to his father and gently prompted him to sit down. He sat himself down opposite the older man and scanned his father's face. Once again, he was alarmed at the changes that he was seeing. The Captain's blue eyes, which were once his most prominent feature, were now cloudy and almost void of all color. Deep crevices had formed around his lips and they, too, were pale. Taking a few moments, Marty carefully formed his words.

"Pop, I know you're scared, I am, too."

His father started to say something in protest, but Marty interrupted him. "I think it would be a good idea if we had someone stay with you while I'm working."

"Look, I don't need no damn babysitter, I…"

Suddenly the older man's words gave way to his emotions. He sat there, saying nothing further, letting Marty know that he wasn't going to argue with him. The last episode had frightened him enough that he was ready to relinquish some control to his son.

Marty thought for a second, trying to think of who would be the best candidate, who his father would be less likely to balk about.

"How about if I get Uncle Brian to come visit for a while? I'll bet he needs a good, long vacation, being surrounded by all those girls. He's probably overloaded on estrogen," he said, referring to the fact that his father's younger brother had recently moved in with his youngest daughter and her five daughters.

His father stood up and walked back to the stove to throw some pasta in the boiling water.

"Fine, just until I see that damn doctor," he said, deliberately avoiding looking at his son's face.

"We'll see…" Marty was about to ask his father for Brian's telephone number when his own cell went off.

"Damn it!" he said aloud as soon as he recognized the number. His father turned and glared at him.

"Keal," he barked into the phone.

He listened intently for a few moments before saying anything.

"I'm on my way." He put his phone back in his pocket and grabbed his coat.

"Sorry, Pop, can you keep that warm for me?" he said, motioning to the dish his father had filled for him.

"What's wrong? What's going on, Marty?" the Captain asked.

"We have another missing girl. Katie Hepburn, the mayor's stepdaughter," Marty told him. "Knox called in, frantic, said they haven't heard from her in hours. I hope it's nothing. I gotta go. I'll be back as soon as I can." He wondered whether leaving his dad alone was a good idea. Frustrated, he felt he had no other choice.

He had a sick feeling that this was not good. Another teenage girl missing was not good. Not good at all.

Chapter Nineteen

After a week of running down false leads, I decided to take a breather. Marty and I had been working thirteen and fourteen hours a day, running down tips that had been coming into a hotline that the chief had set up.

I was exhausted by the time I got home and was so grateful for the warm welcome I received from the only one in the house that didn't think I was some sort of monster. Roxy skidded across the tiles in her enthusiastic manner; one hundred and ten pounds of pure love greeted me with her tail wagging and her rump banging wildly up against my thigh.

I grabbed a biscuit from the ceramic green frog jar on the kitchen counter and handed it to her. As if I no longer mattered, she grabbed it out of my hand with her teeth and walked back to the corner where her bed was. She lay down and proceeded to devour it.

Now I wondered whether it was me that she was really glad to see, or if I was just nothing more to her than a delivery girl.

Bethany was sitting on the couch watching television; she didn't bother to acknowledge my arrival. She was still giving me the silent treatment.

"Did you do your homework?" It was more of a decree then a question. I was letting her know that I was still in charge. She wasn't the only one that was angry.

The air was thick with her attitude, and I was getting ready to perform a very intense surgery on it.

Another few seconds of silence went by before she spoke, still not bothering to look in my direction.

"I can't do research for my social studies report, I need my laptop," she said, staring at the television. I knew she wasn't watching it; she was just using it as a way to avoid me. Bethany was never much one to spend time watching television…but then it struck me—she had changed so much lately, I really didn't seem to know what she liked anymore.

She was probably telling the truth, she couldn't do much schoolwork without a computer. So I relented.

"You can have your computer back to do your homework, but you are not to send emails or go on Facebook...or any other social media sites. Is that understood?"

"Whatever," she answered curtly.

I'd had enough. This attitude of hers was getting on my nerves. She really had not spoken to me since I told her she wasn't to go anywhere near Dylan. I still had my doubts about him, as well as the other four suspects who had been up at the Forester place that night.

I pushed away a pile of schoolbooks and papers and sat down on the couch next to her.

"What the hell is going on with you, Bethany? Why are you acting like this?" I was fighting back tears. I didn't want her to know how frustrated and hurt I was. I didn't want to appear weak.

She turned away from me. I knew that she was trying hard not to cry herself.

I tried another approach. "Honey, please, talk to me!" I gently put my hand on her head, savoring the silky feel of her hair, praying she wouldn't push my arm away like Tiffany did to Mrs. Bennett.

"He didn't do it, Mom. I swear to you. You need to believe me. You never believe me anymore!" She was shaking so hard I grabbed her and held her to my chest. My lips gently kissed her wet face and hair.

It took her awhile to compose herself. She broke away from my embrace, her brown eyes so wet they looked like they were floating above their white background.

"Mom, you used to trust me, when did you stop trusting me?"

"Honey, I stopped trusting you when you started lying and trying to deceive me," I responded. "I know you meant well, but you should have come to me immediately. When did you stop trusting me?" I asked her.

I think it finally sunk in; I finally made my point.

"I'm sorry...I am so sorry, Mom. I should have told you. Then maybe Kimberly would still be alive. I don't want you to be mad at me."

She paused for a moment and then in a faint voice, "I swear Dylan and I didn't…"

I didn't know if I was ready to believe that they didn't have sex, but I needed her to believe that I was willing to trust her. I needed my daughter back, but I also wanted her to know how wrong she had been.

I looked at my daughter's face and my heart just ached. I now knew what unconditional love really was. I didn't know what I would do, how I would feel, if my daughter was held accountable for participating in the cover-up of Dylan's part in this whole mess.

I was now as guilty as she was by not telling my chief. I thought I could trust Marty, but I couldn't say with any certainty that somehow my daughter's participation in this whole incident wouldn't get out.

I wiped away her tears with my thumbs.

"It's okay, Bethany, I believe you. Will you promise me you will stay away from Dylan?" She started to protest. I could see her body language change— her shoulders got stiff and both her hands clenched into tight fists.

I continued.

"Just until he is definitely ruled out as a suspect; until I can say with complete assurance that he has nothing to do with either homicide. Can you promise me that?"

She was obviously reluctant, but she nodded. I felt some relief as I watched her tension appear to diminish.

"Okay, I will give you the computer back, but just for your schoolwork. Are we agreed on that?"

She nodded.

"Baby?" I pushed a lock of her blonde hair behind her ears. She looked at me with those big brown eyes and I could swear that I saw the old Bethany somewhere in there. Her eyes were still moist with tears, her wet eyelashes so black it looked as though she was wearing mascara.

"I'm sorry I hit you, I never should have done that," I apologized.

She gave a curt nod.

I had her attention now. It was as good a time as ever to try and get some answers. I was convinced that getting a better perspective of the dead girls would lead to their killer.

"Bethany, tell me about Jamie and Kimberly. Do you have any idea or feelings about who would want to hurt them?" Does anyone stand out in your mind as being targeted by either of the girls?"

She shook her head. "No, they were equal opportunity bitches."

I winced at her language, but let it slide.

"Sorry," she said, attempting to soften her tone.

"What about the girls who were with her? Dylan said Jamie was pretty bitchy to them."

Suddenly she sat up and I could see the wheels turning in that beautiful little head of hers. I knew exactly what she was thinking. If she could help me figure out who killed the girls, Dylan wouldn't be an issue any longer.

"Jamie was brutal to both Lisa and Tiffany...especially Tiffany, because of that thing she does with her face. I don't know why they even wanted to hang out with Jamie in the first place. I guess because they wanted to hang with Katie, and Katie was friends with both Jamie and Kimberly."

I was entering the country of female adolescence, a territory that I hadn't visited in three decades. I grew up an only child and I was more interested in finding a way to change the world than making paper-thin friendships. I never needed someone else's acceptance to feel good about myself, and I thought I had instilled that in my children. I know I was successful with my son Cliff—he was a leader among his peers. If he got into trouble, it was without a doubt his own idea.

Until last week, I would have believed the same about my daughter. Now I questioned my intuition.

I needed to keep the conversation going.

"What about Katie? Is..." I corrected myself. "Was Jamie mean to her?"

My daughter gave me a look that could only be interpreted as, "Really, Mom, you are clueless," but she was too kind to say it out loud.

"No, Katie is kind of like...well, no one messes with her. She doesn't give anyone a second thought, except maybe for Dylan and that new boyfriend of hers. She's nice, but kind of shallow. You never know what Katie is thinking."

"What about Kimberly? Did she pick on Lisa and Tiffany?" It was a theory that Marty and I had tossed back and forth. We wondered if the two girls formed some sort of alliance to pay back their abusers, but that would mean Lisa had lied to me and that just didn't play right in my mind.

I couldn't put my finger on it, but I believed Lisa Padilla's story. And much to my dismay, if I believed Lisa was telling the truth, it would mean that Dylan couldn't have killed Jamie Camp.

"Yes, I definitely heard Kimberly making fun of Tiffany's tics. Tiffany was so humiliated once she ran into the bathroom at school crying. I was there the day when Dylan found out about it and told her to stop." She immediately gasped, suddenly regretting what she had said. I could tell she was worried that what she had said could implicate Dylan in the girl's murder.

"Mom, Dylan wouldn't hurt anyone, he's always stood up and told people, even if they were his friends, to stop. He might look tough, but he's not mean."

My mind was in overdrive, trying to take in what she had told me. I was willing to let Lisa and Dylan go as possible suspects. I wasn't quite sure that she had convinced me that Tiffany, or Katie Hepburn, couldn't be our assailant, or both of them together.

I was about to ask her to tell me what she knew about Katie when my cell phone buzzed.

I recognized Chief Bergman's number immediately. I glanced at the time. It was seven o'clock. The chief knew I was going to make it an early night. The fact that he was calling now gave me an uneasy feeling.

I touched the green icon on the screen and accepted the call.

I listened intently as he explained about the frantic call he got from Mayor Knox. His stepdaughter hadn't come home from school, and hadn't been seen since early this morning.

Bethany was watching me and trying hard to hear the other end of the conversation. She knew something was wrong, and didn't say a word until I disconnected the call.

"Mom, what's wrong?" she asked.

"Honey, I have to go." I glanced at my watch again. "Dad should be home soon," I told her as I grabbed my car keys.

I wanted to believe that Katie was just pulling some teenage stunt and she was with a friend, or with Cameron. I tried to convince myself that it was just some minor misunderstanding and she would show up.

I wanted to believe it was nothing.

"What is it?" Bethany asked again, this time a little bit more demanding.

"It's probably nothing." I got up, trying not to let her feel my own panic building, but I had to tell her something.

"Mayor Knox called in to report Katie missing." I grabbed my purse.

"Did you see Katie at school today?" I questioned her as I walked toward the door to leave.

"No, we thought she was cutting. Lisa said she didn't answer her texts, she thought maybe her mom took her phone away."

"Bethany, just lock the door when I leave, and do not leave this house. Do you understand?" I instructed her.

I was grateful she didn't argue. She just nodded as I told her I loved her.

I glanced over at Roxy, silently hoping that if there were ever a threat to my daughter, the big dog would rise to the occasion and show some teeth if it became necessary.

~

The mayor's residence was located outside of town on the edge of the lake. The huge, colonial-style, three-story home was constructed mostly of river rock and slate. It had been converted and restored from a once-popular hotel. In the past, it had served as a getaway for young families looking for an escape from the humid summers of the city, until it became more of a status symbol to spend the summers at the Hamptons or the Jersey Shore.

Immediately after Marty arrived, the circular driveway in front of the estate started to light up like a Christmas tree, with blue and red flashing lights from vehicles representing every law enforcement agency for miles around. Every state, county, and city official in the immediate area had been put on notice that Mayor Knox's kid was missing and a serial killer was at large.

News vans were setting up satellite dishes and portable lamps, getting ready to broadcast from the location. Reporters, trying to get someone to make a statement, stuck microphones in the face of anyone who happened to pass by. Radio dispatchers called out codes to unoccupied vehicles. Ringtones would go off and everyone in the crowd would raise their phones to their ears, thinking it was a call for them.

∽

The air was thick with humidity, serving as a reminder that summer was on its way. The moon, not quite full, occasionally peeked out from behind a parade of dark clouds looming in the night sky. It looked as if evening showers threatened to burst out at any moment.

Marty looked around to see if Jean had arrived. Blinded at first by the intense halogen lights of the media, he finally managed to focus on a couple of familiar faces. He caught sight of the red hair of his friend Justin, who was standing on the other side of the crowd, talking to one of the New York state troopers.

Marty carefully made his way around a spider web of cables and camera equipment and walked toward them.

"What a circus," Justin said to Marty, when he got close enough that he didn't have to shout.

Marty nodded in agreement and extended his hand to the short, bulky state cop, who he knew from a softball league they both had played on.

"Terry," Marty welcomed him as they both looked around at the crowd starting to accumulate.

"Think the girl's dead?" the trooper asked, shifting his slightly bulging brown eyes from Marty to Justin.

"If you ask me, the kid's dead," Terry told him. "And we're going to find her just like the other two," he said loudly, not caring who was listening.

Marty flashed back on the memory of the first victim, Jamie, her body lying partially nude in the woods, her charred face still smoldering. He never got a chance to know Jamie, but he did get to know Katie Hepburn. He wasn't terribly fond of the girl, he found her to be narcissistic and self-absorbed. And yet, there was some sort of vulnerability that gave the teenager a type of charm.

He remembered how her personality seemed to adjust to

accommodate the people she was around. He thought about how disappointed she had looked when he told her that her father couldn't be reached. He recalled how uncomfortable she seemed when her stepfather had entered the room.

Marty wondered if her emotional void was nothing more than a defense mechanism the girl had developed. Then he wondered if he was starting to think like a psychiatrist. Had Hope been that much of an influence on him? Before he met her, he never would have even considered something so complex.

Just as Marty was about to ask Justin if he had been in the house, he caught the sight of Jean walking up the circular driveway, pushing a horde of reporters' microphones away from her face.

"No comment," she snarled at Marilyn Tams, the blonde, statuesque, sometime quirky reporter from the local television station.

They kept bombarding her with questions.

Marty excused himself, walked over to Jean, and grabbed her arm, pulling her out of the line of fire. Sometimes, being six foot three and built like a brick wall had its advantages. The crowd opened up like the Red Sea to let them walk through. At least, that's what Marty thought at first.

The truth was, the crowd's attention had shifted. The mayor and his wife had come out of the house and stood in front of a makeshift podium.

Marty and Jean looked at each other, the same thought in their minds. Had Mayor Knox waited to notify them about the girl being missing? Had his first call been made to the media?

"You think this is a media stunt?" Marty asked her.

"No, but I wouldn't put it past that jerk to take advantage of it politically. Let's go," she said, as she pushed her way through the crowd.

The mayor was flushed and sweating. He was in the middle of adjusting the microphone when Marty grabbed him and pulled him away. He ignored the chunky man's protests and pulled him back into the house.

CHAPTER TWENTY

"What the hell do you think you're doing?" Marty asked the mayor. I slammed the double entrance doors behind me, accompanied by Mrs. Knox, obviously upset and disheveled.

"I am trying to save my stepdaughter's life, that's what I'm doing! Your department is worthless! I told you there was a serial killer out there!" Spittle came flying out of his mouth. The man's face became red with anger, blood corpuscles at risk of bursting on either side of his nose.

"Look Paul, calm down," Marty told him. He let loose of the fat man's arm, afraid that the mayor was in danger of having a heart attack. Sweat was pouring down the man's forehead, despite the fact that the temperature in the house was more than comfortable.

"Paul, please." This time it was Katie's mother requesting some decorum from her husband. "Please, they're here to help."

Knox looked at his wife, sadness in his eyes. I was surprised to find myself actually thinking that the man was capable of compassion.

"I'm sorry baby, I'm sorry, I should have protected her." He fell back into a large cushioned chair, defeated. His wife's face was black with mascara-stained tears.

Marty saw a dining room chair not far away. He grabbed hold of it and dragged it over. Facing the chair backwards, he threw his leg over it and sat facing Knox.

"Listen, we are going to find her, Paul," he told him.

I was desperately trying to keep my own doubts from invading my thoughts. I glanced up at Mrs. Knox.

I reiterated what Marty said. "We will find her, I promise." I told her.

The woman closed her eyes and just nodded her head.

Marty turned back to the mayor.

"When was the last time you saw Katie? When did you hear from her last?" he asked.

Mrs. Knox answered.

"When she left for school. She came into my room about seven o'clock this morning. She said she was getting a ride from someone...I...I don't remember who she said—I thought it was one of her friends." She broke down crying again.

I could almost smell the emotion and fear coming from the woman. I had been there just a few days ago. My story had a happy ending. My daughter was safe. I wanted hers to turn out the same way.

A few seconds later, she managed to compose herself. "She never got to school. Her friends said she wasn't in school. She won't answer my calls or texts. Her friends say they haven't heard from her."

She grabbed a tissue and made another attempt to wipe away her tears. They were falling faster now.

Marty looked up.

"What about Cameron? Have you spoken to him, Paul?"

The mayor looked at his wife, trying to compose himself before he spoke.

"He's out looking for her. I called him as soon as we realized. He said...he was going to go look for her. I..." Knox was gasping for breath as he spoke, each word taking a tremendous effort.

Just as Marty was about to ask another question, a loud, musical tone came from a cell phone sitting on a long, narrow coffee table. Donna Knox reached out to grab it, knocking over a glass of wine in the process. Ignoring the mess, she hollered into the phone.

"Hello! Katie?" she screamed in anticipation, only to get quiet as she listened, to the response.

"Hold on..." She handed the mayor the phone, obviously disillusioned. It wasn't the call she had been hoping for.

She made a halfhearted attempt at cleaning up the mess, only to be gently pushed aside by a short, squat, dark-haired domestic worker, who seemingly appeared from nowhere, equipped with cleaning rag and bucket.

Knox mostly listened before informing the caller of the detectives' presence. He handed Marty the phone. "It's Cameron, he wants to talk to you."

Even before Marty put the phone to his ear, he could hear an obviously distraught Cameron.

"I can't find her, Marty, I can't find her. I've looked everywhere. She isn't answering my calls, Marty. Something's real wrong—you've got to find her," he pleaded between sobs.

"Cameron, where are you?" Marty asked, holding the phone slightly away from his ear, allowing me to hear a bit of the conversation on Cameron's end. Marty listened intently for a few moments before speaking again.

"Listen Cameron, just stay where you are, we'll be out there in a little bit."

A loud ruckus was coming from outside. The door opened and Donna Knox became almost breathless in anticipation of seeing her daughter walk in. Instead, she became disappointed again when she realized it was just a police officer. It was Justin. He handed me a piece of paper.

Paul Knox got up from his seat.

"What? What is it? Is it about Katie?" He tried pushing his way past Justin to see what was in my hands.

"It's not about Katie, Paul, it's a phone tip about one of the other girls. It could be nothing, just something we're going to check into," I told him, folding the paper and pocketing it.

I turned my attention back to the lanky redhead, who was almost as tall as Marty.

"Are they running the plate number?" I asked him.

"Yeah, they're doing that now." He watched as Marty finished his phone call to Cameron. He nodded compassionately to Katie's mom and turned back to me.

"I'll let you know as soon as they pull it up. They're having some internal server problems and they have techs trying to solve some issues." Justin offered as an explanation.

Marty handed the phone back to the mayor.

"Look Paul, stay here, give your interview, and talk to the state guys when they get here. We're going up to Cameron's place to talk to him."

He turned to Mrs. Knox.

"We'll find her," he told her, trying to convince himself just as much as her. He turned back to me.

"Let's go talk to Cameron." He walked out and I followed closely behind him.

~

The crowd outside hadn't dissipated. In fact, it had gotten worse, and certainly more chaotic. More media had arrived, and now the area was crowded with ordinary neighbors and citizens trying to find out what all the commotion was about. The scene was starting to resemble a rock concert. I was concerned that now would we have to waste critical personnel on crowd control.

Two canine handlers were waiting off to the side while their four-legged partners sniffed the ground and paced nervously. The canine officers were waiting patiently for instructions, while their dogs appeared anxious to be let loose to hunt down their target. Just as we pulled out, I saw the dogs let go, their noses to the ground, walking in circles.

~

Marty led me toward his car as he explained the content of his conversation with Cameron. I turned back to Justin and handed him my car keys. I arranged for him to have my ride driven back to the station. I got into Marty's car and buckled myself in.

He turned on the lights and siren as he sped away from the mayor's mansion. I started to open the window, but thought twice and changed my mind.

I already felt like I needed a long shower. The humidity was hanging in the air as if we were deep into the summer months, instead of it being a June night. The moon was out, but dark storm clouds floated rapidly past the not quite full bright white disk. An evening storm was brewing, and I realized that whatever rain gear I had left in my car was not going to be an option.

"You think he knows where she is?" I asked.

"No." He shook his head as he answered me. "I think he's seriously worried. I think he may know something, he just doesn't remember what it is. He kept on berating himself...kept talking to himself, repeating, 'Think, Cameron, think,' as if he was trying to pull something out from his memory."

Ten minutes later, we pulled up to the cottage. The door was open and Cameron was sitting on the doorstep, bare chested, wearing only a pair of shorts, his muscular bare legs stretched out before him while moths swarmed, attracted by the light in the room behind him. Totally oblivious to them, he had his hand knotted into a fist, and he was slamming it into his forehead over and over again.

He looked up and watched us get out of the car, but he continued the violent hand motion until Marty grabbed hold of his wrist, forcing him to stop.

If I'd had any doubts up till now, they were now gone. This guy was definitely missing a few crayons from the box.

Shaking his head, he looked up at Marty.

"I should be with her, if I was with her, this wouldn't be happening. They shouldn't have kept her from me, I could have protected her, Marty, I could have!"

I suddenly felt sorry for the man. I don't know; call it a mother's instinct. Either he was a very competent actor or he was in some serious emotional pain.

I was willing to give him the benefit of the doubt, but I remained wary. Besides, my instinctive powers left a little to be desired lately. I was concerned that he was acting like she was dead already. I wasn't ready to go there yet. I knew to be suspicious of anyone that had the girl dead and buried.

I closed the door halfway, in an effort to keep the moths at bay, and sat down next to him, barely fitting in the space of the doorway. I could smell the pungent aroma of cannabis coming from the house. I chose to ignore it.

"Cameron, when was the last time you spoke to Katie? Do you remember?" He had his cell phone in his fist, as if he was waiting for it to ring at any moment, but it remained silent.

He loosened the fingers that held the portable device, his white knuckles turned a pale pink as his circulation began to flow. He handed me the phone.

"She called me this morning, before school. She said something about getting a ride. She told me—I think she did—but I just wasn't listening, I wasn't listening," he sniffled. "I was...I was talking to her, but I was just waking up. I had a rough night."

His nose was twitching and his right hand kept swiping the bottom of it. I wondered if marijuana was the only substance he had indulged in. I suspected he might have ingested something a little stronger than cannabis. I glanced around inside the cottage, and noted an empty bottle of Johnny Walker Red lay empty on the table.

Taking the phone from him, I studied the menu until I was able to find the correct icon that would let me pull up his recent calls. The first call he made to her number was at 12:15 p.m. It went unanswered. He placed another call at 2:30 p.m., about the time school let out. One more attempt at contacting her showed up at 3:00 p.m., then 3:40, then at 4:00. Over the next hour and a half, there were thirty unsuccessful outgoing calls to Katie's cell number, each one closer in intervals, some not allowing a minute between them.

I looked at the incoming calls. There it was, 7:06 this morning—an incoming call from Katie. It lasted three minutes.

I handed the phone to Marty. As soon as he took possession of it, he made a futile attempt to tap in Katie's number. It went directly to voice mail. At the sound of Katie's voice, Cameron's eyes shut tight, his throat made a guttural sound. He reached for the phone. Marty held it away from him.

"No! No! What if she tries to call me?" he cried out in frustration, making a grab for it.

Marty pulled it from his reach.

"Cameron, maybe we can locate where she was when she called you. She might have her phone on, and the techs can hone in on her location with the GPS," Marty told him.

He looked up at Marty with a vacant stare. It must have taken a moment for him to comprehend what Marty was proposing, because he sat there for a few seconds in silence. The words must have made it through whatever brain fog he was experiencing, because he finally shook his head in agreement.

"Look, Cameron," I continued. "I'm going to have one of our men come here and stay, just in case she shows up. Do you have a land line?" I asked him, looking through the opening of the doorway into the house.

He nodded. Marty handed him a blank piece of paper that he ripped off from a small memo pad he had in his shirt pocket. Cameron's hand was shaking badly, but using his thigh for support, he managed to write down the number and handed the paper back to Marty.

We left him there sitting exactly in the same place we'd found him.

Getting into the car, I turned and took a good look at Marty. It struck me that I was seeing him for the first time as my partner, instead of just someone who was taking Moran's place. It had suddenly occurred to me that the past few days, whenever we were together, we easily fell into a sort of natural rhythm.

I was about to tell him my thoughts, when my ringtone—The Beatles' "Hello Goodbye,"—broke the silence.

I hit the speaker button and we listened intently as the Chief Bergman filled us in.

"Whitley, where are you guys?" he asked. Not waiting for an answer, he kept on talking.

"There's no signal coming from her cell, so either she doesn't have it on, doesn't have it, or she is out of the service area."

I glanced over at Marty, who grimaced. I noticed for the first time that both of his dimples were showing. If he was smiling or laughing, only the one appeared.

"What about the partial plate of the car that the witness gave you in the Weston case? Anything?"

"Yeah," he answered me. "Only it wasn't a partial plate number; it's a vanity plate— BETA 1 TOM 3 MARY EDWARD...OR B1T3 ME. It belongs to a 2012 white Lexus, registered to..."

I answered before he could finish.

"Bennett." I glanced over at Marty, who had one eye on the road and one on me.

"Yeah, it's probably nothing, but check it out anyway. You interviewed them, Whitley, did they ever mention anything about giving the kid a lift that day?"

"Never mentioned it, Chief," I told him.

"Well, here's another one for you, Jean, one of the mayor's staff thinks she saw a fancy white car—with the emphasis on the fancy—coming from direction of the mayor's residence this morning. She was just getting to work and she passed it on the road. She can't swear to it, but she thinks she saw the kid in the car. She's an undocumented worker, and it was like pulling teeth getting anything out of her."

By the time I ended the call with Chief Bergman, a host of thoughts popped into my mind, like speech bubbles in a comic book.

First, there was Dylan, alleging that Jamie had been making fun of Tiffany in the car. Then my daughter, saying Jamie and Kimberly had both made fun of Tiffany's nervous tic.

Tiffany was the one who had discovered Jamie's body. Tiffany had access to Father Murphy's drugs and lighter fluid. Kimberly, and now the missing Katie, had both been seen getting into a white vehicle similar to the ones parked outside of the Bennett's home.

I was about to tell Marty to head toward the Bennett home when I realized he was way ahead of me. I felt my seatbelt dig into my shoulder from the abrupt turn the car made as he was in the process of doing just that.

I closed my eyes. I almost did damage to my bottom lip as he cut off and narrowly missed hitting an SUV. I looked over at the driver and mouthed an apology. The wave of the driver's hand did not give me comfort that he was accepting of my gesture.

Seven minutes later, we arrived at the Bennett home.

Chapter Twenty-One

Marty knocked on the door, maybe the correct terminology, was banged. The door opened and the Hispanic woman who had taken groceries from Mrs. Bennett appeared on the other side.

"Chyez, may I ..."

I didn't wait for an invitation. I pushed my way passed her.

"Where's Tiffany? We want to speak to her," I demanded.

I could hear someone coming toward us. Whoever it was definitely was not wearing the four-inch heels we had seen earlier. From the sound of the heavy steps, I wasn't surprised when I heard his voice.

"What the hell?" he asked angrily as he met us entering the front room.

"Where's your daughter, Bennett? Where's Tiffany?" I called out to him, my hand ready to draw my weapon.

"That's none of your damn business, now please leave," he answered angrily. He stood there, his chest puffed out like a football player guarding his quarterback.

"Look, Bennett..." I pointed a finger at him. "I have two dead girls and now another one is missing. Where the hell is your daughter?"

"Daddy?" a voice called out from above us.

Tiffany stood at the top of the stairs, her arms extended. On top of them sat some neatly folded laundry.

"Daddy, Maria was putting these away with my clean clothes," she told him, a puzzled look on her face.

He didn't look up at her.

"Honey, please, not now," he told her, sounding impatient, as if he was dismissing her.

"Daddy...they're not mine, Daddy," she told him, her voice quivering.

The pieces of clothing fell from her arms and over the banister. We all watched as they floated through the air toward us.

The next words she spoke seem to float down with them.

"Daddy, it's Jamie's. It's the shirt Jamie was wearing." She stood at the top of the stairs, as if she was frozen.

Now I was confused. I'd thought I had it all solved. It had to be Tiffany. Both girls were seen getting into a car registered to her family. She was alone in the woods when Jamie was found. Both girls teased her unmercifully.

Maybe I was wrong; maybe it wasn't Tiffany at all, but this S.O.B. standing in front of me…I looked over at Marty and I knew we were in sync; he was thinking the same thing.

We both started to pull our cuffs out and I was about to arrest and read the bastard his rights.

"Dustin Bennett, you are under…"

All the color drained from his face. He turned ashen and fell back, landing on a red velvet chair. His hand grabbed his face and he pulled on his leathery skin as if he wanted to pull it off.

Something was out of place. This was not what I was expecting. I had been ready to take him down, but the look on the man's face had me doubting myself.

It was Marty who figured it out first.

"Your wife, Mr. Bennett? Do you know where she is?"

Bennett looked up at me. Pewter-gray eyes matched the color of his hair perfectly.

"Which one? Which girl is missing? You said another girl was missing."

"Katie Hepburn. She hasn't been seen since getting into a white Lexus this morning," I told him.

I could hear Tiffany gasp. She was still standing at the top of the steps.

Her father looked up. "Tiff, go to your room." She started to protest, but he stopped her. "Tiff, please."

He didn't have to repeat himself. She turned with some reluctance, but walked back into a room and shut the door behind her.

Marty turned to him.

"Do you want to tell us what's going on, Mr. Bennett? Do you know where your wife is?"

Mr. Bennett looked up and shook his head. As big a man as he was, it must have been intimidating looking at Marty who stood six foot three, positioned in front of him, his Glock resting snuggly in the leather holster next to his broad chest.

I'd had enough, time might have been running out for Katie. I knew it was imperative to get to her fast. I was hoping that she was still alive; that for some reason she was being kept alive.

"Look, Bennett, where do you think she is?" I asked.

He turned and faced me. He looked like he was having trouble focusing.

"My wife has some problems. She's had a tough time. Gail is a good mother and she loves our kids, she loves my daughter. She's..." His eyes dropped down to the floor.

"Do you have any idea where she may be? Does she have a cell phone? The car—does it have a GPS system?" I grabbed my phone, ready to call in the answer, to find the woman, track her down.

He looked up. "Yes, she has a cell, and we have OnStar on the Lexus."

He got up and we followed him into the room where we had spoken to his wife earlier in the week.

He grabbed his iPhone from the coffee table and punched in some numbers. I glanced out the wall of windows again. If I wasn't so agitated, I would have been able to appreciate the scenery.

He held out the phone for me to see. A small thumbtack type icon pointed to a spot on a map.

"She's on the property, she's here somewhere." I could feel a sense of relief in his words.

I looked out the window again, this time with a purpose. The scene was the same, except the horses were missing. The waterfall, the rocks, a few spruce trees, the little cottage, it was a breathtaking view.

The cottage! I looked closer, trying to see if I could spot her car. I wasn't sure, but I thought I could make out the front end of a vehicle hidden by an evergreen that was on the north side of the building.

"Is that the only building on the property, besides this one?" I asked him.

"No, we have a building that houses occasional help, and a stable for the horses, but she never goes there, she hates horses. She's deathly afraid of them."

Marty had already called in an APB on her Lexus and was patiently waiting for me to call the next shot.

I looked back at Mr. Bennett.

"You said she had problems—what kind of problems, Mr. Bennett?"

It was all just conjecture up till now. We didn't have a motive, I mean, why would the woman want to harm these girls? She may have seemed a bit stuffy, but she looked and sounded normal. She definitely didn't look like a psychopathic serial killer.

"My wife's mother was burned badly in a fire, resulting in her death. Gail was only thirteen at the time. The woman was insane and was very abusive to my wife. Everyone in town knew it, so Gail immediately became a suspect."

"Did she do it?" Marty asked him.

"What happened? Was she arrested?" I asked him, impatiently waiting for his answer. I was ready to go.

"She was, but because of the abuse, her attorney used the insanity defense. Gail was acquitted, but the judge had her committed to Armistace Mental Institution for Children. She lived there until she reached the age of majority, and then was released."

I'd heard enough. I wanted to find Katie, and now I was positive we were headed in the right direction. I'd had enough of the history lessons.

I turned to Marty after another quick glance at the small building in the distance.

"Let's go." I turned back to Mr. Bennett. "Stay here, and keep your daughter here." He nodded, giving up without a fight.

I called for backup as we were leaving the house and getting into our car. We drove down a gravel road through the property until we had in our view the building I had seen from the house.

Marty parked the car and we made our way on foot through a narrow, wooded area covered with spruce trees, until we hit a clearing.

The building that we had seen from the Bennett house appeared before us. It looked like something out of a child's storybook. A human-sized dollhouse is the only way I could describe it. The white cottage with rounded corners had roof shingles that were created to look like pieces of a chocolate bar. A round-edged door with large wooden slats had a brass knocker shaped like a lion. White wooden shutters accented real glass windows, set in the same wood as the front door. Below the windows were red flower boxes filled with giant vinyl lollypops of various colors. It was obvious to me that the building had once served as a playhouse for the child of a very wealthy parent.

When we first entered the clearing, I first thought my instincts had been wrong. The building appeared to be unoccupied. Still keeping a safe distance, we quietly made our way around the west side .We could see the Lexus, partially hidden by some trees.

Marty put his finger up to his lips as we stopped to listen.

There must have been either little or no insulation in the walls of the cabin, because we could hear her voice.

We were about twenty-five feet away, but we were able to decipher what was being said. Not all the words were clear, but I could make out most of them. It was clear from the woman's tone that she was frantic. Her words would fade in and out, as if she was pacing back and forth in the small structure.

"This is your fault. You know that, don't you? I wouldn't have to be doing this if you would have protected her. You were supposed to be her friend." Her voice faded out, and we strained to listen.

A feeling of relief came over me like a warm wave. As long as she was talking to someone, there was a good chance that Katie was still alive. Unless this woman was totally psychotic and delusional, there was a good chance we were in time.

I saw Marty speaking quietly into his radio. He was getting the ETA on the backup and requesting they come in with no lights or sirens.

We had no idea what the situation inside was at this point. We both knew we had to proceed with caution. We knew what this woman was capable of, and neither of us wanted her to catch the scent of what was right outside the door.

"You let them torture her. You let them tease her without mercy. Why didn't you stop them? My baby, my Tiffany, would call me, crying. Crying about the cruel things Jamie and Kimberly called her. And you...you called yourself her friend. You were too busy with your new boyfriend to be her friend."

Her voice began to fade in volume, her tone going from anger to despair. She started out ranting and ended up with her voice cracking in sobs. If it was Katie she was talking to, the girl was either unable to answer or too afraid to do so.

Marty must have noticed a spot where he would be able to see inside without taking a chance of alerting the woman to our presence.

He put a finger to his lips and circled around the building, his movements as careful as a cat hunting prey. He stopped and positioned himself up against the wall of the building, just below one of the windows. He peeked through the window, whose sides were adorned with a delicate taupe lace curtain, pulled back with a narrow braided rope.

Suddenly I could see the tension leave his body, like air escaping from a balloon. He nodded, and I let my own anxiety dissipate as I became convinced that Katie was still alive and, I hoped, unharmed.

But I didn't know how much longer that would be the case.

I was now the closest one to the front door. Convinced that we were running out of time, I pulled out my Glock and motioned for Marty to cover me. I was going to try and open the door. I waited for Mrs. Bennett to start ranting again, hoping her own voice would cover my attempt to enter. I watched Marty with my peripheral vision as I made my way to the entrance. I watched for any sign from Marty that Mrs. Bennett had become aware of us.

I put my hand on the brass handle and turned it slowly. I could see Marty out of the corner of my eye, nodding, letting me know it was still safe to proceed. I drew a deep breath as the knob turned easily. As soon as I felt the latch become undone, I thrust open the door and screamed "Stop!" as I saw the madwoman dousing the frightened girl with fluid from a small gas can.

In her other hand was a box of matches.

"Drop it!" I shouted at her, aiming my weapon on the target I was trained to hit, the spot right between her eyes.

I glanced over at Katie, she was sweating profusely and her olive complexion had turned sheet white. Her mouth was covered with a strip of gray duct tape. The girl's arms and legs were tightly bound to the wooden chair she was seated in.

It still wasn't over for her. I could still see the desperation and fear in her eyes as the liquid made its way down her face. She shook her head to avoid getting the flammable substance in her eyes.

My sudden appearance startled Bennett, who jerked her head in my direction. I saw the movement of her eyes when she realized I wasn't alone.

"You understand, don't you? You have a daughter?" she asked. Her eyes, haunted and vacant, targeted mine. "She put up a brave front, but she wasn't brave. What would you do if your daughter came home crying every day, pleading with you, begging you to just let her die?" The hand that held the matches shook uncontrollably as she waved it in an exaggerated motion.

She continued to plead her case.

"Those girls thought they were so pretty." She spat on the ground. "They weren't pretty, they were horrid, wretched creatures. I just made them look on the outside like what they were really were on the inside."

I nodded my head in agreement, trying to contain her attention solely on me. My own eyes were starting to burn. The caustic fumes of the flammable liquid that I recognized as gasoline became overpowering in the confines of the small room.

"She was supposed to be her friend." She briefly turned her attention back to Katie, whose eyes pleaded with me for help.

Gail Bennett's hand suddenly became steady as she struck the match against the box. The smell of sulfur dominated all the other odors and I knew immediately we no longer had time. My hand gripped my firearm, my finger, now trembling, began to bend against the trigger.

I yelled one more time for her to stop, hoping she wouldn't drop the match. I glanced down at the floor, looking for puddles of the liquid. I tried to calculate how I was going to reach Katie and get her away, just in case it ignited.

She must have become aware of my scream at the same time she realized Marty had made a move to grab her arm. Startled, she dropped the lighted match.

Time stopped for all of us. It was like watching a film clip in slow motion. The match hit the floor and a puff of smoke and a soft "psst" sound occurred simultaneously. The gasoline ignited and a ball of flames shot up. Gail Bennett watched, as if hypnotized.

Marty grabbed hold of her arm and was able to overcome and restrain her. He immediately pulled her away from the flames as I ran to Katie. I knew I would never be able to loosen her binding, so I didn't even attempt it.

Instead, I grabbed hold of the back of the chair she was tied to and pulled it backwards. The chair crashed to the floor as it fell, causing Katie's head to smack against the floor. I grabbed hold of one of the wooden strips on the back of the chair, lifted it a few inches, and dragged it as far from the fire as I could.

Suddenly the chair and Katie became weightless as Marty appeared beside me. His hands found a place next to mine as we pulled Katie out of the house to safety.

∽

Backup had arrived and the scene became a series of isolated moments. Men and women in different uniforms had converged on the grounds. Someone pulled me away from the smoke and began to ask me questions. It took me a few moments to clear my mind and shake the fog that seemed to envelop my thoughts.

The sound of burning lumber splintering and falling to the ground reached my ears as if I was under water.

"Are you okay, detective?" a female paramedic asked me as she shined a small flashlight in my eyes.

The smoke had reached my throat and caused it to burn as I swallowed, but I nodded my head in response to her question.

"Yes, yes, I'm fine," I told her, finally finding my voice.

I looked around for Marty, who was also being attended by a paramedic. They were cutting away one of his sleeves and examining his arm. We made eye contact and he smiled, exposing that one dimple.

Somebody threw a jacket over my shoulder, probably because I had begun to shiver.

I looked around to see if I could see Katie, and make sure she was all right. She was on a stretcher, being loaded into the emergency vehicle.

"I think she'll be okay," The soft-spoken medic with the flashlight informed me. "She may have a little smoke inhalation and a bump on her head, but she should be okay. We need you to get checked out though, to make sure your lungs aren't damaged."

I wasn't going to argue, I was just glad that this whole ordeal was over and another family wouldn't have to suffer the same fate as Jamie Camp and Kimberly Weston.

I turned and made my way toward the ambulance. I saw Mr. Bennett standing in the distance, his arm wrapped around his daughter. They just stood there, watching, as his wife—the mother of his children—was taken away in handcuffs. I wondered to myself if they would ever be okay again.

CHAPTER TWENTY-TWO

Marty suffered second-degree burns on his forearm. He was treated at the hospital and was released three hours later, with instructions on how to care for the injury at home.

Justin had picked up Marty's car and had driven it to the hospital. He was waiting in the lobby to bring him home.

Once they were in the car, Justin asked him, "Where to?"

"My house," he answered curtly.

"Hope working?" Justin asked. It was his way of making an indirect attempt at asking why she wasn't there.

Marty shrugged his shoulders, causing the pain of the burn to intensify. With one hand, he managed to open a small vial that contained four prescription painkillers, which the hospital pharmacy had dispensed to him. He built up a mouthful of spit, then popped one into his mouth and swallowed.

The silence that followed was too much for his redheaded friend.

"What's going on with you two? I thought we were going to start looking for tuxedos, and now I'm getting vibes that you're ready to scan the Match.com ads."

Marty remained silent, but Justin wasn't the type of friend to let it slide.

"What the hell is going on, Marty? Two weeks ago, you were going to ask the woman to marry you. Now you act like she was just another roll in the hay."

Marty eyes focused on the road before him. He let a moment pass before he replied.

"Can you just drop it, Justin?"

Feeling sorry for his friend, he decided to let it go. Justin knew that Marty would eventually bring him up to speed. Pushing the issue would slow up the process.

"Fine," Justin replied, with a touch of hurt in his voice. Not a word more was said until they reached Marty's house.

"Just take the car home with you, I'll arrange to pick it up tomorrow," Marty said as he maneuvered his way out of the passenger seat, taking care not to make any sudden moves.

Still feeling the sting of Marty's mood, Justin nodded.

"Yeah, don't worry about it. Just get some sleep and take care of that arm." He managed a weak smile.

"Sleep yeah. Justin...thanks," Marty told him as he shut the car door and walked slowly toward his house.

The door opened just as Marty was inserting the key in the lock. He was taken aback when he found Hope facing him instead of the Captain.

He immediately thought his father was in trouble. He started to panic.

"What's wrong?" he asked, stretching his neck and looking past her, trying to catch sight of his father.

She gently took his hand, examining the gauze bandage that took up most of his forearm.

"Justin called. I was going to go to the hospital, but he said he would bring you home. It looks like it hurts," she told him sympathetically.

"You have no idea," he replied sharply, not holding back the attitude. He dropped her hand as he walked farther into the house.

"Where's my dad?" he asked, still avoiding any eye contact.

"He went to the store to pick up some chicken stock. He decided that you were going to need some of his homemade soup." She followed closely behind him.

"Can I get you something? Why don't you sit down and I'll get you a glass of wine?"

"No, I just took a painkiller. Look, I really appreciate it, but I'll be okay, you can leave."

He was having a harder and harder time avoiding her eyes. Her voice was tugging at his heart like a magnet. He missed being with her, but he would be damned if he'd let her know it.

He moved one of the pillows on the sofa and carefully sat down, trying to keep his arm from making a sudden movement.

"Marty, please, just listen to me." She sat down next to him.

Marty turned and looked at her. The painkillers must have affected his vision, because her eyes appeared greener as they reflected the lamplight in the room.

"What?" he asked impatiently. He just wanted her to say what she had to say and leave. He wasn't in the mood for her usual excuses of blaming her mother or her ex-husband Richard for her emotional shortcomings.

"We never finished our conversation the other night. You never…"

"Look, Hope," he shifted his body so he was facing her. He took a deep breath and made the conscious decision to stop acting like a child and accept the inevitable. He was going to let her off the hook.

"Let's just forget it. I'll return the ring, no harm done. You don't want to get married? Fine."

As the words were coming out of his mouth, he was praying that his body language wasn't betraying what he was feeling.

"For heaven's sake, Marty, will you stop making assumptions on what I want and how I feel? How can someone who is so loved and respected be so damn insecure? You know what your problem is? You are spoiled rotten! You have gotten everything you ever wanted, and the minute you have the slightest inkling that something isn't going the way you want it, you run. Marty Keal, you are a chicken. You are too damn scared to sit here and hear me out!"

He sat there, dumbfounded. The last thing he had expected was a tongue lashing.

She caught her breath after the rant and her expression dared him to talk. He remained silent.

"Yes," she said softly.

He looked at her confused.

She repeated it.

"Yes." She put her hand over the hand of his injured arm, wrapping her fingers around his thumb.

"'Yes?' I don't understand what you're saying." He scratched his forehead with his good hand.

"Looks like I am going to have to spell it out. Yes, I'll marry you." She squinted, and the skin on the top of her nose wrinkled. "Am I speaking a foreign language?" she asked him, breaking into a broad smile.

Suddenly they realized they weren't alone. The Captain's voice filled the room.

"Are you deaf, boy? The girl just told you she's accepting your proposal," his father said, and headed into the kitchen with his groceries.

He glanced up at his father and then to back to Hope. "Yes? Are you sure?"

She nodded her head.

He looked back in the direction his father walked. Suddenly he had another concern.

"Maybe this isn't a good time, Hope. I can't leave him now. We don't know what the doctor is going to say."

Now he wondered whether it just wasn't something that was supposed to happen. Maybe he was better off when she hadn't answered him.

She stood up.

"Marty, who said anything about leaving him?" She looked around the room.

"I think this house can accommodate one extra person. I don't take up that much room, and we already know that it's a great place to raise a brood of children."

"You would do that? You would give up your home? You would move in here with us?" He ran his hand through his hair with a look of disbelief.

Hope gently bit down on her bottom lip as she once again nodded a yes.

"Yes?" he asked her again, not quite believing what was happening.

This time when she repeated the "yes," he lifted her off her feet with his good arm and she wrapped her legs around his hips.

"Yes!" she said once more, as their lips met.

They were so lost in the moment; they didn't hear the Captain yell out.

"Does this mean we get to have that sixty-inch flat-screen television?"

∽

When Marty and I walked into our squad room, I immediately noticed almost everyone was milling around in front of the chief's office.

Kathy jumped out of her seat and walked over to me.

"Joe's here, he's in with the chief."

I looked at her, expecting her to elaborate, but she just shrugged her shoulders, as if she had no clue what was going on.

A good twenty minutes later, while I was trying hard to concentrate on some paperwork, but failing miserably, the door to the chief's office opened. Joe and the boss walked out.

I was shocked. He looked like a man does after a long, hot shower. The two weeks he had spent in Florida had given his pale Irish complexion a rich color. His skin was sunburned in a few spots, but his face had turned a healthy-looking bronze and he was clean-shaven.

These last few months since Connie died and Annie had gotten hurt, his hygiene had taken a dive, but now he looked well groomed and neat. It looked as if he had even had his haircut and styled, something that used to be a regular ritual for him, but had gone by the wayside in his grief.

I was still furious with him, and I was going to let him know it. I had rehearsed a million and one verbal lashings to give him, but the minute he walked over to me, I felt a lump the size of an apple suddenly appear in the back of my throat.

I expected the smell of Jack Daniels to seep into my nasal passages, something that had been becoming more and more obvious and frequent these past few months. Instead, I smelled the familiar aroma of Old Spice, the cologne my daughter insisted on buying him every Christmas since she was old enough to dictate her preference in gifts.

"Hey, Jeannie!" He planted his butt on my desk, just as he had done a zillion times before. "I hear congratulations are in order. You put a lid on the Faceless case. Nice work."

I nodded, accepting his compliment.

"What's going on, Joe? How's Annie?" I tried to keep my anger out of my voice, but I was having trouble with that.

"She's better, she's...well, she's doing better. Look, I'm sorry I didn't tell you and just took off, but things just got out of hand for me. Okay?"

I turned to look away so I wouldn't burst out in tears. I knew that he would make an issue of it and tell everyone that I was crying, and I just wasn't in the mood to be embarrassed.

"So?" I asked him "When are you coming back to work?" I was moving papers around for no apparent reason and he knew it. He grabbed my hand to stop me.

"I'm not, Jean, I just came from Human Resources. I put in for my retirement."

I looked up. He must have seen the surprise on my face, and he broke out in a smile. I had thought he was going to tell me he was going to AA meetings or rehab for cops with substance abuse problems and he would be gone a few weeks.

But retiring? Gone for good? No, I couldn't get a handle on that. We had been partners for seven years now, and we fit like a glove. Joe was as important to me as my husband Glenn was. I trusted him, I knew he had my back, and I knew that he trusted me with his. It takes a lot of time and effort to build up a rapport like the one we had with each other. I wasn't worried anymore about Marty, but losing Joe was like losing a family member.

"Jeannie, I rented a condo down in West Palm Beach, just a few minutes from the hospital. This way, I can spend everyday with Annie, give her some encouragement. I spoke to her doctors and they think that if we can get her out of there, she'll do better. There's a gym and swimming pool in the complex, and once she is able to come home, she can do outpatient therapy. They say if she doesn't start getting stronger emotionally, she just is not going to get any better. They think she'll get worse. She needs me, Jeannie, and frankly I need her."

I saw tears welling up in his eyes, and I pretended not to notice when he wiped them with the back of his hand. I knew that my wanting to keep him there was selfish of me, and he needed me to not fight him on this.

I stood up and threw my arms around him, just relishing in the aroma of Old Spice.

"We're going to miss you, I'm going to miss you. When is this going to happen, Joe?"

"Hey, you're embarrassing me." He placed his hands on my forearms and held me at arm's length.

"I'm leaving tomorrow morning. I got some movers coming this afternoon." He glanced at his watch. "Damn, I gotta go. Look, when you go to visit Cliff in college, just take some extra time and keep going south. Gainesville is only five hours or so north of me."

"You're not going to stop at the house and say goodbye to Glenn and Bethany?" I asked him, a little annoyed. I knew that my daughter would be crushed if he left without saying goodbye.

"I already did. I went to your house first. I explained everything to Bethany. She says she understands. She's a good kid, Jeannie. You're a lucky woman, remember that." He gave me a quick kiss on the cheek. There was nothing more for him to say.

I didn't say anything else…just watched as he shook a few hands and said goodbye to everyone in the room. Then I heard him when he turned to Marty and spoke loud enough for me and everyone else to hear.

"Just remember Marty, when she wears a skirt, it's 'cause she bloated, she's on the rag. She gets cranky when she's on the rag. She's wearing pants—you're safe!"

I looked down. It dawned on me that I was wearing a skirt. *Damn it*, he was right.

THE END

ABOUT DAWN KOPMAN WHIDDEN

Dawn Kopman Whidden is a native New Yorker and successful author who grew up in the close-knit community of Little Neck Douglaston during the baby boomer era. She graduated from Queensboro Community College.

Twenty years ago, she traded in her days of living in the bustling city for a more serene and tranquil life on a small farm in the town of Bell, located in North Central Florida.

She is retired and shares her life and love with her husband of fourteen years and an adopted stray dog she named Casey. She has also been blessed with two beautiful grandchildren.

Her previous work, *A Child is Torn "Innocence Lost"* was published in 2012 receiving great acclaim in the literary market.

A Child is Torn

When dependable Evan Madison fails to show up for work, police are dispatched to his home. His ten-year-old son, Brad, is discovered inside, unharmed and seemingly alone. He is stoic, sitting in front of the television playing his favorite video game, Super Mario—*and he's covered in blood.*

Veteran Police Officer Marty Keal is the first on the scene. With his many years of experience, he thinks he's seen it all. That is, until he discovers Brad's not really alone after all. Upstairs in their bedroom lies the brutally bludgeoned and deceased bodies of both his mother and his father. When questioned, Brad confesses to the horrific murders.

When Brad is transferred to a local mental health institution for children, Dr. Hope Rubin is brought in to evaluate and treat the child. A preliminary investigation shows no evidence of any kind of mistreatment in his past. She must determine the disturbing truth— Is Brad telling the truth? Or, is he covering for someone else?

Detective Jean Whitley rounds out the investigative team, and she suspects there is much more to the case than what meets the eye. The happily married mother of two is unwavering in her determination to uncover the real truth about Brad. Was he abused? Or, is he the product of an evil seed born to kill?

As the layers of truth about Brad are systematically peeled away, you will be compelled to ask yourself, *Which is the more dominate factor in contributing to who we are—NATURE or NURTURE?*

FACELESS: A MYSTERY ~ DAWN KOPMAN WHIDDEN

A FEW OF THE MANY READER REVIEWS

A plot so suspenseful it will make your teeth clinch!

"Dawn Kopman Whidden utilizes her exceptional insight into child abuse and mental illness to deal properly with the common misunderstandings and stereotypes. She is a true craftsman capable of developing sympathetic characters, vivid and descriptive settings, and a plot so suspenseful it will make your teeth clinch."

A must read!

"A Child Is Torn is a must read book. It is well-written and keeps your interest from the beginning. The characters are so realistic that they could be your neighbors or friends. Although it is a murder mystery, it is not easy to figure out who did it, as there are a lot of red herrings. If you like Jodi Picoult and Alafair Burke, you will enjoy this book. There are similarities, but Whidden has her own unique style. Once you start reading it, you will not want to stop."

Amazing!

"A Child is Torn: Innocence Lost, was amazing! I've never read a book so fast. It kept me on the edge of my seat from the first page to the last. The author, Dawn Kopman Whidden, really knows how to write! I can't wait to read her next book. Don't ever stop writing Dawn! Great Job!"

Hard to put it down!

"This book is a great read! It will hold your interest from the first through the last chapter and it's hard to put it down once you begin. Great work Dawn! When will the next one come out?"

A Child is Torn is a wonderful read!

"I couldn't put it down. If you like mysteries and psychological thrillers, you will love this book! Can't wait for the author's next book to be published."

FACELESS: A MYSTERY ~ DAWN KOPMAN WHIDDEN

An amazing read!

"I recommend this book to everyone. Ms. Whidden has taken a controversial subject and woven it into a "not to be put down" book. I can't wait for her to write more, hopefully with the same unforgettable characters."

Could not put it down!

"*A Child is Torn* had me hooked from the very first page. So relevant to events that have happened recently that I wonder if this was fiction or based on a real-life event. I actually read this book in less than two days. Kept me in suspense from the beginning to the end. Can't wait to see more from this author."

A Child is Torn, well worth reading!

"I really liked the book very much and felt an immediate affinity for the characters. I found myself concerned about them and thinking about them when I wasn't reading the book. That didn't happen too often as I finished the book within three days!"

One of the best I've read in a while!

"Dawn Whidden astounded me with the plot, amazing attention to detail, and brilliant concept in *A Child is Torn*. This book instantly grabs your attention. It's impossible to put down. Whidden is absolutely incredible. With one novel, she's the same caliber as Mary Higgins Clark. Clearly Whidden is a dedicated writer and I expect to see many more great novels from her."

Awesome read!

"Absolutely loved this book. It was an easy read I could not put down. The characters were interesting and the mystery kept me reading."

Will keep you up all night reading!

"*A Child is Torn* is one of those books you just cannot put down. One twist after another, and what a surprise ending. Nature or Nurture is the repeated question of the book. And it truly makes you think about nurturing—what we learn as children, our experiences in life, and how they affect us an adult. Or, do we have no control of ourselves as nature takes its course? The burning question that can be debated forever as long as there is mankind and circumstances that suggest either can be the answer. I am so looking forward to Ms. Whidden's next book—her writing reminds me of Lisa Gardner—same can't-put-down thrillers that keep you up all night reading. Well done for a first published book. I highly recommend this one."

A gripping story!

"This book is really hard to put down. The author brings you right into the story and keeps you wondering."

Awesome book!

"This book was awesome! I was hesitant to read it. I am an avid reader and I thought, How good could a first-time book be? Boy was I fooled. Once I started it, I couldn't put it down. I tried to make it last 'til my vacation, but I just couldn't. BUY IT!!! GREAT JOB!!! Looking forward to your next book! I give this SIX STARS!!!"

A Child Is Torn is a must read!

"This is a can't-put-down read. The writer draws you into her characters so you know them like your next-door neighbors and your family. She makes you want to know what is going to happen to each of them, and leaves you guessing until the end."

Great read!

"This story was a page turner from the start. I couldn't put it down. Great first novel. I can't wait to see what she comes out with next."

Fantastic read!

"Dawn Kopman Whidden has written a "page turning, can't-put-down" murder mystery. As her characters develop, you feel as if you are there...watching them...you are part of their lives. Her book is better than a 5 star movie. I found myself thinking about the story during the day, trying to figure out what would happen next. The ending will absolutely surprise you. BRAVO!"

A great book!

"Dawn, I just finished *A Child is Torn: Innocence Lost*. It was a good read! The characters were thoroughly developed. As I came to know them and began to empathize with them, I found myself looking forward to see how their lives and loves would unfold. I'm excited to

FACELESS: A MYSTERY ~ DAWN KOPMAN WHIDDEN

find out what happens to them next! A great book!"

A page turner!

"From the very first paragraph, Dawn Kopman Whidden's storytelling and character development skills are evident. She has a natural talent for building suspense from the very first page. I highly recommend this novel!"

Totally entertaining and thoughtful!

"A Child Is Torn is a deep, emotional book about a little boy's struggles and grief. It goes beyond the subject of the loss of loved ones. It takes the reader inside the lives of so many people that they become a part of your own life. This is one of those books that you just can't put down. The story is so true to life, even though it falls into the "fiction" category. You will fall in love with Brad, and you will weep for him. You will be transformed and find yourself rooting for a lasting love for Hope and Marty, the psychiatrist and police officer who are involved with the case of the brutal murder of Brad's parents. There is so much going on within the pages of this book, you will not be disappointed. The author of this book has brought her characters to life, each with a story of their own and she keeps you wanting to know more. Totally entertaining and thoughtful. I look forward to reading more from the author, Dawn Kopman Whidden. She truly has a gift!"

Gripping tale of innocence and savagery!

"A book you will not be able to put down. Absolutely riveting. A must read for murder mystery aficionados and those who simply enjoy good intrigue. A spellbinding novel from start to finish."

5 out of 5 Stars—Psychological Stunner—Don't Miss this Novel!

"In her own way, Dawn Whidden has emerged on the scene to open our bewildered eyes to the mystifying world associated with mental illness and childhood abuse. Written with a masterful attention to detail, similar to works by authors such as Kurt Vonnegut, Ms. Whidden guides the reader into a hidden world that we haven't seen—or thought of—since the case of the Menendez brothers. This is truly an eye-opening novel."